# In My Sister's Shoes

## SINÉAD MORIARTY

**ISIS**
LARGE PRINT
Oxford

First published in Great Britain 2007
by
Penguin Ireland,
a division of
Penguin Books Ltd.


Published in Large Print 2008 by ISIS Publishing Ltd.,
7 Centremead, Osney Mead, Oxford OX2 0ES
by arrangement with
Penguin Books Ltd.

**British Library Cataloguing in Publication Data**
Moriarty, Sinéad
    In my sister's shoes. – Large print ed.
    1. Sisters – Ireland – Dublin – Fiction
    2. Large type books
    I. Title
    823.9'2 [F]


ISBN 978–0–7531–8090–7 (hb)
ISBN 978–0–7531–8091–4 (pb)


Printed and bound in Great Britain by
T. J. International Ltd., Padstow, Cornwall

# In My Sister's Shoes

For Geordan

One, two, three, four, five, six, seven, eight, nine, TESTOSTERONE . . .

I waited . . . nothing. Bollox. I still wanted to kill them. I thought the counting was supposed to calm me down, make me Zen, stop me wanting to murder them.

The letter T flew by me, hit the wall and slid down, leaving a trail of tomato sauce behind it. An F hit me right in the face, splashing tomato sauce into my eye. They screeched with laughter.

I wiped my eye with my sleeve and sighed. How, in God's name, had I ended up here? Where was my old life, the glamorous one, the independent one, the nice, clean, non-food-smudged, non-snot-covered one?

Maybe if they were my own kids it wouldn't be so difficult. Maybe if they were my own kids I wouldn't want to kill them right now. Maybe if they were my own kids I'd know what the hell I was doing.

But they weren't and I was drowning in a sea of alphabet spaghetti.

# CHAPTER
# ONE

As I strutted up the pathway to my sister's house, I realized I felt really happy for the first time in ages. I was on top of the world. I, Kate O'Brien, was a television presenter. After eight years of living in a studio apartment in London, making tea for other presenters, I finally had my own show and it felt fantastic.

I rang the doorbell and heard squealing from the other side. The twins were obviously very excited about being five.

The door opened and a very harassed-looking Dad pulled me into the hall.

"Guess what?" I asked, dying to tell him my good news, but he cut across me.

"Thank God you've arrived. Mark's been boring me rigid about some new mathematical theory or other. I'd rather nail my balls to the mast of a sinking ship than listen to another word of it," he hissed.

"Charmingly put. Nice to see you too, Dad." I laughed, and looked at my brother-in-law, Mark, who had his back to me and was now busy showing the twins how to multiply three apples by three pears. They gazed adoringly at their father as he prattled on.

"That dude needs to get out more," drawled Derek, my younger brother, from the couch. "It's bad enough that he's a maths professor but he doesn't need to inflict it on his kids. They're going to be total nerds. No one wants to hang out with kids who are good at maths!"

"You could have done with a bit more focus on your studies, instead of pie-in-the-sky dreams about being a musician," grumbled Dad. He had been funding Derek's dream of becoming a famous rapper for years and was clearly fed up.

"When I'm playing sell-out gigs in Wembley, you'll eat those words," said the confident artist.

"Seeing as you haven't made it outside the garage yet, I won't hold my breath."

"Where's Fiona?" I asked.

"She's in the kitchen putting the candles on the cake," said Dad. "If you can call it a cake, it's a rotten looking organic carrot yoke. Sure you wouldn't feed it to a rabbit."

As if on cue, my elder sister came through the door carrying the birthday cake. "Kate, I'm so glad you made it," she said, coming over to kiss me.

"I wouldn't miss the boys' birthday," I said, winking at the twins, who ran across to say hello.

"Except last year when you forgot," said Mark, as I glared at him. I could never figure out what Fiona saw in him. I suppose because she was a maths genius too, they had numbers in common.

"Never mind, you're here now," said Fiona, smoothing things over as she always did.

"Where's our present, Aunty Kate?" Bobby demanded.

"It's in here," I said, handing him the bag.

"I hope it's more suitable than their Christmas present was," said Mark.

I blushed. Riddled with guilt at having forgotten their fourth birthday I had spent a month's wages on a PlayStation that came with two games — Big Mutha Truckers 2 and Airforce Delta Strike — which I'd thought was a really cool present. How was I to know that they were violent games and that the boys were too young for PlayStation? I didn't have a clue about kids. Fiona was speechless and Mark kept shaking his head, saying how totally unsuitable it was and didn't I know that these games corrupted children's minds? I had felt about two feet tall.

Jack held up his present, looking confused. "What is it?" he asked.

"Burberry ear-muffs — to keep your ears warm in the winter when you go to the park," I announced.

The twins looked blankly at me.

"Look, you put them on like this," I said, placing them on Jack's head.

"Yucky," he said, and pulled them off.

"What's this?" asked Bobby, trying to put a little jacket over his head.

"That's a little Burberry coat for Teddy, so he can keep warm when you take him for walks," I said, grinning at Teddy, the cocker spaniel, who was curled in a ball in the corner.

Everyone was staring at the ear-muffs in silence.

"Lovely," said Fiona, bemused.

"What's Bunberry?" asked Dad.

"It's, like, totally bling designer gear," said Derek.

"I thought tartan went out of fashion in the sixties," said Dad, laughing.

"Well, it's better than last year's fiasco," said Mark.

Bobby peered into the bag to see if anything else was in there. Finding nothing, he fixed his eyes on me with raw disappointment.

"Sorry, guys, I thought you'd like them," I said, feeling like a total moron.

We heard a yowl and turned to see Jack wrestling Teddy into the dog coat — clumps of his fur were stuck in the zip.

Mark ran over to save him.

"Guess what?" I said, still bursting to tell them my news.

"You're up the duff," said Derek.

"You've met a nice lad," said Dad, hopefully.

"I've got my own show!" I said, ignoring them both.

"Kate, that's fantastic!" said Fiona.

"Ah, sure what good is that to you?" said Dad. "You need to focus less on that auld job and more on meeting a nice boy."

"So, are you going to be earning mucho *dinero?*" asked Derek, perking up.

"Well, it'll be a lot better than what I'm on now, although that wouldn't be hard. But don't be expecting hand-outs — get your own job."

"Is it an entertainment show?" asked Fiona.

"Yes, pretty light stuff — interviewing rising stars, reviewing music, movies and TV shows. It's on the

Lifechange channel, not exactly the BBC — but it's up and coming and at least I finally get to present. I've taped the first three shows already. It's going well."

"Mark," Fiona called, "did you hear the good news? Kate has her own show. She's going to be famous."

"Finally. Well, at least now you won't have to worry about her so much," he said, sitting down beside his wife and putting his arm round her.

"Fiona! What are you doing worrying about me? I'm thirty, for God's sake, I'm fine."

She shrugged. "I can't help it. It's habit."

I smiled at her. She'd been worrying about Derek and me since Mum had died twenty-two years ago. Dad, heartbroken, had thrown himself into work and left Fiona, aged twelve, to look after her younger siblings. I was eight and Derek was only four, so Fiona had become our surrogate mother. I always felt guilty that she had given up her youth to make our sandwiches and do our homework with us. She had been twelve going on forty.

"Well, you can stop right now," I said. "I'm an overnight success after eight years' grafting."

"So, like, can Gonzo and me come on your show and try out some of our new material?" asked Derek.

"No."

"What happened to families helping each other out?"

"She doesn't want the show to be cancelled," said Dad.

"Your stuff isn't good enough yet. It needs more work," I said, trying to be tactful.

"We've been working on some new songs. You'll be blown away when you hear them. We're recording a CD on Friday so I'll send you a copy and you can slot us into your show," said the wannabe rapper, as he headed out the door. "Thanks for the grub, Fiona, I'll catch you later."

"Oh, God." I groaned. "How am I going to get him off my back? He's going to hound me about this every day."

"Couldn't you put him on the show for a few minutes?" asked Fiona.

"No way — he's brutal."

"Is it that bad? I thought some of the lines rhymed well," said the ever-supportive oldest sibling.

"It's absolute tripe. The lad needs to cop on to himself and get a proper job," huffed Dad.

"Well, Bill, you're the one who's funding his delusional music career," Mark pointed out, and Dad bristled.

"I've told him, next year when he turns twenty-seven the finances will dry up. Besides, he's working part-time at the moment so I'm helping him less. I can tell you now, when your two boys grow up and beg you to support their pipe-dreams, you'll find it a lot harder to say no than you think."

"Our boys will be mathematicians, like their parents," said Mark, as we watched Jack rubbing birthday cake into Bobby's hair.

"Now who's delusional?" muttered Dad.

"So, how've you been?" I asked Fiona, changing the subject as quickly as possible.

"Good, thanks. You know, busy with teaching and the boys. Actually, we have some exciting news too. Mark's been asked to submit a paper for the Goldwin Prize."

"Sounds great," I said.

"Tremendous," said Dad.

Mark nodded. "It's a big honour. It's for the conference on statistics, mathematics and related fields."

"What do you get if you win?" Dad asked, in his usual blunt manner.

"A huge grant for the department, and worldwide recognition of his work. It's a really big deal — there's a lot of pressure on him," said Fiona, smiling proudly at her husband.

"Wow! Well, good luck with it all," I said.

"Thank you, Kate," said Mark. Then, to Fiona, he said, "Actually, darling, speaking of the prize, I need to slip away and do a couple of hours' work, if that's all right?"

Fiona looked a bit crestfallen.

"Now? On the boys' birthday?" I asked.

"It's fine, Kate," said Fiona.

"This paper's going to make a difference to the way people think. Not as important as interviewing teenage singers, perhaps, but important none the less. I'll be back to read the boys a bedtime story," he said, kissed Fiona and walked out.

"Who'd like tea?" asked Fiona.

"I'd love some," I said, as she went into the kitchen to boil the kettle.

"Imagine how insufferable he'll be if he wins this prize." I sighed.

"Perish the thought," said Dad, with a shudder.

The phone rang. Fiona mustn't have heard it in the kitchen so I picked it up. "Hello."

"Hello, Mrs Kennedy, your biopsy results have come through and Dr Summer needs to see you right away. I've scheduled you in for nine tomorrow morning."

"OK," I said, as the phone went dead.

What the hell was going on?

# CHAPTER
# TWO

I sprang up from the chair and went to find Fiona, who was in the kitchen with the twins.

"Hey, boys, will you go to Granddad? He wants to talk to you," I said, and ushered them out.

I took the teapot out of Fiona's hand and led her to the table to sit down. "What's going on?" she asked.

"My question exactly. You've just had a phone call from Dr Summer's secretary. Your biopsy results are back and he wants to see you at nine tomorrow morning." Fiona's face crumpled. "Are you OK? Why are you having biopsies?"

"You should have called me. That was a private phone call," she said, trying to compose herself.

"The woman didn't give me a chance to say I wasn't you. Anyway, that's irrelevant. Are you sick?"

"If they're calling me back first thing tomorrow it must be bad news," she said, fighting tears.

"Jesus, Fiona, what is it?"

"A lump."

"Oh, God, where?"

"Breast."

I stared at her, speechless.

"Freaky, isn't it?" said Fiona, laughing bitterly. "She was exactly the same age as me when she died."

"Don't think about that. It was a long time ago and the treatment now is much better. Besides, Mum's was very advanced. Yours is probably just a little lump that they need to take out," I said, grabbing at straws.

She sighed.

"Does anyone know?" I asked.

She shook her head. "I didn't want to worry Mark unnecessarily."

"I'll go with you tomorrow."

"You're flying back to London in the morning."

"I'll change my flight."

"Don't you have to work?"

"Yes, but I can sort something out. Come on, I'd like to go with you."

"No, it's fine. I'll tell Mark tonight and he'll come with me."

"Well, if you change your mind I'm happy to stay."

Fiona smiled at me. "You'll break out in a rash if you stay in Dublin for more than twenty-four hours. It's OK, I'll be fine."

"Rash?"

"Come on, Kate, you're allergic to Dublin."

"No, I'm not."

"Yes, you are. You always look uncomfortable and edgy after a couple of hours."

"Do I?" I asked, knowing fine well I did. "I don't mean to. I love catching up with all of you."

I did like the idea of coming home and seeing my family, but after an hour or two I always began to feel claustrophobic. In the last three years I'd only come home for Christmas, and once during the summer for a weekend. I could never wait to get back to the airport. A weight lifted off me when I boarded the plane to London. I was always glad to see my family, but after the initial catching up, I never knew what to do with myself. I didn't seem to fit in. Dad, Fiona and Derek had moved on with their lives and were closer to each other than they were to me. I felt like an outsider as they told stories about things that had happened while I was away. I spent most of my time lurking about the house, clock-watching.

"Maybe if you came home more regularly it'd be more comfortable for you. I know Dad would like to see more of you. I would too."

"Sure, absolutely, I'll try and do that," I lied. "Anyway, what are we talking about this for when there are much more important things going on? How are you feeling? Have you been sick?"

"No, not at all. I only noticed the lump a few weeks ago, so I decided to get it checked out and they sent me for a biopsy."

"It'll be OK, Fiona. You've caught it early."

"What if I haven't? What if the boys end up like us, with no mother? I couldn't bear that, Kate. Life can be so unfair. I hated not having Mum around. It meant having to grow up so quickly. I want the boys to be children for as long as possible."

I tried desperately to think of something reassuring to say. I owed her so much. She had given up her youth to raise me and Derek. While we were playing with our friends on the road, Fiona was cooking dinner or doing our laundry. Because of her selflessness, Derek and I had had a very stable upbringing. She was the one who made all the sacrifices.

"Fiona, the boys will be fine and so will you. Women are always having lumps removed and go on to live long, healthy lives. I bet when you see the doctor tomorrow he'll tell you it's nothing to worry about."

Before we could continue the conversation, Dad barged in, with the twins hanging off his back, screeching with laughter. "Jesus, did you go to India to pick the tealeaves?" he puffed, as Fiona and I peeled the boys off him. "My God, Fiona, they're very lively. I don't know how you do it. I'm worn out after ten minutes," he said, plonking himself down on a chair while the twins chased each other round the table.

"You get used to it," she said.

"Well, you look tired to me," said Dad. "I hope Mark's doing his fair share, Goldwin Prize or no Goldwin Prize."

"Yes, Dad, he is. Mark's a very hands-on father."

"Here you go," I said, pouring his tea to shut him up.

"Well, *have* you met a nice lad yet?" he asked, ricocheting from one interfering question to the next.

"No, I'm too busy with work to meet men," I said.

"You've always been far too focused on your career. You should spend more time trying to meet a nice fellow like your sister and settle down. You're no spring chicken any more."

I almost choked on my tea. Mark had never been Dad's idea of a great son-in-law. He had hoped Fiona would meet someone who'd spoil her and pamper her and take away all her worries and responsibilities. Give her back some of the childhood that had been robbed from her. But you can't turn back the clock and change the past. Fiona was responsible, efficient, reliable and dependable, and she wasn't going to change regardless of whom she married. Besides, she really did seem to love Mark and he adored her.

They had met at a chess competition — Mum had taught Fiona how to play. When she was too sick to get out of bed, Fiona would go up to her room and they'd play for hours. After Mum had died, Dad signed Fiona up to a chess club and made her go every week. At first she didn't want to, but then she began to enjoy it, especially after she met Mark.

For Fiona it was love at first checkmate. She had finally met someone who was passionate about chess and maths. Living with Derek and me must have been torture for her — we could barely add. They spent hours discussing linear programming, genetic algorithms and differential equations. Fiona thought she had died and gone to heaven. After years of trying to teach me and Derek to play chess — I got bored after five minutes and Derek tried to shove the pieces up his nose — she had found a true kindred spirit.

"Thanks for reminding me of my age, Dad," I said. "And, by the way, in case you ever meet anyone I work with, I'm twenty-six," I said.

"What?"

"In my line of work once you reach thirty you're over the hill, unless you're hugely successful. So, I'll be twenty-six for a couple of years."

"What kind of a job is that? You should come home and —"

"Get a real job," I said, finishing his sentence for him. "No, thanks, Dad. I love my job and I'm where I want to be. If I have to starve myself and go to the gym five days a week to look younger, so be it. It's worth the effort."

"You're looking very thin," Fiona said.

"I have to be. TV adds on ten pounds — and you should see the girls I'm in competition with. They're stunning and rail thin. It's dog eat dog out there."

"Who's eating dogs?" asked Jack.

"That's mean," said Bobby, putting a protective arm round Teddy.

"No one's eating dogs, sweetie, it's just an expression," said Fiona, giving Jack a hug.

"Mummy, will you light the candles again?" he asked.

"Of course. Will we sing 'Happy Birthday' again too?" Fiona asked.

"Yes, please," they said, jumping up and down.

"OK, here we go." She lit the candles and we sang "Happy Birthday" for the fifth time.

I watched Fiona's face looking lovingly down on the twins as they blew out their candles, and remembered my mother lighting my birthday cake and felt a pang of emptiness. I prayed that everything would be all right with Fiona's lump. Children need their mothers, and

**16**

Fiona was incredible with the twins. They were lucky to have her, and she deserved to be their mum for a very long time.

# CHAPTER
# THREE

I sat smiling tersely at the teenager sitting opposite me and watched the clock tick. I had ten minutes with her and was supposed to air the interview on the show later that week. Some interview, I thought glumly. So far the kid had answered every question with either a shrug or a barely audible monosyllable. The bolshie Hollywood starlet scowled and pulled on her cigarette, exhaling smoke into my face. I took a deep breath and tried again: "So, did you find the role of Amy challenging?"

"*No.*"

"Is Louisa May Alcott your favourite author?"

"Who?" said the star, frowning.

"The author who wrote *Little Women*, the book of the film you've just made," I said, beginning to lose the screed of patience I had left.

"Dunno, never read books."

"So you made a film, based on a classic tale, and didn't read the book?"

She shrugged.

"Are you as good at reading as you are at conversing?" I snapped.

"What?"

"Talking. You know, having a conversation," I said, letting my temper get the better of me. "Is that concept alien to you? Because I'd like to know why you've wasted my time today. I've spent five hours waiting in a draughty hotel corridor to interview you for ten minutes and all you can say is, 'dunno', 'yes' and 'no'. Do you not understand English?"

As my cameraman, Gary, sniggered, the PR woman, who had been nodding off in the chair behind him, leaped to her feet and said that the interview was over. How dare I speak to her star like that? She called Security and I was promptly escorted out of the hotel by two large bodyguards.

"Bloody hell, Kate, what's got into you today?" asked Gary.

"I'm sorry. I'm in a really bad mood and I'm sick to death of interviewing mind-numbingly stupid child actors with attitude."

"Yeah, but Donna's going to do her nut when she hears about this."

"Fuck Donna," I snapped. Gary stared at me in shock. I never lost my cool in interviews — I had plenty of experience with uncooperative stars. He knew something was up.

"Sorry, Gary, I didn't mean to be so grumpy. Look, I've got to go. I'll see you back in the office. We'll sort something out," I said, smiling weakly at him.

Gary shrugged and walked off to his van.

I sighed as I watched him go, then set off for the tube, putting my sunglasses on to hide my tears. What was I going to do? For the first time in my life, my sister needed me. I knew going home to Dublin was the right thing to do but I also knew that the sick feeling in my stomach wasn't just concern and fear for Fiona. If I was being totally honest, a big part of it was selfish anger. I knew that by leaving London I'd lose everything I'd worked so hard to achieve.

I went over that morning's disastrous phone conversation with Mark.

"Hello, Kate. Are you alone?" he asked, sounding strained.

"Yes, what's up?"

"I'm afraid I've got some bad news. Fiona's biopsy has shown the lump to be malignant. She has breast cancer. She's having the lump removed and then she's probably going to need chemotherapy."

My hands began to shake violently.

"Kate?"

"Is she going to be OK? Is it bad?"

"We won't know until after the lumpectomy, which she's having on Thursday."

"How is she?"

"Not good. She seems to have fallen apart."

"Can I talk to her?"

"No. She's gone to drop the boys to music lessons. Besides, she doesn't know I'm calling you. You know what she's like, never wants to worry anyone."

My head was throbbing. "Does Dad know?"

"She's too afraid to tell him. Especially with your mother's history."

"Oh, God — poor Dad! This'll kill him. Do the boys know?"

20

"Not yet," said Mark, choking up. "We're going to need help with them, so I don't want to say anything until we've arranged something. Actually, that's why I'm calling. Could you come home and look after them?"

"Sure, I'll come home tomorrow for the day and try to get back every chance I have between recording the show."

"The problem is, Fiona's going to need full-time help for the foreseeable future. It could be three months, it could be six."

"But if I come home every opportunity I can, and if you work part-time, we should be able to manage."

"Unfortunately the timing couldn't be worse. I'm completely swamped with this Goldwin Prize paper and Fiona won't hear of me giving it up. She became hysterical when I mentioned it. She said my work on the paper would keep her going, that it would be a really positive focus for us in the middle of this nightmare. She thinks she can manage on her own, but she can't, Kate. She's struggling already. She needs someone to be there all the time for the boys, someone she trusts and who knows them," he said getting emotional again.

"But, Mark, I can't give up my job and move back. I've only just got my own show after eight years' hard slog. I'll help in any way I can — I'll come back at every opportunity — but I can't be there full-time. You can work on your project when the boys are asleep and I'll be back every week and Dad can pitch in. We'll muddle through."

"Muddling through isn't good enough," said Mark, suddenly sounding angry. "We have a crisis on our hands. Fiona has cancer. She's always been there for you — she gave up her youth to bring you up when your mother died. You owe her, Kate."

"Look, I've said I'll do what I can and I —"

"I have to go! She's back, and she'd kill me if she knew I was asking you for a favour," whispered Mark. "Kate, I need an answer within the hour, or I'll have to start calling nanny agencies. She's going into hospital on Thursday. Call me back as soon as you've made your decision."

I stared at the phone in shock. I wasn't Mark's biggest fan, but he'd never been rude before. I understood that he was upset, but he didn't have to try to blackmail me into moving back. Who did he think he was, telling me I owed Fiona? Telling me she'd given up her youth for me. I knew exactly what Fiona had done — she'd been amazing and I *did* owe her. But I loved my job. It had taken me so long to get to this point in my career. Why did *I* have to give everything up and not Mark? He was her husband. They were his children. Stuff his stupid prize. He'd have to put his foot down and tell Fiona she came first, not work. I'd help as much as I could. He needed to understand that my presenting job was a one-in-a-million opportunity and as important to me as his Goldwin Prize was to him.

I called him back and told him as much. There was a deathly silence at the other end of the line.

"What you don't seem to be grasping here," he said coldly, "is that your sister has begged me to continue with the prize paper. Of course I'd give it up if I thought it would help, but she made me promise not to. I realize your job means a lot to you, but you're young, you'll pick up another job as soon as all this is over. Right now, you need to focus on Fiona."

"I *can't* give it up. It's my life! I don't have a husband or kids — this job is it for me. I'm sorry, but giving it up just isn't possible. I'll talk to my producer and see if I can come back for two days a week or something."

"Do you have any idea what's been going on here while you've been chasing your career in London? For the last eight years Fiona's nursed your father every time he's had the flu or a cold and she's the one who always boosts Derek's confidence when he gets yet another knock-back for his music. She's spent her life looking after your family but she can't do it any more. She's sick and it's your turn now. It's time for you to step up and be responsible. She needs to concentrate on getting better. You owe her, Kate."

I really wish he'd stop saying that. It had got to me because he was right — I owed Fiona a lot and she had never asked me for anything.

"Well?" he asked.

"I can't decide now. I need time to think about it. I *can't* give up my job and move home. I'll see if I can work round it."

"Your sister has cancer, the same cancer your mother died from at the same age. How *can* you put your job first? She never put herself first when it came to *you*. She gave up everything to make sure you and Derek had a happy childhood. Do you have any idea how difficult that was for her? You have to come home and help her with the boys."

"Why can't *you* look after her? To hell with your stupid maths prize! Your wife and children are more important," I snapped, panicking as reality hit me. I knew now I'd have to move back. I couldn't leave her.

"How eloquently put. I can see why you appeal so much to the dumbed-down television generation. Much as I'd love to sit here and argue with you, I have to sort out care for my wife and children. If you're not going to help, I need to start calling agencies."

"Wait!" I said, and my heart sank. "Don't call anyone else. I'll come back."

"Thank you," said Mark, sounding relieved.

When I hung up I realized I was shaking, with shock about Fiona and fury with Mark for having forced my hand. Why was it up to me to look after his wife and kids? Hadn't he married Fiona in sickness and in health? Why did responsibility for his family fall on my shoulders? How long would it be for? Would I ever work again?

How would we get on living in each other's pockets? Fiona and I were very different. She was responsible, *über*-organized and happy for her career to take second place to Mark and the twins. I was restless, ambitious and impulsive. Fiona craved a secure family unit, while the thought of settling down made me feel claustrophobic.

24

She had been a child genius and member of Mensa, while I had struggled to pass exams of any kind.

Fiona had spent her life being my surrogate mother, worrying about me, fussing over me, but as I got older and she continued to mother me it had become a bit suffocating. Moving to London had been incredibly liberating. How would Fiona react to me taking care of her and her children? It wouldn't be easy.

I took a few deep breaths and tried to process the information: Fiona had cancer, the same cancer Mum had died from.

Mum had only lived eight months after she was diagnosed. If Fiona only had eight months to live, how could I not be there for her? On the other hand, she might get better and live to be ninety. But could I take that chance? In my heart I knew I only had one choice. My sister needed me and Mark was right: I did owe her.

I had twenty-four hours to tape the new show and beg my producer, Donna, for leave of absence. I was doing the right thing, the only thing, but I was terrified. I had left Dublin eight years ago in search of fame and fortune and had just reached D-list fame, with the fortune yet to come — but at least I was free, anonymous, away from the goldfish bowl of Dublin and Fiona's lifelong habit of trying to fix me. I dreaded going back. I knew it would be as if the last eight years had never happened. I'd have to try and persuade Donna to keep my position open. I had to able to come back. It was the only thing that'd get me through.

# CHAPTER
# FOUR

I got through to Fiona later that day.

"Hi, Kate," said my sister, sounding tired.

"Fiona, Mark told me about the result, I'm so sorry. I'm coming home tomorrow to help. I'll stay as long as you need me. I'll look after the twins and you and . . . Oh, Fiona, I can't believe it's happened to you," I said, and began to sob.

"Don't do that. No tears, it'll be fine. The lump is there and it has to come out, and then I'll have the chemo and it'll all be over. You don't have to come back. I'm fine," said Fiona, sounding hollow.

"I'm coming home and that's the end of it. I'm catching a flight tomorrow night. What time is the lump-thingy?"

"It's a lumpectomy and it's scheduled for Thursday morning. It's unnecessary for you to be here, Kate."

"Look, I'm coming and it's non-negotiable. Have you told Dad?"

"No," said Fiona, her voice catching. "I can't seem to find the right time," she said, and broke down.

"You're going to be fine," I said, as much to reassure myself as her. "Do you want me to tell Dad?"

"Yes," said Fiona, regaining her composure. "I have to go now. It's time for the twins' bedtime story."

"What are you reading them?"

"Mark found a book called *Inventors and Inventions*, which they love."

"But they're only five!"

"It's never too early to stimulate the brain."

Those poor boys, I thought, having to listen to some boring story about inventions. I'd rather boil my head! For once, though, I decided to bite my tongue. Fiona didn't need me to stick my oar in. Besides, what did I know about kids? I had little or no interest in them. Although I was fond of the twins, I found that after an hour with them I'd had enough and so had they. Fiona, on the other hand, had the patience of a saint.

"Fiona?"

"Yes?"

"Just, you know, it'll be OK and —"

"Goodbye, Kate," she said, cutting me off before I could get soppy on her.

After hanging up I decided to call someone and go out for a drink. I needed to talk. I thought about all the friends I'd made over the last eight years. I'd met some lovely people but none of them was a friend I could offload to about this kind of personal problem. The only person I could really talk to was Tara, my best friend from home.

Tara knew me inside-out and upside-down. Our mothers discovered we were the same age when Tara's family, the Dennys, had bought the house across from ours and we'd been inseparable from the age of six. When Mum died, Mrs Denny had been really good to me. I spent more time in the Dennys' house than I did in ours. It was fun over there, cosy and homely. Our house was run like an army camp, with Fiona constantly making charts that Derek and I had to fill in after each chore we'd completed.

I think the reason Tara and I got on so well was because we were fundamentally different. She had never felt the urge to run away from Dublin. She loved it. She liked the fact that everyone knew everyone: it was nice, safe and familiar. I found it small and claustrophobic. Tara was comfortable with who she was, and I'd always envied her that. She had always been happy with her lot, while I was always searching for something better.

Tara was the only friend I'd stayed in touch with. She and I had kept up to date with each other's lives — the good, bad and ugly bits. I was always totally honest with her and had often rung her in tears, frustrated and fed up that it was taking so long for my career to get off the ground. I was the first person she'd called after she'd met Tom and realized he was "the one". We shared everything. She was the person I needed to talk to now.

I picked up the phone and dialled.

"Hello?"

"Hi, Tara, it's me."

"How's it going?"

"Uhm, not so good, actually."

"What's wrong?"

"It's Fiona. She's got breast cancer."

"Oh, my God, Kate! Is it bad? Is she OK?"

"They're doing a lumpectomy on Thursday and she'll probably have to have chemo, but they don't know yet if it's spread."

"Oh, Kate, that's terrible. Poor Fiona. How are Mark and the boys?"

"Don't talk to me about Mark! He demanded I give up my job and move home for six months to look after everyone while he focuses on work. He was very heavy-handed with the emotional blackmail."

"Are you?"

"Coming home?"

"Yeah."

"I have to. I owe Fiona."

"What about your show?"

"I'm going to ask for leave of absence, but I won't get it. I'll probably lose the job for good," I said, trying to sound as if I didn't mind all that much. "Hopefully I'll get something else in six months' time."

"That can't be easy. You worked so hard to get that job."

I fought back tears. "I know, but sure it's only a job, and Fiona needs me so I don't have a choice."

"I guess it's your kind of payback to her. How's your poor dad?"

"He doesn't know yet. I'm going to ring him after this. Fiona's too scared to tell him because of —" I stifled a sob.

"Your mum."

"Yes."

"Oh, Kate, don't worry. Lots of women with breast cancer get better now. And Fiona's a fighter — she'll be fine and I'm sure she'll really appreciate you coming home. You're doing the right thing. And it'll be nice to spend some time with your family. You see them so rarely now."

"Tara?"

"Yes?"

"I'm scared of that."

"What?"

"Spending all that time at home. I feel as if I don't know them any more. I mean, obviously I know them, but sometimes I feel like a bit of an outsider."

"That's because you haven't spent any length of time with them in the last few years. This is your chance to get back into the fold. It'll be good for all of you. And I'll be here if they start driving you round the twist."

"Thanks, Tara."

"So you'll be looking after the twins?"

"I suppose so."

Tara began to laugh. The very *idea* of me looking after two five-year-olds was enough to set her off. "Who would have thought it, Kate? You — Mary Poppins!"

"Don't. I've no idea what to do with kids. Though, knowing Fiona, I'll be left a rigid timetable so, hopefully, it won't be too bad."

"As long as she doesn't expect you to teach them maths," said Tara, giggling.

"I doubt Fiona would leave that up to me after the fiasco with the Rubik's cube."

"How long did it take you to figure it out?"

"A mere nine months," I said, laughing. "It took Fiona about nine minutes and Derek still can't do it."

We laughed at the thought of Derek with a Rubik's cube. He was so laid-back he almost sleep-walked through life. He'd sauntered through school, failing most of his exams because study came under the banner of stress — and Derek didn't do stress. Besides, he was convinced his future lay in music, and all knock-backs and criticisms only made him more determined. He had a band, which consisted of him and his best friend Gonzo whose real name was Frank Murphy: he'd been nicknamed after Gonzo from *The Muppets* because he had a hook nose — he'd tried to change it to Maverick after he'd seen Tom Cruise in *Top Gun* but his friends had laughed at him and told him to look in the mirror. The band was called Rap-sodie and was so bad it was almost funny.

"I'd better call Dad," I said, as the laughter faded and a knot formed in my stomach.

"Good luck."

"Thanks, I'll need it."

I decided I needed some Dutch courage before calling Dad so I knocked back a glass of wine. I've always wondered why they call it Dutch courage. Surely it should be Irish courage — aren't we the most famous nation for drinking? Or are the Dutch all secret alcoholics?

Anyway, the wine calmed me down and I dialled home.

Derek answered. "Yo."

"Hi, Derek, it's me. Is Dad there?"

"Hey, sis, whazzup?"

"Has it ever occurred to you that you are neither black nor American?" I said, taking my nervousness out on him.

"What has you in such a good mood?"

"Just get Dad, will you?"

"OK, keep your hair on. By the way, did you ask your producer if me and Gonzo can come on your show?"

"No, Derek, I didn't. Your stuff is crap and you'll have to come up with something a lot better if you want to get on the show."

"Right. Thanks for the support. I'll go and get Dad so you can abuse him, you grumpy cow."

"Derek, I'm sorry —" I said, as Derek shouted at Dad.

"*Daaaaaad* — Kate's on the phone. She's in great form, a regular ray of sunshine. She just ate the face off me, so watch what you say."

"What's he on about?" said Dad, picking up the phone.

"I was a bit mean about his music."

"Jesus, don't talk to me. It's the worst tripe I've ever heard. That lad needs to accept that he's not going to end up in Madison Square Garden. Anyway, how are you, pet? Did you get back all right?"

"Dad, I need to come home for a bit, if that's OK," I said, as my voice broke. Just hearing him made me want to weep. He'd been through so much and I was about to land him with more heartbreak.

"Hey, now, Katie. What's wrong? What's happened? Was some bastard mean to you? Did you break up with a boyfriend?"

"No, Dad, you need to have a boyfriend before you can break up with him. It's Fiona, she's kind of sick and I have to come home to help out."

"Sick?" said Dad. I could tell he didn't like the sound of that. Fiona was never sick. "What do you mean? What's wrong with her?"

"She's found a lump, Dad. It's not a good one."

Silence.

"Dad? Are you all right?"

"Jesus Christ, I think I'm having a heart-attack. Hold on till I sit down. My heart is pounding. *Derek*," he roared, "get me a drink, I'm having a heart-attack."

"Do you not think an ambulance would be more useful?" I heard Derek drawl.

"Get up off your lazy arse and get me a drink."

"Dad, I hate to interrupt your shouting-match with Derek, but Fiona's sick so I'm afraid you can't have a heart-attack right now."

"I'm all right now. Sorry, pet. What exactly is it?" asked Dad, still panting from the near coronary.

"It's a little lump. They want to take it out and examine it. It's probably not that bad at all," I said.

"Where's the lump?"

I winced. "It's on her breast."

"So it's breast cancer?" Dad whispered. I knew he was thinking his beautiful Fiona couldn't have breast cancer. This couldn't be happening to him again. God couldn't be so cruel as to take his wife and his daughter.

"It looks like it. They're going to cut it out and examine it," I said, as my father shuddered. "I'm sure it'll be *fiiiiine*." I burst into tears. This wasn't how the conversation was supposed to go. I had planned to be strong and reassuring and already I was failing miserably

Dad forgot about his heart and went into organizing mode. "OK, don't get upset. Have you booked your flight?"

"Yes."

"What time do you land?"

"Seven."

"I'll be there to meet you and we'll get the best doctors in the country to look after her. We'll fix this, Katie, don't you worry. We will sort this mess out. Fiona is not going to die. Not from that bastard of a disease. Just you get home and I'll take care of everything else," he said.

"Dad?"

"Yes, pet?"

"I won't be working for a while so I might need you to help me with my rent."

"For God's sake, Kate, you're thirty years old. You need to take responsibility for your life. I thought you were getting paid a fortune on this new show."

"The salary was better but I'll have to give it up to come home, so I'll be broke again."

"At your age! It's ridiculous. How many times did I say it to you? You have to put something aside for a rainy day —"

"Dad! Can you save the rainy-day speech for another time? I don't need you shouting at me. I'm stressed enough as it is."

The extension phone clicked. "Yo, I don't know what's up with you two, but the ambulance is on its way for you, Dad, and FYI, I don't think you're supposed to be shouting when you're having a heart-attack. If you need CPR, can you hurry up and let me know coz I'm going out to a gig with Gonzo in ten momentos," drawled Derek.

# CHAPTER
# FIVE

Sleep evaded me that night: I woke up time and again from a recurring nightmare of giant breasts chasing me down a street. Finally I dragged myself out of bed and made a large cup of strong coffee. I shuddered as I remembered Fiona's voice — so lifeless.

On automatic pilot, I showered, dressed and went to work. I got there before anyone else did and found two large Post-its stuck to my computer screen. One was from my producer, Donna, wanting to know why the hell I'd freaked out during an important interview, and the other was from Gary, the cameraman, telling me that Donna was doing her nut.

I went through the tapes of the interview with the teenage star. There was very little we could use, but maybe if we interspersed it with trailers from the film, we'd get away with it. I sat down to write a grovelling email to the PR lady who had evicted me from Claridges. I decided to try the woman-to-woman approach and explained that I was having some personal problems and that I'd never meant to insult the wonderful Anna-Lisa and I was planning to give the film a rave review. By the time Donna arrived in, I had managed — with the help of super-editor Gordon — to piece together a usable five minutes of footage. I spent the rest of the morning compiling the other segments of the show, then went to tell Donna I was leaving.

I knocked on her office door and popped my head in. "Hi, Donna."

"What the bloody hell's going on? I've had the PR woman from Warner Brothers screaming down the phone at me because my presenter abused her precious star."

"Donna, calm down. I can explain."

"It'd better be good."

"I found out yesterday that my sister has breast cancer. I was upset and a bit distracted during the interview, but it's all sorted now. I've apologized and pieced together a decent segment for the show. The thing is, though, I have to go home and be with my family for a while. It'll just be for a month or so," I lied. "I was thinking maybe I could tape the show from Dublin or something." I was grasping at straws.

"Look, Kate, I'm really sorry to hear about your sister, but we can't shoot the show from Dublin," said Donna, cursing under her breath. She had a show to air and no presenter.

"I'll be back before you know it," I said, trying to sound *blasé*. "Why don't you get Colin to fill in for a few weeks?" I was desperate not to have some younger, fitter girl take over my precious show.

"Yeah, maybe. I'll have a think," said Donna. "How many weeks will you be gone? We need to know."

"It's hard to say exactly, but it'll probably stretch to a couple of months," I said, and watched Donna's face fall.

"Two?"

"Maybe three or four," I said, hating the words.

"Bloody typical! I manage to find someone really good and now this happens. You're one of the best we've had and, let's be honest, the male audience doesn't just tune in for your accent or your one-liners — your legs were a big asset. Anyway, I'd better get on with finding someone to take your place. Good luck, keep in touch." Donna already considered me old goods.

In this business you get one shot and you work hard and cling to it until a better offer comes your way. You never, ever walk away from a good job in the limelight and hand your profile over to someone else on a silver platter. My heart plummeted. I'd be forgotten in no time. I felt sick.

I thanked Donna and went into the bathroom and wept — for Fiona, my mother and myself.

# CHAPTER
# SIX

As I sat on the plane, looking out the window, I thought about Dad and the difficult life he had led. Born and reared in a small town ten miles outside Galway, he was the eldest of seven children. His father had died when he was thirteen and his mother was barely able to make ends meet. So, aged fourteen he left school and went out to find work. His first job was as an usher in a small cinema in Galway. There and then he fell in love with the movies. Within three years he was manager, and two years later he took out a loan to buy a run-down building in the centre of Galway, which he transformed into a three-screen cinema — the first in the city. A few years later, he was in Dublin, looking at the way the big cinemas were run, when he met and fell head over heels in love with Sarah Boland, a beautiful nurse. He was a plain, working-class man, but he was funny and made her laugh like no one else could. Within a year they were married. He sold up in Galway and bought the George cinema in Dublin. Nine years later they had accumulated two daughters, a son and two more cinemas.

From what I can remember they were happy together. So, when Mum died, not only was he heartbroken but he had been left alone to raise three young children. Poor Dad had no idea how to cope with two growing daughters, not to mind a baby son. When Fiona had come into his room aged thirteen to say she had just got her period, Dad had turned a deep shade of purple, then taken her to the chemist and asked the assistant to show her what products she needed while he waited outside. By the time I got my period, at twelve, Dad was used to seeing Tampax and sanitary towels on the shopping list.

However, he had struggled with the sex-education issue. He knew what it was like to be a horny teenager and he didn't want pimply youths with raging hormones near his girls. So he gave Fiona and me a book on how the body works — which he discreetly wrapped in brown paper so that we wouldn't be embarrassed when he handed it over. Then he told us that boys were off limits until we were thirty. He regularly mentioned how wonderful he thought Mother Teresa was and how she seemed to be in desperate need of helpers: would we not think of becoming nuns and helping the poor? This was met with much eye-rolling and "As if!" from his healthy, heterosexual teenage daughters.

When I decided I wanted to go to discos, Dad was at a loss. When I asked, he said no.

"Why?"

"Because I said no and that's the end of it."

"You have to let me go. Everyone's going. I'll be the only person in my class not there."

"It's good to be different. It'll make you stand out from the crowd."

"Different! I'll be the laughing-stock of the school. Do you want me to be the class loser? The person everyone feels sorry for because she's never allowed out? Do you want me to have no friends?" I screeched.

"Jesus, my eardrums. Calm down. No one's going to think you're an outcast because you don't go to this dance."

"It's a disco, not a stupid dance, and I have to go. Give me one good reason why I can't go."

"Because I said so."

"Everyone else's parents are letting them go."

"Good for them."

"Dad, you can't do this to me! I have to go! I don't want to be the class nerd! Do you want me to be bullied and cast out of my group?"

"Your sister's never gone to a disco and she's plenty friends. Now, stop your nonsense, you're not going."

Bloody Fiona, I thought bitterly. All she did was study. She had been the school super-brain and was now in her first year at university, studying pure mathematics. She'd never wanted to go to discos when she was still at school because she spent her spare time at chess or maths clubs.

"Fiona and I are different," I reminded him, determined to wear him down. "Different people have different needs. Fiona likes playing chess with other nerds, I want to go and dance with my friends."

"You'd be much better off playing chess."

"Dad, Fiona was born with brains, I was born with . . ." I wasn't sure what I'd been born with. Average height, average looks, and average ability in sports and schoolwork. I didn't shine at anything. My friends told me I was funny, but who wanted to be funny when guys were only interested in looks?

"I'm waiting with bated breath. What were you born with, apart from a big mouth?" said Dad, grinning behind his newspaper.

"Pizzazz," I announced, delighted with myself for having thought that one up.

"Pizzazz!" snorted Dad. "And is that going to get you into college?"

"Liza Minnelli has it, Judy Garland had it, uhm . . ." I racked my brain to come up with other successful movie stars.

"Judy Garland died of drugs and poor Liza's been on a rocky road. A bit less pizzazz from you, madam, and a bit more studying. This conversation is over," he said, muttering that I was a handful.

"Dad," I said, voice quavering, "if you don't let me go to this disco I will never forgive you."

"Kate," said Dad, "if you don't get out of my sight I will send you to a boarding-school where they only let you out to go to mass and pray for your lost soul."

I never made it to that disco, but after a weekend of following Dad around in my pyjamas crying, and asking him to drive me to the Samaritans so I could get counselling on how to cope without friends, he let me go the following month. Anything for an easy life.

As I walked through the Arrivals door, I felt nervous. I had no idea what the next six months would hold. Would Fiona get better? How would I cope with the twins? What was I going to do when they didn't need me any more? I had no job, no life. I wanted to turn round and run. "Get a grip," I muttered angrily to myself.

I took a deep breath and walked through the Arrivals door, dragging my enormous suitcase. Dad was at the barrier, hopping from one foot to the other, with Derek beside him, eyeing up the young bronzed chicks coming back from their holidays.

Earlier, Dad had told Derek that I was moving home because Fiona was sick and asked him to come to the airport because he was afraid he might have a heart-attack in the car. He didn't want to die on the way to the airport, and have me arrive with nobody to collect me. Derek pointed out that if he did have a heart-attack while he was driving the car, the chances were that Derek would die in the crash, too, or end up paralysed, so maybe they should get a taxi. But Dad said he needed to drive: it would keep his mind occupied and stop him panicking about Fiona.

"So what exactly is wrong with her?" asked Derek, clutching the dashboard as Dad skidded out of the driveway on two wheels.

"She's found a lump and they think it's cancer."

"Bummer," said Derek, exhaling deeply.

"I've just told you your sister might have cancer and all you can say is 'bummer'. That's all you can come up with after I spent thirty thousand shagging pounds on a private education for you?"

"Chill, Dad, she'll be fine."

"And tell me, Einstein, how do you know that?"

"Cos," said Derek, as if it was the most obvious thing in the world, "Fiona *is* this family."

"How right you are," said Dad, marvelling at the fact that, once in a while, when you least expected it, Derek would come out with something that made sense.

He looked at his son, who was dressed, as usual, in baggy black T-shirt and jeans with the backside hanging down to his knees. His shaggy black hair stuck out in tufts from underneath a woolly hat. He spoke like one of those American rappers and half the time Dad didn't understand what he was saying. All Derek wanted in life was to make it in the music business, and if he had one prevalent characteristic it was his eternal optimism. He firmly believed that he was destined to be a famous rap star and no amount of criticism was going to sway him.

On his twenty-sixth birthday Dad had sat him down and told him that he had one more year to make it and after that he had to get a real job. He said he was sick of all this messing about. Derek would have to face reality at some stage and this time next year, if he wasn't on M-bloody-TV morning, noon and night, he was going to work for Dad full-time. Not part-time as he did at the moment, to earn money to pay for studio bookings: he was going to learn the ropes and take over as manager of the cinemas. Derek had nodded and smiled and told Dad not to sweat it: he was on the cusp of fame.

Now Dad rushed over to hug me. I snuggled into his jumper and we tried not to cry. Derek was staring lustfully at a young blonde in a very short denim mini.

"Hi, Derek," I said. "Sorry for being a cow on the phone. I was a bit stressed out."

"No worries. Dad told me Fiona's got the big C. He's totally freaking out, he nearly crashed, like, fifty times driving out here," he said.

"Don't mind him, I'm fine. Come on, let's get you home. Derek, grab Kate's suitcase there, will you?" said Dad, trying not to look at my swollen red eyes.

When we got to the car, Derek tried several times to lift my suitcase into the boot and eventually had to ask Dad for help.

"I can't with my back," said Dad.

"Dad! It weighs more than I do. I need some help."

Dad bent down and tried to pick it up. "Jesus wept! What in God's name is in here, Kate?"

"I didn't know what I'd need, or how long I'd be staying, so I brought pretty much everything."

"Oh, God, oh, no — I think I've slipped a disc." Dad staggered around in a circle, gripping his back. Derek and I glanced at each other and tried not to laugh. Dad was obsessed with his back. He had slipped a disc fifteen years ago, and although it had mended itself perfectly, we had been hearing about it ever since. Everywhere you sat in the house you were attacked by some form of orthopaedic support. They would thump you in the spine as you sat down in an armchair to

45

watch TV, and in his car was a veritable treasure trove of back support cushions: he had rattan cool covers, lumbar-support and doughnut-pillow cushions, inflatable pads . . . If you wanted to know anything about backs, Dad was your man.

"Here, give it to me," I said, and hauled the suitcase into the boot, much to Derek's amusement. Meanwhile Dad was sitting in the driver's seat, inflating his back pad for the journey home. I climbed in behind him.

Home sweet home.

# CHAPTER
# SEVEN

I always liked the first five minutes of arriving into the house. The familiarity of my bedroom, the photos on the wall in the hall, the warmth of the kitchen . . . The brief period before I began to feel claustrophobic and edgy was the best part of coming back.

As I began to unpack there was a knock on the door. I opened it and came face to face with Derek's best friend and bandmate, Gonzo.

"Any chance of some lovin'?" he asked, grinning.

"Zero," I said, ducking as he lunged.

Gonzo had been trying to have sex with me since his considerable hormones had kicked in when he turned twelve. Fiona, at eight years older than him, was out of his league so he focused all his energies on me — with the mere four-year age gap. He had spent his teenage years skulking around the house behind me, even though I had slapped him, thumped him, kicked him, roared at him and once even resorted to hitting him over the head with a saucepan. He never stopped trying.

Like Derek, Gonzo was an eternal optimist. Unlike Derek, he was only interested in the band because he thought it would attract girls and get him laid. So far it hadn't been working very well — and I could tell, from his lunge, that he was badly in need of a shag. Hell would freeze over before I'd oblige. Apart from being my little brother's friend, Gonzo was smaller than me, thinner than me and had some serious personal-hygiene issues.

He sat down on my bed and picked up a bra. "Ooh," he said, holding it to his face.

"Stop it, you pervert," I said, grabbing it back.

"So, like, Derek tells me you're home for good."

"No, just for a few months to help out."

"Cos Fiona has the big C."

"Yes."

"Great ass."

"What?"

"Oh, sorry, did I say that out loud? I was just admiring your *derrière*."

"Jesus, Gonzo, we were talking about Fiona being sick — can't you stop thinking about sex for ten seconds?"

"Not with that kind of perfection in my face."

I ignored him and carried on unpacking.

"So I totally watch you all the time on your show."

"Do you think it's good?"

"I think you're good. I like the short skirts — great pins should be shared with the world."

"Oh, God, Gonzo, how long has it been?"

"Too long, dude."

"There must be some girl your age who'd take pity on you."

48

"That's the problem. Girls my own age are too immature. I need an older woman."

"Well, you're barking up the wrong tree here. It's been fourteen years now. It's time to look elsewhere."

"Perfection is worth the wait. Besides — you complete me."

"Get some original chat-up lines and stop quoting from movies. Everyone knows that line from *Jerry Maguire*. Tom Cruise is the only man who can get away with saying it."

"Are *you* getting any?" Gonzo asked.

"None of your business."

"Well, if you get lonely while you're home, you know where to find me," he said, and winked as he stood up to leave.

"Knickers, please," I said, holding out my hand for the red thong I'd seen him hide in his pocket.

Derek arrived at the door as his friend handed it back. "Dude, she's my sister."

"Sorry, dude, I'm in love," said Gonzo, and walked out of the room.

Derek rolled his eyes. "Dad told me to tell you Fiona rang. She wants you to call over now."

"OK."

I was dreading seeing Fiona. I knew the minute I clapped eyes on her that I'd want to hug her and cry, but she hated displays of emotion. Having been dragged into adulthood at twelve, she had learnt to deal with everything that came her way calmly and efficiently.

When we were younger Dad had tried to help out, but he had a business to run. In the end he'd hired Molly, who came in to clean and cook from Mondays to Fridays, but Derek and I hated the food she prepared and refused to eat it, so Fiona ended up with the cooking. Molly stuck to cleaning, ironing and telling us sad stories about her ten brothers and sisters and their thirty-two children.

Over the years we heard about relations who "suffered terrible from their nerves", others who had gone down the slippery slope of gambling, drinking, cavorting outside wedlock, drug-taking, teenage pregnancy — but the final straw for Molly was when one of her nephews turned out to be "queer". This apparently was worse than all the rest put together.

We had no idea what it meant, but from the look on Molly's face it was very bad news. Fiona looked it up in the dictionary when Molly left and read out: " 'Strange, odd, eccentric, ill, homosexual.' "

"What's that mean?" I asked.

Fiona shrugged and turned to "homosexual." " 'Feeling or involving sexual attraction to people of same sex.' " She went red and shut the dictionary, but I still didn't understand. She told me to forget about it and left the room.

When Dad came home later, I decided to ask him. "What's 'queer'?"

"Strange," he said, shovelling mashed potato into his mouth.

"What's homosexual?"

"*What?*" he spluttered. "Where did you hear that?"

"Molly said it. What's it mean?"

Dad put down his fork and chose his words carefully. "It's when a boy likes a boy or a girl likes a girl."

"I like Tara so am I homosexual?"

"No, pet, it's more than that — it's when a boy wants another boy to be his, uhm, well, I suppose to be his boyfriend. So instead of a boy and a girl being together it's a boy and a boy or a girl and a girl together."

I wasn't sure how to process this. "Like Derek and Frank?" (This was before Frank was renamed Gonzo and developed hormones.)

"No. It's when a boy loves a boy and wants to marry him. Or two girls want to marry," said Dad, floundering.

I frowned. Boys getting married was news to me. For some reason I wasn't so bothered by the idea of girls doing it. Tara and I were always playing husband and wife. "Do they kiss other boys?"

"Yes, they do."

"Yuck."

"Well, I'd have to agree with you there. It wouldn't be my cup of tea."

"Do we know any?"

"Rock Hudson," said Dad, deciding to use someone I idolized as a positive role model.

"But he kisses Doris Day and they're married."

"In the films they are, but not in real life. In real life, Rock likes to kiss boys."

I was devastated. I had planned to marry Rock when I grew up and spend my days in yellow headscarves driving around in open-top cars drinking martinis and generally having a swell time. This was long before I saw *Dirty Dancing* and gave my heart to Patrick Swayze. Molly had done untold damage to my future by bringing queerness into my house and ruining my marriage prospects. I never fully forgave her and decided to write Doris Day a letter to inform her of Rock's sexual leanings — after all, the poor woman was making a fool of herself in all those films as his wife. Dad promised he'd post it for me, and produced it eleven years later on my twenty-first birthday when he read it out to Fiona and Derek's hysterical laughter.

I took a deep breath and rang the bell. Fiona answered the door, looking wretched. Her eyes were in the back of her head and her face was a shade of pale I'd never seen before. I hugged her and blinked back the tears that were forming in my eyes.

"Good to see you, Kate," she said, prising herself away from me.

"You too. Now tell me what you want me to do," I said, in an over-cheery voice.

"I'm feeding the boys," she said, leading the way to the kitchen where pandemonium was taking place.

Jack was trying to throw his carrots on to Bobby's plate and he in turn was chucking broccoli on to Bobby's. Teddy, meanwhile, was lapping up the bits that fell on to the floor.

Mark's surname was Kennedy and he had insisted on naming the twins Jack and Bobby and the dog Teddy. I suppose it showed he had a sense of humour — although he kept it well hidden.

"Say hello to Auntie Kate," Fiona said, as the boys stared at me. They saw me only twice a year and, truth be told, I wasn't exactly full-on then. I never knew what to say to or do with them, so I did the usual adult thing and asked them questions, which they tired of pretty quickly. Now I felt nervous — I had absolutely no idea how to relate to or look after these two little boys.

"Hello, Auntie Kate, do you have more presents for us?" shouted Jack, the more boisterous of the two.

Damn, I should have brought them something. Mind you, with my track-record of present-buying they'd probably have hated it. "Sorry, boys, no presents today, but I'll get you something tomorrow."

"Don't be silly. They don't need any more presents," said Fiona, firmly. "Jack, it's rude to ask for presents. Now eat your dinner." Jack fed Teddy another broccoli floret.

"Are you going to take us to school tomorrow?" asked Bobby.

"Yes, she is," said Fiona. She turned to me and said, in her best teacher's voice, "I've been telling the boys you'll be looking after them when I'm feeling a bit tired from the medicine that's going to make me better."

"Mummy's sick," said Jack. "She has a cancer."

"She's got a bad lump," said Bobby.

"But the doctor's going to take it out and throw it in the bin," said Jack.

"And then she's going to get medicine to kill the bad cells," said Bobby.

"And then she'll be better."

"Wow," I said. "You guys have it all under control." Then, to Fiona, "So they know about everything?"

"It's important for them not to be afraid. Information takes away fear," she said, then kissed them and told them how clever they were for remembering all the information. They basked in her praise. Then, pointing to me, she said, "Now, you know that Kate will be putting you to bed tomorrow night while Mummy goes to the hospital. It's only for one night, so you're to be good for her."

The boys nodded.

"Will we show Kate what we do at bedtime so she can follow the routine?" asked Fiona. "Let's start with our bath."

With that the two boys raced up the stairs and flung off their clothes.

# CHAPTER
# EIGHT

After a noisy bath, which left both Fiona and me drenched, I helped her put the twins into their pyjamas and then she read them a story from *Inventors and Inventions*. The way she read it made it sound interesting even to me. I leant back against the wall and watched the two bent heads hanging on her every word. She was a natural-born educator — maybe if I'd had a maths teacher like Fiona, I wouldn't have been such a dunce with numbers.

After she had qualified with a first in pure maths — Mark got a first too, but Fiona's marks were higher — Fiona decided to devote her life to teaching. Having seen how bad Derek and I were at maths, she was determined to make it more interesting and appealing to young people. She had landed a job teaching at an all-girls school and, by all accounts, was liked, respected and feared by her pupils. Maths was a vocation for Fiona. She wanted to rid it of its nerdy-and-boring reputation and spent a lot of time and energy making her classes interesting.

To be fair, she also loved teaching because it afforded her so much free time with the twins. They meant the world to her and she was determined to be with them as much as she could. To be a mother on her own terms, as opposed to having the role foisted on her at twelve, was a completely different experience. She had found it a chore to bring up Derek and me but raising the twins was pure joy. She relished her role and, as usual with Fiona, she became the best she could be — cooking them home-made organic meals, reading to them every night, teaching them the piano and playing stimulating games with them when she was so tired she could barely keep her eyes open. She had the patience of a saint — a virtue that had passed me by. Clearly she had got my share too. But all this, plus looking after Mark, preparing and correcting classwork had left little time for Fiona to look after herself. As a result she seemed tired and older than her thirty-four years.

Mark had chosen a more ambitious route and gone on to become a college lecturer. He had spent nine years playing the political game like the chess master he was, which had led to his recent appointment as head of mathematics at Dublin University. At thirty-five, he was the youngest person ever to hold the post — which he wasn't shy about telling you.

It was all very well for him to focus on his career, but it left Fiona to do the lion's share of parenting and home-making. No wonder she was tired: it was a one-woman show. Whenever I had raised this with her in the past, she had laughed and said marriage was about compromise and that Mark's success provided them with a lifestyle they wouldn't otherwise have had. Because of him, the boys would be going to the best private school in Dublin and would have all the extra-curricular lessons and tutoring they needed. When I said I thought they'd be better off going to the local national school she shook her head and said that gifted children needed special guidance. The twins seemed bright enough, but I wasn't sure about gifted. High-spirited, maybe, but I didn't see any signs of genius, but then, hey, what did I know? I was single and in a job that required little or no intellect.

Once the twins had nodded off, I asked Fiona when Mark was due home. She looked at her watch. "Oh, probably not for another hour."

"How come he's so late?"

"He's busy with the paper for the Goldwin Prize. He's flat out, poor thing."

I resisted the urge to tell her that I thought it disgraceful that her husband was showing up at nine o'clock on the night before her lumpectomy. Surely his stupid paper could have waited until tomorrow. "Can I get you anything?" I asked.

"No, I'm fine. I'll just clean up here and then we can go through the boys' routine for tomorrow."

"I'll do that. Go and sit down — you look exhausted."

"I'm fine, Kate. Leave it," she said, grabbing the plates from my hand.

"Fiona!" I said sharply. "Sit down and relax. I'll clean this up. Stop trying to be Superwoman. Let me help."

She looked surprised at my outburst, but for once she did as she was told. She *must* be feeling rotten, I thought, as I stacked the dishwasher. She'd never normally let me boss her around.

When I had finished clearing up, Fiona said, "I don't want the boys' lives to be interrupted by my being sick. It's absolutely vital that they have a normal routine. It'll make them feel secure."

She was right. It made sense. Suddenly I felt very grownup. I was about to be allowed to look after the twins — gifted and all as they were.

"Should I be taking notes?" I asked, fishing in my bag for a pen and paper and coming up with an eyeliner and the back of a cigarette pack.

Fiona sighed and handed me a folder titled "Routine". In it was a colour-coded timetable, covering every detail of the twins' day, including what music to play in the car on the way to and from school.

"Wow, that's impressive. You'll have to give me the CD," I said, looking down at the list: Beethoven, Symphony No. 5; Pachelbel, Canon in D; Mozart, *Eine Kleine Nachtmusik*; Bach, *Jesu, Joy of Man's Desiring*; Brahms, Piano Concerto No. 1; Mendelssohn, Symphony No. 4; Beethoven, *Für Elise*; Mozart, Violin Concerto No. 3; Tchaikovsky, *Waltz of the Flowers*; Schubert, *Trout Quintet*. "I somehow doubt that Derek will have it in his collection."

Fiona didn't seem to find this amusing.

"Don't kids listen to nursery rhymes any more?" I asked.

"Classical music has been proven to develop motor and rhythmic skills. Before we get into the car the boys pick a song and I tell them a little fact about the

58

composer. They really like it and already have preferences. Bobby loves Mozart, and Jack leans more towards Schubert."

I stared at Fiona. Was this for real? Did she really believe the boys knew the difference between Mozart and Schubert? She was beginning to sound like one of those home-schooling parents whose kids wore dickie bows and went on *Mastermind* aged five and studied at Oxford at eleven. They were always total loners and most ended up having nervous breakdowns because they hadn't had a normal childhood. I was concerned for the twins.

"It seems a bit hectic and intense," I ventured.

"Kate," said Fiona, glaring at me, "they are my children and they like their routine. They are very happy and well balanced. Don't swan in here and criticize me. You've always done exactly what you want to. That has to change now. You don't come first — the twins do."

I felt as if I'd been slapped in the face. In the past when Mark had implied that I was selfish, Fiona had always defended me and said I was self-sufficient and that it was a good thing. I was the type of person who needed to spread my wings, she'd said. I knew that sometimes, like when I forgot the twins' birthday last year, she got fed up with me and told me I was thoughtless, but she'd never snapped at me like this before. And the way she'd said it, with so much anger, I could see it had come from deep inside. I was tempted to defend myself and tell her that I was just trying to get on with my life and make something of myself, instead of staying in Dublin, marrying the guy next door and having children. What was wrong with being ambitious and wanting more? I craved excitement, independence, freedom and new experiences. She didn't. We were different. Different strokes for different folks. Besides, it had been better for her when I moved away because she was able to get on with her own life and stop thinking she had to look after me and fix me. I didn't need fixing. I needed room to breathe. And, besides, hadn't I just moved home, lock, stock and barrel, to help her out? I'd given up the life I'd made for myself and a job I loved.

The new mature me decided to bite my tongue. She was sick and scared.

"OK. Well, I'll let you get an early night. I'll go home and study the timetable and read up the information about the composers so I can tell the boys tomorrow. I'll see you at eight."

I'd be up all night at this rate, reading about Mozart and the gang — I hadn't counted on having to study to look after my nephews. Maybe I could rent that movie about Mozart. I wondered if they'd made one about Schubert. If so, I hoped the actor who played him was cute — it'd be so much easier to watch.

"Fine, thanks," she said stiffly.

I looked at her worried face. "Fiona, it's going to be OK. You're not Mum."

She looked away. "Right . . . I'll see you tomorrow, then."

I reached out to touch her shoulder but she moved away, so I left her standing in the kitchen, arms wrapped around herself in an effort to find warmth and comfort.

As I was leaving, I bumped into Mark getting out of his car. He came over to say hello. I could smell beer on his breath. "Have you been drinking?"

"Welcome back, Supernanny."

"Have you?"

"I had a beer with the dean."

"Couldn't it have waited? Your wife is inside having a nervous breakdown about tomorrow."

"Did you reassure her? Is she OK now?"

"I was too busy putting your children to bed and learning their routine off by heart while you were downing beers. You should have taken Fiona out for dinner, and pampered her and told her how wonderful she is. She's got cancer, Mark, in case you forgot while you were choosing between Heineken and Budweiser."

"I am well aware of Fiona's condition. I really don't think someone who has been back all of five minutes is in any position to tell me about my wife."

"I didn't give everything up to come back here and look after your family so that you can go out and get pissed whenever you feel like it. I thought you were supposed to be busy preparing some world-altering paper," I hissed, venting my general frustration on him.

"Which was exactly what I was talking to the dean about. Really, Kate, there's no need to turn into a fishwife. I hope you won't be talking like that in front of the boys. If I hear them cursing I'll know who to blame."

"Well, Mark, that makes two of us, because I hold you responsible for my sister's happiness and so far you're doing a pretty crummy job. You might want to remember the 'in sickness and in health' vow you made when you married her. Now, get in there and comfort her," I said, and stormed off before he could respond.

It was only when I was half-way down the road that I realized I had forgotten to call a taxi. It had started to rain so I called Derek to come and pick me up.

"I don't drive."

"I thought Dad got you lessons for Christmas."

"Yeah, but I flogged them to one of the chicks in work for cash to buy some new equipment."

"Jesus, Derek, it's bucketing down. Is Dad there?"

"Nope."

"Bollox!" I roared, now at the end of my tether.

"Tone it down a million. Gonzo's here. He's just offered to pick you up."

I really didn't feel like being groped all the way home, but the rain was beating down and I was damned if I'd go back and ask Mark for a lift. "OK. Tell him to hurry up."

Five minutes later Gonzo came hurtling up the road. I squeezed my soaking frame into his Mini.

"Oh, yes — I love the wet look," he said, and placed a hand on my thigh.

"Gonzo, if you value your life, you'll keep your eyes on the road and your hands on the steering-wheel. I'm cold, wet and in a very bad mood," I said, putting his hand back.

"Feel free to rid yourself of the wet clothes," he said, with a grin.

I lit a cigarette and inhaled deeply. What the hell was I doing here?

# CHAPTER
# NINE

When I had finally extricated myself from Gonzo's lunges, I went in and poured myself a glass of wine to steady my nerves. Derek was sprawled on the couch watching MTV's top ten rappers of all time and shouting along to the lyrics. I closed the kitchen door, sat at the table, lit a cigarette and opened my folder. Homework time.

Fiona's timetable was detailed to say the least. When I had ploughed through all the stimulating games I was supposed to play with the boys — including some maths ones that I wasn't sure I was up to — I found a handwritten note.

*Kate, thanks for coming home. It means a lot to me. I know how hard it was for you and I really appreciate it. I'm only holding it together by a thread, so I can't say this to you face to face. Anyway, you know me: I've always been hopeless about showing my emotions. I know the boys will enjoy spending time with you, but please follow the routine. I want their lives to continue as normal. I don't want them to know how sick I am. I don't want them to be scared. I don't want their childhoods to be snatched away like ours was. See you tomorrow and thanks again. Fiona*

This was Fiona all over. She had a heart of gold and always believed that actions spoke louder than words. She'd show you she loved you by doing things for you. Since Mum died, she had found it hard to show her emotions, probably because she had to suppress her grief while comforting Derek and me. I sniffled into my glass of wine. My sister was glad I was home, and that was all that mattered. Mark and his snide remarks were irrelevant.

The door opened and Dad came in. "How many Oscars did Katherine Hepburn win?"

"Three."

"Name the films."

"*Morning Glory. Guess Who's Coming to Dinner. On Golden Pond.*"

"Wrong. She won four, and you know the other one. Come on, Katie."

I racked my brains. This was Dad's and my favourite game, and one that I was actually good at. I shared his obsession with films. As far back as I could remember he had sat me down to watch all the classic Hollywood films — it was our way of bonding. Fiona had been too busy with chess and Derek had had the attention span of a flea, so Dad focused his love of cinema on me. I had spent many a rainy Saturday afternoon with him, watching spellbound as Henry Fonda, Gregory Peck, Bette Davis, Lauren Bacall and many others strutted their stuff.

"*The Lion in Winter*," I shouted.

"Well done. Good to see you haven't lost it," he said, beaming at me. "Now, how did it go with Fiona?"

"She's stressed and scared but, all things considered, she seemed OK. As for that husband of hers, though — God, Dad, he's so patronizing! He didn't get back till nine and then he started giving me grief. He's behaved like a total tosser since she got sick."

"Careful, Kate, you can't go around criticizing Mark. He's Fiona's husband and you have to respect that and put up with him for her sake — even if he is being a pain in the arse," he muttered.

"Who's being a pain in the arse?" asked Derek.

"Mark," I said.

"Wanker," said Derek. "He called me up yesterday and told me to stop asking Fiona for advice and stuff. He said she doesn't need to be worrying about me when she's sick. As if I'd offload on her now! I'm not a total moron."

"That's a relief," said Dad, winking at me.

"How is she anyway?" asked Derek.

"Being brave."

"Sure that girl was born brave," said Dad. "How are the twins?"

"Fine. They seem blissfully unaware that anything's wrong. I've a list of things to study for tomorrow, though. They have a very precise schedule."

"Don't talk to me about *that*," groaned Dad. "I'd to look after them one afternoon and I learnt more than they did. We were doing sums and all. They'll be going to college next year at this rate."

"Cool, like the little dude in *Little Man Tate*," drawled Derek.

"Didn't he have a breakdown at the end of the movie?" I asked.

"Yes, he bloody did," said Dad. "Those kids need to kick a ball around and climb trees."

"Well, there is forty-five minutes allocated for 'outdoor activities'," I said.

Just as Dad was about to reply, the door opened and a girl wearing baggy jeans — which showed off her boxer shorts — with a yellow bra top strolled in. "Yo, Derek, you should have woken me up. I've gotta hit the road."

Dad and I, decked in woolly jumpers, stared at Derek.

"This is Roxanne," he said proudly.

"I thought it might be Daisy," said Dad, pointing to her nose-ring, as I choked on my wine.

"No, I'm named after the Police song," said Roxanne, staring blankly at Dad.

"Well, isn't that lovely?" said Dad, and then, unable to resist, he added, "I see you don't feel the cold, which is great, especially in this climate."

"You have to freeze for fashion," said Roxanne, winking at him, as I nodded sagely. She had a point there, especially if you lived in Ireland. You had to freeze at some point or you'd never get out of woolly jumpers and boots.

Derek put his arm around her.

"And what do you do with yourself when you're not freezing?" asked Dad, cutting to the chase.

Roxanne sighed. "I'm an artist."

"Could you be more specific?" asked Dad, as Derek groaned.

"I create body art."

"I'm not with you," said Dad, looking puzzled.

"Tattoos."

"Lovely," said Dad, trying to hide his shock.

"She's the best in Dublin," said the loyal Derek. "Show them your cobra."

Roxanne pulled her boxer shorts dangerously low to reveal a large, colourful snake's head with a tongue leading downwards.

"Jesus," said Dad, not knowing where to look.

"I know," said Derek, smiling. "Impressive, isn't it?"

"That's one word for it," said Dad.

"Wasn't it painful?" I asked, wincing at the thought of how far down the tongue went.

"Oh, yeah, I passed out twice, but it's worth it," said the painted lady.

"So, are you two an item, then?" asked Dad, looking concerned.

"We're fuck-buddies," said Roxanne, shrugging. "No ties, no drama."

Silence filled the room. No one knew what to say, least of all Derek, who, judging by his face, was under the impression that they were a lot more than that, and was none too pleased at having this news broadcast to him in front of his father and sister.

"Have you any older sisters?" asked Dad.

When the alarm went off at half six the next morning, I felt as if I'd been asleep all of five minutes. I dragged myself out of bed and into the shower. Not having had time to buy shampoo and shower gel, I washed in Head and Shoulders shampoo, which looked as if it had been there since the eighties, then pulled on a pair of jeans and a sweatshirt. Having seen what messy eaters the twins were, I chose not to wear anything I actually liked.

Dad was waiting for me in the hall. "Come on, I'll give you a lift. I want to see Fiona to wish her luck . . . DEREK," he roared.

"WHAT?"

"Get your lazy arse down here — we're leaving." Then Dad turned to me. "I've organized a rental car for you. It'll be here tonight when you get home. We can't have you being molested by that eejit every time you need a lift for the next few months."

I smiled gratefully. "Thanks, Dad."

"*Derek!*" he bellowed. "I'm not waiting any longer."

As we were pulling out of the drive, Derek hurtled towards the car, barefoot. "Jesus, Dad, where's the fire?"

"Your sister's having an operation for cancer. That's the bloody fire," snapped Dad.

We drove the rest of the way in silence.

Fiona answered the door. She looked dreadful. She clearly hadn't slept a wink and her hand was shaking as she tried to stir the boys' porridge. Gently I took the spoon from her and led her to a chair. I returned to the porridge.

Dad was doing his best to be super-cheery. "Derek brought a lovely girl home to me last night, Fiona. I don't know if you've met the charming Roxanne."

"No, I haven't," said Fiona.

"Like Audrey Hepburn, she is. A class act."

"Wow! Good for you, Derek," said Fiona.

"She showed us a lovely tattoo of a snake she has down to her crotch and informed us that Derek is her fuck-buddy."

Despite herself, Fiona laughed.

"Granddad said fuck! Granddad said fuck!" screamed Jack, as Mark walked in, immaculately turned out in a suit and tie.

"Bill, can you please watch your language in front of the boys?" said Mark, frowning.

"It was worth it to see Fiona laugh," retorted Dad.

"Are you OK about the sleeping arrangements?" Fiona asked Derek, always looking out for him.

Derek shrugged. "It was news to me. I thought we were mutually exclusive. The bummer of it is that I'd just written this wicked song about her and now I'll have to change it."

"Why can't you find a nice sensible girl to go out with, instead of these half-wits?" said Dad.

"Creative people are drawn to each other, Dad. It's not like I have any control over it."

"Fiona, we'd better go," said Mark, pointing to the clock on the kitchen wall.

70

My stomach sank. Please, God, let it be OK and let the cancer not have spread.

Fiona bent down to hug the twins. "OK, boys, remember what I told you? Mummy won't be sleeping here tonight and when I come back I'll have a sore tummy for a few days. But I'll see you tomorrow and Auntie Kate is going to look after you today." She had opted for "tummy" rather than having to go through the breast chat with two five-year-olds who thought that boobies were hilarious.

"No, Mummy," said the twins in unison, having picked up on the tension in the room and their mother's drawn face. "Don't go."

"I have to, boys, but I'll be back tomorrow. Now, be good for Kate," she said, then wrapped her arms round them and whispered, "I love you," into their hair as they clung to her. It was the first time she had ever been away from them for a night, and they knew it wasn't good news. They began to cry and clung to her legs, which made her cry too. Even Teddy looked sad, sitting in his basket, whimpering.

"Boys," said Mark, "Mummy has to go now or she'll be late. Go back and finish your breakfast. I'll be home to read you a story and tuck you in. Come on, now, let go of her legs."

Reluctantly they did as they were told, but ran after their parents as they climbed into the car.

We all hugged Fiona, and as Dad clasped her to his chest, I heard him whisper, "You're going to be fine, my darling girl. Don't worry, we'll get through this."

We waved them off, all of us fighting tears but trying to look cheery for the boys' sake.

"Why does Mummy look so sad?" asked Bobby, as Fiona turned to wave.

"Because she'll miss you tonight, so you've to be very good and give her lots of hugs tomorrow when she comes back," I said.

"Why will she have a sore tummy tomorrow?" asked Jack.

"Because . . ." I was floundering.

"Because the doctor is going to take out the bad stuff inside and it will be sore for a few days until the scar heals. Like when Bobby got glass in his hand and the doctor took it out — it was sore first and then it got better," said Derek.

That made sense. The twins nodded.

"Nice one, Derek," I said, smiling at him. Then, turning to the boys, I said, "OK, come on, eat up, we don't want to be late for school."

"I hate yucky porridge," said Bobby, turning his spoon upside-down on the table.

"Me, too," said Jack, flicking a lump, which landed on Teddy's nose. They both squealed with laughter as the poor dog leapt up in shock.

Bobby jumped down and began to chase Teddy around the kitchen, shoving his bowl under the dog's nose.

"Leave that poor dog alone," said Dad. "Come on, now, do what Kate says."

Grudgingly, the twins sat down.

"My porridge has dog spit in it," said Bobby.

"I want Frosties," roared Jack.

"Well, I've a meeting at nine, so I'll leave you to it," said Dad, backing out the door as fast as he could, followed by the fastest-moving Derek I'd ever seen.

"Thanks a lot!" I called after them.

I heard a screech and turned back to the boys. Jack had upturned his bowl of porridge on Bobby's head. I had been in charge for precisely six minutes.

# CHAPTER
## TEN

Having chased the boys around the house for half an hour, trying to get them dressed, I eventually resorted to rugby-tackling them to the floor and dressed one while I sat on the other. They were none too pleased to be squashed into the carpet by their supposedly "fun" aunt and I was told in no uncertain terms that I was "mean and nasty".

I bundled them into Fiona's jeep, but as we were about to drive off, Jack said, "*No!* We can't go till we pick our music."

Bollox, the bloody music.

"OK, whose turn is it?"

"Mine," said Bobby.

"What would you like to listen to?"

"Kakosky flowers," he said, decisively for a five-year-old. Maybe Fiona was right and this classical-music playing *was* brain-inducing. I might try it myself.

I grabbed a bunch of CDs from the glove compartment and riffled through them. "It's not here. Can you choose something else?" I asked impatiently, as I glanced at my watch. We were already running late and Fiona had specifically told me that Mrs Foley liked her pupils to be on time. What difference it could possibly make to a bunch of kids running around or playing with Lego if one was late was beyond me. But I wanted to do everything right and prove myself a responsible, reliable sister. So far, it wasn't going to plan.

"I want Kakosky flowers," Bobby whinged.

I looked again. Who the hell was Kakosky? Some stupid bloody Russian composer, no doubt, who'd spent his life freezing his arse off in a wooden hut in the middle of a snowy field with no heating and all his family killed in some revolution or other. So he wrote music that reflected his sad depressing life and no one appreciated it because it was so dark and grim. So we had been spared it, until a century later when some music critic determined to make a name for himself had decided to find an obscure composer and convince us that the music wasn't depressing, it was "moving and stirring", and now we had to pretend to appreciate it. Because to say you think it's a pile of horse manure shows you're an ignorant fool, even though most people probably agree with you.

My patience was running out. "I'm sorry, Bobby, it's not here."

Bobby grabbed the CDs and waved one at me. "It's the one with the butterflies on it. It's number three," he said.

I looked down: Tchaikovsky, *Waltz of the Flowers*. "Sorry, Bobby, I see it now." I felt like a prat. These kids could run rings round me in the brains department. "OK, let me tell you something about

Kakosky," I said, shuffling through my notes. "Here we go. His name was Peter."

"We know that," said Bobby.

"And we know he was from Russia," Jack piped up.

"OK. Did you know he had twin brothers, just like you two, whom he adored?"

"Cool," said Bobby.

I looked down at the sheet I'd printed off the Internet in Dad's office the night before. "It says here he was married but he was actually a homo — Oh!" I said. I didn't think the boys needed to know about Kakosky's sexual preferences.

"Homo what?" asked Jack.

"Home a lot where he composed all his lovely music," I said, cranking up the volume to drown any more questions.

When I dropped the twins off at school, I received a stern lecture from Mrs Foley about tardiness being unacceptable, until I cut across her and told her to give me and the boys a break as Fiona was in hospital and very unwell. She sniffed, then said she hoped my sister would recover soon, but if I was in charge for the moment, I must make the effort to be on time in future. Then I was informed that if I was late to pick them up at lunchtime I would incur a charge of five euro for every half-hour, except under very exceptional circumstances. In being late I was teaching the boys a bad habit, which could lead to sloth in the future. And sloth, as we all know, is a deadly sin.

I backed down the driveway as fast as my legs could carry me before Mrs Foley could list any more sins I might inflict on the boys. Where did Fiona find these people, I wondered, as I drove back to the house to clear up.

When I got in, the kitchen was a mess. Porridge was stuck to the floor and the table. Milk had spilled down the side of the chairs and Teddy was licking the honey jar, which had fallen on to the floor.

He jumped when he saw me and looked mightily relieved when he realized I was alone. The poor dog was tormented daily by the twins with their over-zealous displays of love.

"I know how you feel," I said, patting his nose. I made myself some coffee and sat down to have a cigarette before I did the cleaning. As I lit up, I saw a bright red sign on the fridge: "No Smoking — Our Kids Breathe Clean Air." I sighed and put the cigarette back into the packet. I made myself two slices of toast, which I lathered with butter to compensate for my lack of nicotine. I hadn't eaten bread or butter for four years. Since I'd got my first five-second slot on TV, I'd been starving myself every day. Bread, potatoes, pasta, rice and chocolate were all things of the past. When I was hungry, I smoked. Pretending you're four years younger than you are requires a lot of discipline and permanent hunger.

The toast tasted fantastic and I decided to have another slice to treat myself. What the hell? I didn't need a flat stomach. I wasn't going on TV. Besides, I'd starve myself before I went back to London. For now, I was on a time-out.

Reinvigorated by the food, I cleaned the kitchen thoroughly, let Teddy out for a run in the garden and by the time I'd finished it was eleven o'clock. Fiona was due out of theatre at about eleven, so I called the hospital. The nurse said she was in the recovery room and still very groggy but the operation seemed to have gone well. She wouldn't give out any further information until the doctor had spoken to Fiona himself.

After pacing up and down, praying that the news would be good and biting my nails, I decided to hop into the car and drive to the hospital. I wanted to be near Fiona physically; whatever the news, I wanted to be there.

When I arrived, Dad was in the visitors' room, pacing like a caged tiger.

"Any news?" I asked.

"No," he growled, "they'll tell me nothing. The surgeon is in with her and Mark now. Jesus, Kate, let it be good news. Don't let it have spread."

I squeezed his hand and we sat watching the clock for twenty more minutes, until the nurse came in and told us we could see Fiona, but only for a minute as she was still very tired.

She looked very small and frail in her hospital gown, but she was smiling. "It's good news," she said, and began to cry.

"The surgeon said he was confident he'd removed all the cells and that it doesn't appear to have spread to her lymph nodes," said Mark, taking over.

"But we won't know for sure until the test results come back in three days," added Fiona.

"Fantastic news," said Dad, and kissed Fiona's cheek.

"She has invasive ductal carcinoma," continued Mark, as if he was addressing a conference of cancer specialists.

"In English, please," I said.

He glared at me. "IDC is the most common form of breast cancer in those with breast tumours. The treatment for early detection has a very high success rate. Fiona is going to have chemotherapy and radiation treatment, but she's going to be fine."

"Excellent," said Dad, beaming.

I looked at Fiona, who was smiling weakly. It was good news, but she still had to wait for the test results and then faced a pretty horrendous few months with no guarantee of success. I went over and held her hand.

"I'm dreading the chemo," she whispered.

"Don't worry, sis. We'll get through it. One day at a time."

She squeezed my hand, and then, looking at Mark, she said, "You'd better go, you don't want to be late. Good luck."

He bent down to kiss her, and left.

"Where's he off to?" asked Dad, trying to sound casual when it was as clear as the nose on his face that all he wanted to do was go out there and box his son-in-law for leaving Fiona.

"He's got a conference call with an expert from China who can help him with his paper. He's been trying to get in touch with him for weeks."

"I see," said Dad, not seeing at all. I could tell he was thinking of what to do with Mark's important paper and it didn't have anything to do with prizes.

The door opened. Thank God! Mark's seen sense, I thought. He's come back to put his wife first rather than some Chinese mathematician.

But it was Derek, looking a bit flushed. "Yo, howzit going?" he asked.

"Good, thanks. It doesn't appear to have spread and it's a very treatable form of cancer so I'll be fine," said Fiona.

I looked at her in amazement. She was so concerned not to upset Derek that she'd made it sound like a walk in the park.

Derek looked at the drain in Fiona's side, then at her pinched face and winced. "So, like, was it savagely painful?"

"Well, I was out for the count during the operation, but it is a bit sore now," she admitted.

"Like, really bad pain?"

"About as sore as having a big lump sliced out of one of yours balls," I said, losing patience with Derek's need for gory details.

"Chill, I was just asking. I wanted to do something for you, like, make a gesture, and I couldn't think of anything, but Roxanne came up with a brilliant idea. While you were having your operation I was having one myself. It was total agony, but it looks deadly," said

Derek, turning round and pulling up his T-shirt to reveal a large tattoo on his lower back, which read "CARPE DEIM".

I began to laugh. Fiona joined in, then Dad.

Derek glared at us. "It's not supposed to be funny. Don't you know what it means?"

"I think, Derek, you'll find that your fuck-buddy suffers from dyslexia. 'Diem' is spelt backwards, you turnip." I giggled.

"What the hell? Are you having me on?"

"No, Derek, she isn't," said Fiona. "You now have a huge misspelt tattoo on your backside. But I appreciate the thought."

"Roxanne's a legend. She'd never get it wrong," said Derek.

"In all fairness, Derek, she didn't strike me as a Latin scholar," said Dad.

Derek ran into the bathroom to check it in the mirror. "I don't fucking believe it. I suffered two hours of torture for this. I'm outta here. Man, I'm gonna kill her."

"It's proud moments like these that a father dreams of," said Dad.

"Hey, Derek," said Fiona, as he was storming out the door.

"What?" he asked grumpily.

"Thanks for cheering me up."

# CHAPTER
# ELEVEN

I left the hospital and was on my way to pick up the twins when my phone rang. It was Tara. "How's Fiona?" my friend asked, full of concern.

"She's OK. We still have to wait for the test result but they don't think it's spread to her lymph nodes, so they say that the chances of her recovery are good but she has to go through chemo."

"Poor Fiona."

"I know, and she's trying to be brave, but I can tell she's terrified. I feel so sorry for her."

"At least the diagnosis is good, that's the most important thing, and I'm sure you being home to help is a relief to her. How are you getting on with the twins?"

"Not great. They were late for school and I got a bollocking from the teacher. I'm on my way to pick them up. They're hyper — and it's going to be a long afternoon. Seven and a half hours to be precise."

"Do you want to hear something that'll distract you?"

"Is the Pope Catholic?"

"I bumped into an old pal of yours today."

"Who?"

"Sam," said Tara, then paused for dramatic effect.

"Oh, right. How is he?" I said, trying to sound casual as I narrowly missed slamming into the car in front.

"Very well . . ." said Tara, and she told me the story, leaving nothing out.

She was sitting in the café around the corner from her office, munching her sandwich, when she heard, "Tara? Hi."

She looked up. It was my first love — Sam Taylor. She hadn't seen him in at least five years.

"Oh, my God! Hello, stranger, how are you?" she said, and got up to kiss him. They smiled at each other with a mixture of awkwardness and familiarity — the way people do when they used to know each other very well but haven't met in a long time. "Will you join me for a coffee?" she said, pointing to the chair opposite her.

"I'd love to. How the hell have you been? What's new?" asked Sam.

"I don't even know where to begin." Tara laughed. "It's been so long since I saw you. Well, the short version is that I got married and settled down. What about you?" she asked, pretending not to know that Sam had married Nikki Jennings four years ago, a fact she had dissected in minute detail with me for weeks, months and even, possibly, years. Nikki Jennings had been in the year below us at school — she was all blonde hair, big tits and sunbed tan.

She sipped her tea and waited for Sam to tell her about his marriage. He hesitated, then said, "Well, I was married for three years, but we've been separated for almost a year now."

Tara choked. She hadn't seen that one coming. Separated? "God, Sam, I'm sorry. I had no idea. Are you OK?" She was, trying to figure out a way of asking him what had happened without appearing nosy. Wait until Kate hears this, she thought.

"Yeah, I'm fine now, thanks. It's been a rough year or two, though," he said, looking up at her.

Wow, he still has those killer eyes, thought Tara. "And is there no possibility of a reconciliation?" she asked, congratulating herself on her subtle questioning.

Sam shook his head. "Well, considering she's now living with her boss — the man she was having an affair with while she was with me — I'd say the chances are slim," he said, smiling ruefully.

"Yikes! I'm sorry, Sam."

"Yeah, me too. So, anyway, how's married life with you?"

"Is it OK for me to say that it's great?"

"Absolutely. I'm glad it's going well."

"Tom, my husband, reads your column religiously. He thinks you're the best sports writer around."

"And what do you think?"

"You know me and sports — even Kate had more of an interest than I do."

"How's Kate? How's her high-flying career going?" he asked, with just the slightest hint of sarcasm. "Has she married some hot-shot TV star yet?"

"No, she's single, actually," said Tara, archly. "But her career's going really well. She just landed her own show."

"She finally got what she always wanted, then."

Tara was annoyed with Sam for being flippant. "Well, it was great until last week when she found out Fiona has cancer and had to move home to look after her," she said.

"What?" said Sam, staring at her. "Did you say cancer?"

"Yes, it's breast cancer, but I shouldn't really have told you. Don't say anything to anyone. They don't want people to know yet."

"Jesus, is she all right? How bad is it?"

"They'll know after today how bad it is. She was operated on this morning. Look, Sam, I shouldn't have said anything, just forget it. I have to go back to work now."

"No, wait," said Sam, grabbing her arm. "Take my card and please call me when you know more. I'd really like to know how she gets on — I was always a big fan of Fiona's and . . . tell Kate I was asking for her. God it must be hard on her with her mum and all."

"So I took the card," said Tara, "which I have here in my pocket, in case you're interested. I'm sorry I told him about Fiona but I wanted to show him that you'd put your family first. Are you annoyed?"

"No, it's fine. I'm glad you did — I bet he was shocked to find out I've put my job on the back-burner.

I can't believe his marriage broke up. Mind you, he never should have married that cow."

"So he's single," said Tara, "and you're back in Dublin for the foreseeable future . . ."

"Tara! We broke up eight years ago. It's dead and buried."

"If you say so," she said. "Look, I've got to go. My boss is glaring at me. I'll call you later."

I leant back on the head-rest and sighed. Even now the mention of Sam's name brought a knot to my stomach. I didn't know if it was down to guilt because I'd broken up with him when I went away to London, or regret, or simply because I hadn't had a serious relationship since him — unless you count six months going out with a producer at Channel 4 who only called me when he was bored or horny. The men I dated were never right, and I was always so busy with work that I never felt lonely — well, not often. Also, I didn't want children so the biological-clock thing wasn't an issue.

Sam was my first love, the guy I lost my virginity to, and the nicest guy I ever dated. When I met him I was nineteen, and itching to finish my degree in media studies then get the hell out of Ireland to seek fame and fortune in London. I talked incessantly about leaving the backwater that was Dublin. Sam was studying journalism in the same college, although we never actually met. When we were introduced by Tara's cousin Conor — who was also studying journalism — we had the most enormous row.

I had asked Sam what newspaper he aspired to write for and when he said the *Irish Independent*, I laughed.

"Yeah, right! Come on, you must want to write for *Sports Illustrated* or one of the big English papers. I mean the *Irish Independent*'s a bit lame. You'll spend your time writing about local football. How dull is that?"

"It depends what you find interesting. Maybe in your world talking to arseholes who think they're God and won't give you the time of day is fascinating, but in my world that's sad. Half the sports journalists in the UK have to make up their interviews because none of the sports stars will spit on them. Why would I want to waste my time chasing Alex Ferguson around for weeks only to be told to fuck off?"

"Well, I'd rather spend my time chasing a great interview than waste my talent standing on the sideline of some sad local hurley match in the pissing rain talking to spotty seventeen-year-olds."

"What the hell would you know about it?"

"It doesn't take a rocket scientist to figure out that writing for the *Guardian* or *The Times* would be a lot more exciting and challenging than some crappy Irish daily. You'd be working with really talented journalists on Fleet Street where you might actually learn something. I wouldn't dream of wasting my time working in Irish television. The UK is where it's at for people with ambition and drive."

"Two very overrated virtues in my book."

"There's nothing wrong with ambition. Some men are intimidated by women who strive to succeed."

"There's a subtle difference between being intimidated and being turned off. And, believe me, a woman behaving like a pit-bull terrier is a real turn-off."

"How dare you speak to me like that? Just because you —"

"Down, boy, there's no need to bite."

"Listen, you . . ." I said to Sam's back, as he walked away, laughing.

I was furious. Who the hell did this guy think he was, speaking to me like that? What was wrong with being ambitious and wanting a successful career? God, some men were pathetic. What a loser.

Later that day when I met up with Tara I ranted about Sam for at least an hour. Eventually Tara cut to the chase. "So, is he cute?"

"What?"

"Well, is he?"

I had to admit he was very attractive, in a scruffy kind of way. He had that just-got-out-of-bed look. Tousled brown hair and crumpled clothes. At first glance he wasn't much to look at, but up close his eyes got you. They were emerald green, and when he'd looked directly at me — as he had that afternoon — they had seemed to pierce right through me. Although I had spent the day seething because he had been so rude, I couldn't get those eyes out of my head. "He has nice eyes, but the personality of a pig."

"I dunno, Kate, I think you like this guy. He's the first person to challenge you in ages. You're always saying how boring the guys we know are and now you've met someone who in one conversation has managed to totally wind you up."

"I'm not attracted to him. He's a loser," I lied, picturing the gorgeous green eyes again. "See what you can find out from Conor about him. I'm not interested, just curious."

Tara duly called her cousin and found out the following:

Sam was paying his way through college by working part-time as a hotel porter. He had one sister, Caroline — who was a real looker and Conor was hoping to hop on. Sam never mentioned his father but lived with his mother and sister. He had just broken up with a girl called Alice, whom he had been dating for a year. She was absolutely devastated and, according to Conor, had taken a bitter pill and was now telling everyone that Sam was awful in bed and had a very small penis. Tara was a bit alarmed to hear this — was Alice being catty or was it the sad truth? Conor was not very helpful in this department as he hadn't slept with Sam.

"Well, does he have a small willy?" asked Tara, going for the Best Friend of the Year award.

"Tiny," said Conor.

"Shit."

"Why do you care? I thought you were going out with Damian?"

"I am. I just feel sorry for anyone with a small penis."

"Sure you do. It's OK, Tara, I'm kidding. You can tell Kate that his nickname is Horse and there's a very good reason for that."

"Why would I tell Kate? She has no interest in Sam."

"I was there yesterday when they were sparring. She's keen."

"She is not. In fact, she thinks he's a pig."

"Yeah, right. Whatever you say."

While Tara relayed all the information to me, Conor told Sam that he had been grilled by his cousin, who happened to be my best mate, and as far as he could tell, Sam was well in. The next time we met was a week later at a party. I knew Sam was going to be there and had spent ages getting ready — eventually opting for a very short denim mini-dress.

The minute I saw him, my heart jumped. He looked even better the second time. He glanced up and waved, so I made my way over to talk to him, but as I got close he turned his back on me and began to chat up some girl with a really annoying laugh. He studiously ignored me for the entire night. Eventually as everyone was leaving he came over to me.

"Look who it is! The girl who thinks she's too good for Ireland."

"You owe me an apology."

"For what?" asked Sam, raising an eyebrow.

"For being so rude to me last week when we met."

"I think you're the one who should be apologizing. You insulted my career aspirations."

"I did not."

"I think you'll find that you did."

"Apologize to me and I'll apologize to you," I said, flicking my hair back and giving him my best pout.

"The mini-dress and pouting might work for some guys, but I find it a bit obvious."

"Fuck you."

"My sentiments exactly," said Sam, walking away.

I was left open-mouthed, shaking with rage, embarrassment and lust. No one had ever wound me up like that before.

A week later, we crossed each other again, outside the college gates.

"Hello," said Sam.

"Hi," I said, wishing I'd made more of an effort to look good. The woolly-jumper look was not exactly *femme fatale*.

"I'm surprised to see you here. I thought the BBC would have head-hunted you by now."

I smiled, then burst into tears. Sam was unprepared for that, although, having lived alone with his mother and sister all his life, he was not as uncomfortable around tears as most guys. "Shit, I'm sorry. I didn't mean to upset you. I take it all back."

I shook my head. I was mortified. "It's not you, I'm fine."

"We can safely say that that is one thing you're not. Can I buy you a coffee or a stiff drink? Would thumping me help?"

"Coffee would be great. It's my mum's anniversary today," I said. "I never seem to get used to it."

We spent the afternoon together and never looked back . . . until I broke up with him when I moved to London three years later.

# CHAPTER
# TWELVE

I arrived exactly ten seconds early to pick up the boys. I walked into the room and was met by a happy-looking Bobby, whose hands were covered in paint. "Hi there," I said. "You look like you've had a good time. Where's Jack?"

"He's in the corner cos he was bold."

I looked up and saw Jack facing the wall, looking very small and forlorn. I went over to Mrs Foley. "Hi," I said. "Remember me? Kate O'Brien, the twins' aunt?"

"Yes, you dropped the boys off late this morning."

"That's right and you made a big song and dance about it. Well, I'd like to know why Jack is standing in the corner."

"He bit Max on the arm. Biting and violence are unacceptable and children must learn the difference between right and wrong. So when they are bold they stand in the bold corner for five minutes."

"I see. And tell me, Mrs Foley, do you not believe in making allowances for little boys who might be acting up because their mothers are in hospital with cancer?"

"Mrs Kennedy has never questioned my use of gentle discipline on the boys. I realize that she is in hospital and that the boys might be out of sorts, but biting another child, whatever the reason, is wrong and must be dealt with."

"Well, maybe my sister would disagree with you on this rather exceptional day. I think Jack could have done with a cuddle and a chat. I'm taking him home now."

"Jack has a minute left in the bold corner."

"Get a life, you insensitive cow," I snapped, ruining any hope of a friendly relationship with the boys' teacher.

I went over to Jack and bent down. "Hey, buddy, it's time to go home now. Are you OK?"

He shook his head. "I was bold today. I bit Max."

"Listen, Jack, everyone is bold sometimes. It's OK, as long as you said you're sorry to Max."

"I said sorry. Please don't tell Mummy. She told me to be a good boy today."

"Of course I won't tell her. As far as I'm concerned, it's all over and forgotten about. And I've got good news about your mum. She's feeling much better and the doctor got all the bad stuff out and she'll be home tomorrow. So don't you worry about anything."

He nodded, and bit his lip to stop himself crying. Bobby came over. I kissed them both and told them they were the best boys in the school. Bobby squirmed and wiped the kiss off his cheek, but Jack seemed to find it comforting.

Mrs Foley glared at me as I was leaving. She followed me out to the car and assured me that she would be having a word with Mrs Kennedy, who had chosen someone completely unfit to look after the twins.

I spun round. "I'm her sister. What do you think she's going to do? Fire me? Get used to it, Mrs Foley. You'll be seeing a lot of me over the next few months. 'Bye now." With that, I screeched out of the driveway with the twins kicking each other in the back of the car.

When we got home, I checked Fiona's instructions for lunch.

Proper nutrition: should include eating three meals a day and two nutritious snacks. It's important to limit high-sugar and high-fat foods. Eating fruit, vegetables, lean meat and low-fat dairy products, including three servings of milk, cheese or yogurt to meet their calcium needs, can also prevent many medical problems down the line.

She had picked out a menu for me to follow, which was in one of her fifty cookbooks on food for children, by someone called Annabel Karmel. I opened to page fifteen as instructed and read: "Pasta with Tomato Sauce and Hidden Vegetables."

Ms Karmel described the recipe as a great way to disguise vegetables so children would eat them unwittingly with the tomato sauce. I had to sauté onions and garlic, then add the vegetables — courgettes and carrots and mushrooms — the tomatoes, chicken stock and sugar, and then there was some simmering followed by some blending. It all sounded pretty complicated and time-consuming.

Fiona had added a footnote to tell me that the boys hated courgette but in this wonderful recipe they'd never notice it. I wasn't to chop it in front of them because if they saw it they'd know it was in the sauce and then they wouldn't eat it.

I sighed. Whatever happened to ham sandwiches? Take one slice of processed ham, put it between two slices of bread and eat. I took the vegetables out of the fridge. Thankfully, Fiona had left a jar marked "chicken stock", because I had no idea how to make it.

While I chopped the courgette, blocking the boys' view, they played with their toys and tormented Teddy. Suddenly everything was quiet. I looked around and they were gone. Fiona had said if I only remembered one thing it was that silence was deadly.

"If the boys are being quiet they're up to *no good*," she had stressed.

I went upstairs. "Boys? Where are you?"

They weren't in their bedroom, and it was only when I was passing the bathroom that I heard a whimper. I opened the door and there stood poor Teddy, wrapped from head to toe in toilet paper. Beside him, my bag lay open, makeup all over the floor. Jack was spraying Teddy in the face with my expensive and much treasured Jo Malone perfume while Bobby was shoving my Lancôme Juicy Tube lip-gloss up the dog's backside.

"*Stop!*" I shouted, as I pushed the boys aside to rescue poor Teddy, who was looking at me through perfume-poisoned bloodshot eyes. I pulled the lip-gloss from his bum, but the top didn't come with it. "Shit."

"You said 'shit'," shouted Jack, who was back to his old boisterous self.

Ignoring him, I looked at Bobby. "Was the top on this when you pushed it in?"

"Dunno."

"Bobby, I need you to think. Was it or wasn't it?"

"*Dunno!*" he shouted. And then, bored with tormenting Teddy, they ran into their bedroom to jump on their beds.

I looked at Teddy. If the lip-gloss top was up his bum he'd be in pain. He looked in pain. Would he poo it out? Or did I have to — Oh, God — did I have to try to get it out? Teddy shuffled over to me. He was walking like John Wayne. Clearly the lip-gloss top was lodged in there.

"OK," I said to Teddy, "I can sort this out. I just need to calm down and think. I can either try to fish it out myself or take you to the vet."

Teddy rested his head on my knee. I decided to opt for DIY. I went downstairs and put on Fiona's Marigold washing-up gloves. I went back into the bathroom, followed by the twins, who were fed up with jumping, and turned Teddy round. I tried not to gag as I put my finger up his bum to dislodge the lip-gloss top.

"*Yuck!*" shouted Bobby. "You're putting your finger up Teddy's bum!"

"Smelly," said Jack, as they dissolved into giggles.

I fished about, withdrew my hand and leant over the bath to retch. Even Fiona couldn't have prepared me for this particular drama. I'd have to take Teddy to the vet.

I ushered the boys downstairs and into the car, where they started to complain that they were hungry. I ran back into the house, grabbed a couple of slices of bread and a banana. I mushed the banana between the bread and sprinkled sugar on it, like my mum used to do when I was little. I cut it in two and handed the boys a sandwich each.

Then I put Teddy in the front seat beside me and drove off.

"Banana!" squealed Jack.

"And sugar?" said Bobby, in shock.

"Yes." I had no patience for complaints. "Delicious banana sandwiches. Now eat up."

The vet, thankfully, was able to fit us in and was extremely kind and patient. He didn't give out when the twins pulled off his stethoscope and ran around bashing it on the surgery walls, and just nodded when I explained Teddy's delicate problem. He had clearly seen it all before, which was a relief, as I was worried he would report me to the RSPCA for cruelty to animals. He expertly removed the lip-gloss top from Teddy's bum and told me to make sure he had a soft cushion to sit on for the rest of the day, then suggested that I keep the boys away from him until he had had time to recover. He also gave me a tip. "Little boys can be very energetic. It's all the testosterone. When it gets too much I recommend counting to ten. We have three boys and my wife swears by it."

I thanked him and when we had climbed back into the car I gave the boys a lecture. "What you did to

Teddy was very bold and mean. He was in a lot of pain. You cannot push things up his bum or spray him with perfume. How would you like it if I sprayed you in the face and made your eyes sting? It's not fair. Teddy needs lots of gentle cuddles and pets. Do you understand? You have to be nicer to Teddy and not shout at him or pull his tail or wrap him in toilet paper. OK?"

"Are you going to tell Dad?" Bobby asked, his eyes like saucers.

"Well, if you promise to be kind and gentle to Teddy then I won't tell him this time."

With that my nephew undid his seatbelt and lunged at Teddy. The poor dog cowered in the front seat as Bobby smothered him.

"Gently, Bobby!" I said, pulling him back. "Look, just pet him like this. It's what he likes best."

Bobby thumped Teddy's head, then climbed back to his seat.

I spent the rest of the afternoon protecting Teddy and trying to stick to Fiona's routine. We did some maths problems and then we went to the park for some fresh air, but I had to leave Teddy in the car because he wasn't up to it. When we got home I cooked the pasta with hidden vegetables, but Jack spotted the courgette and freaked out, so Bobby refused to eat it too. After I had argued pointlessly with them for fifteen minutes and faced with clamped lips, I gave in and handed them toast and jam . . . at which point Mark sauntered in. "Hi, boys — what on earth are you eating?" he said, looking at me accusingly.

"Yummy toast and jam," said Bobby, licking off the jam to demonstrate his enjoyment of this particular *cordon-bleu* meal.

"Well, that's not very healthy," said Mark, then whispered to me, "What's going on here? I thought Fiona left you instructions on what the boys are to eat. They have five portions of fruit and vegetables every day."

It was now seven o'clock and my eyes were stinging with exhaustion. I had never been so tired in my life. I took a deep breath. "They wouldn't eat the vegetable pasta that I spent an hour cooking, because they hate courgette, so rather than let them starve I've given them toast and jam. OK? It's not exactly battered cod and chips."

"What did they have for lunch?"

"Uhm, I gave them raw carrots and cheese and —"

"Banana sandwiches with sugar," announced Jack, who had snuck up behind me.

Pesky kids.

Mark raised an eyebrow. "If you're finding preparing their meals too complicated, just say so and I'll get someone else to do it."

I turned to Jack. "Can you please go and play with Bobby for a minute? I need to talk to your dad." As he slouched off, I rounded on Mark: "Who did you have in mind? Dad? Derek? Fiona? If you're so concerned about their nutrition, why don't you cook the meals

**99**

yourself? It's called pitching in, helping out, lending a hand."

"I was thinking of buying in bulk from a delicatessen and freezing them," he said catching me off guard.

"Oh, well, that might be a good idea, but I don't think Fiona would approve. I don't want to wind her up. It'll make her sicker."

"Fiona's going to be fine. She'll be back to normal in a matter of weeks."

"She's going to get a lot sicker before she gets better and you have to face that fact and deal with it, instead of sticking your head in the sand. She's about to embark on months of chemo and radiation treatment that will make her incredibly ill. And then, if she's really lucky, she'll go into remission, but she will never be clear of the cancer because it can come back at any time. She needs all the support she can get," I said, feeling tired and emotional. "And if the boys eat a banana sandwich once in a blue moon then so bloody what? Now, instead of giving me a hard time with your rules and regulations, take your coat off and help me put them to bed."

"I'm well aware of how sick the chemo will make her. I'm just trying to be positive instead of pessimistic, which is the attitude you seem to have taken. Thinking the worst isn't going to help Fiona either."

"I'm too tired for this crap," I snapped, fed up with his criticisms.

"Daddy, are you and Auntie Kate fighting?" asked Jack, appearing from nowhere and looking as if he was about to cry.

"No, you silly billy," I said, feigning a smile. "We're saying how excited we are about Mummy coming home tomorrow."

"Yes, it's going to be wonderful," said Mark. "Now, come on, let's find your brother and get you to bed. I've got a fantastic story to read to you tonight about a man called Archimedes who was a mathematician and inventor from ancient Greece . . ."

They'll be asleep in no time, I thought, as I watched the boys heading upstairs with Mark. Two minutes of Archimedes would put anyone into a coma.

# CHAPTER
# THIRTEEN

By the time I got home I was as tired as I ever hope to be. I heard Derek and Gonzo talking in the TV room so I went into the kitchen for some peace and quiet. I didn't have the energy to talk. I flopped down at the kitchen table and ate my way through a packet of chocolate biscuits. Cooking was not an option: it required too much effort.

I could hear Derek and Gonzo lusting over some girl on the TV.

"Dude, check out those tits."

"She's a fox."

"Do you reckon they're real?"

"Who cares? They look sensational."

Whoever this girl was, she had two big fans. Marginally revived by the sugar rush from the biscuits I wandered in to the boys. They were staring at a blonde girl with enormous boobs, enhanced by an obscenely low-cut top. Something looked familiar. I peered at the television . . . Hang on a minute . . . I know that set. That's my show.

"*Noooooooooooooooo!*" I shrieked.

Derek and Gonzo jumped.

"What's up with you?" asked Derek.

"That's my show! That tart is presenting my bloody show! Oh, God, what have I done?" I said, dropping to the ground and wailing like a banshee.

"Fuck, Kate, I'm sorry I didn't realize," said Derek.

"Dude, you're like way better-looking," said Gonzo, trying to do some damage limitation. "She's just tits and ass."

I sobbed uncontrollably as the two boys hovered around me, not knowing what to do.

"She's a total bimbo and you're a . . . an older, like, more serious chick," said Derek.

"Yeah, totally. You're the Trevor McDonald and she's, like, the Jordan," added Gonzo.

"You are so Trevor," repeated Derek, confirming my likeness to a seventy-year-old, knighted newsman.

I managed a watery smile. I had to give them an A for effort. "Thanks, guys," I said. I dragged myself off to bed to lick my wounds, then cry over my lost career and current position as an unsuitable, unqualified childminder.

My alarm went off at six thirty. I had been asleep for thirty seconds — or so it felt to my tired body and puffy eyes. This was worse than boot camp. Fiona told me that Mark liked to get to the office early so I needed to be at the house at seven to give the boys their breakfast and dress them. I staggered into the bathroom and stood under the shower, hoping it would revive me. It didn't. I threw on a sweatshirt and jeans, drank a cup of extra strong coffee and headed for Fiona's house. It was still dark. This day two weeks ago I had been in Paris, interviewing Drew Barrymore about her new film.

When I arrived Mark was ready to leave.

"The boys are just waking up. Please make sure they're on time for school today. Bobby told me they were late yesterday. I'll be picking Fiona up at lunchtime and bringing her straight home. Could you put fresh sheets on the bed and maybe get some flowers for her bedside locker. Right, I'm off," he said, darting out the door before I had had a chance to open my mouth.

"Good morning to you too," I hissed after him. "I hope you have a rotten day and the Chinese mathematician is a phoney who makes you lose your stupid prize, you selfish prick."

"Why do you want Daddy to lose the prize?" said a voice behind me.

I spun round to see Jack in his *Bob the Builder* pyjamas, frowning at me. It was seven-oh-one and I had already messed up.

"I wasn't talking about your dad, silly, I was talking about the other man who's trying to get the same prize and I want your dad to win."

Jack looked unimpressed.

"Where's Bobby?"

"In bed and he says he won't get up."

"Well, let's go and see if he's OK," I said, glad of the distraction. I climbed the stairs with Jack hot on my heels.

Bobby was lying in bed with the duvet round his ears. "What's up, lazy-bones?" I asked, going over to pull down the duvet.

"No," Bobby shouted.

"Are you all right? Do you not feel well?" I asked, praying he wasn't sick. I was really looking forward to the three hours when they were at school. It was the only thing keeping me going.

He shook his head.

I sat down on the bed and leant over. "Are you worried about your mum?"

He shook his head again.

"Are you worried about Teddy?"

He shook his head a third time.

"Do you not want to go to school?"

He rolled away from me and as he did I got a strong whiff of urine.

"Oh, honey, did you wet the bed?" I asked.

His little head nodded sadly.

"That's OK. Everyone does it sometimes. It's nothing to worry about," I said, leaning in to hug him.

"*I* don't. I *never* wet the bed," said Jack.

"Shush now. Go and brush your teeth and I'll be in to you in a minute. I want to speak to Bobby alone."

Jack ran out of the room, shouting, "Bobby peed in his pants."

I rolled Bobby over so he was looking at me. "It's OK. Come on, let's get you out of those nasty wet sheets and pyjamas and we'll have a nice bath and then we'll get dressed."

"Will you tell Mummy?"

"Not if you don't want me to."

"I had a bad dream that she was really sick and then I woke up wet."

"Oh, sweetheart, you mustn't worry about your mum. She's going to be fine," I said, and hugged him.

As I did, I remembered my father doing the same thing to me when I was nearly eight. I had woken up in the middle of the night, screaming, and he had come in to me. I'd had a dream that Mum was being eaten alive by monsters. Dad had rocked me in his arms and told me not to worry, Mum would be fine. But she wasn't fine. She died three months later. Was I lying to Bobby? Would Fiona be OK? Were we all being over-optimistic about her recovery?

I looked down at his worried little face and kissed it. I'd said the right thing. He needed to believe — just as we all did — that Fiona would get better and things would return to normal.

"OK, Mister. Off with those stinky jim-jams and let's get some big bubbles for the bath so you smell all nice and clean for school."

As I was stripping the bed, and Bobby was taking off his pyjamas, he came over and hugged my leg. "Auntie Kate."

"Yes, pet?"

"I'm glad you came back from Ingerland."

I turned round so he wouldn't see me cry — if the sheet hadn't been so smelly, I'd have buried my head in it. I had done the right thing. This family needed me.

Jack insisted on getting into the bath with his brother and chaos ensued. I ended up wetter than anyone. Then I got them dressed and fed, and somehow managed to be at school two minutes early. Mrs Foley barely acknowledged me as I dropped them off. "Be good, boys. I'll see you later. By the time we get home, Mum will be back."

Their little faces lit up. I could tell my popularity was going to be short-lived.

I drove back to the house, put Bobby's sheets into the washing-machine, changed Fiona's bed linen and tidied up. I wanted everything to be nice and organized for her return.

Mark's car pulled up at exactly twelve, and I watched him help a frail Fiona out of the car. She winced as she stood up, clearly still in pain. I ran out to help her in. "How are you feeling?"

"Not too bad," she said bravely.

"She needs to take her painkillers," said Mark.

"I'll just have a cup of tea first," said Fiona, and sat down at the kitchen table. I put the kettle on. "How are the boys?" she asked.

"Great," I said. "They've been as good as gold. Although I'm not sure Mrs Foley is my biggest fan."

"What did you do?" Fiona asked, sighing, which I have to say ticked me off, considering I'd been running around like a blue-arsed fly for the past twenty-four hours looking after her kids.

"I didn't *do* anything. I just dropped them off ten seconds late yesterday and she gave me this big lecture on tardiness as if I was five years old."

"She has to be strict about parents being late, otherwise people take advantage and treat the school like a hotel. It's important for children to learn about good time-keeping."

Clearly the pain hadn't done anything to reduce Fiona's ability to lecture. I bit my tongue. "What are your doctor's instructions? Lots of rest, I suppose?" I asked.

"She's to rest and she'll start chemotherapy in three weeks' time," said Mark, as if he was reading a shopping list.

"Yikes! So soon," I said, looking at Fiona, who was glaring at Mark.

She nodded.

"Do you think you'll be able for it?"

She shrugged, as Mark said, "It's what the doctor recommended."

"Well, we'll all be here to help, so don't worry." But I was frightened by the dread on Fiona's face.

"Thanks," she said.

Mark cleared his throat and said he had to get back to the office. He asked Fiona if she wanted to be carried up to bed.

"No, thanks. I'd like to be up and dressed when the boys come back so they don't worry," said the saintly mother, as her selfish husband got ready to slink back to the office, away from his responsibilities.

"Fine. We can discuss that other matter later," he said, as he left.

When he had gone, Fiona slumped in her chair.

"What's he talking about?" I asked.

"Oh, Kate," she said, her eyes filling with tears. She told me about the conversation she and Mark had had with the doctor. He had asked if they wanted to have more children and Fiona had said, yes. He explained that chemotherapy can cause infertility and that Fiona needed to consider whether she wanted some of her eggs to be preserved for the future. But he added that he wouldn't recommend that she go down this avenue, first, because it would delay her treatment, and second, because of the high doses of hormones she'd be given to induce ovulation. But, he added, it was entirely Fiona's decision and something she needed to think seriously about.

"Mark said I need to focus on getting better and we can think about having more children later."

For once I agreed with him. "Well, the priority now is that you get better. It's only a possibility of infertility, and if the worst came to the worst, you still have two beautiful boys."

"But I really want more kids for Mark," Fiona said, welling up. "He's such a brilliant dad. We were going to start trying again before all this happened."

"And maybe in a year or two you'll get pregnant, but I don't think postponing your treatment is an option at this stage. You have to take the doctor's advice. He said he wouldn't recommend it."

"But I love kids."

"Look, if you need eggs, I'll give you mine. They're shag-all use to me so you might as well have them. Problem solved. Now, I've to go and collect the boys or that witch will have the police out looking to arrest me for tardiness."

As I drove to pick the twins up I thought about Fiona wanting more children. Having spent half a day with the twins I couldn't imagine how anyone would want to add to the pandemonium. Where would you get the energy from? When would you have any free time to go shopping or read a magazine in peace? She must be mad. But, then, she had always been maternal. I seemed to lack that gene. I liked the twins but, God, was I glad to hand them over to Mark last night and leave! The responsibility was too much. I liked my own space and being able to do what I wanted, when I wanted. No, kids were definitely not for me. Fiona was welcome to my eggs.

I skidded to a halt outside the school just on time. The twins came sprinting out, impatient to see their mum. I was irrelevant now — a mere chauffeur — as they quizzed me on what time she'd got back and was she all better and would she be staying at home for ever . . .

When we arrived, Fiona was leaning against the front door. She smiled when she saw her sons and they ran into her arms. I saw her catch her breath with pain as they threw their arms round her, but she hugged them and gave an Oscar-winning performance of someone who was in full health. When she had the chance she told me that the hospital had called to confirm that the cancer hadn't spread to her lymph nodes. I hugged her too, but gently, and told her it was the best news I'd ever heard. She laughed and said Dad had used the same words.

After an hour with the twins, she looked exhausted and I made her go up to bed for a nap. It was only when she didn't protest and didn't quiz me on what I

**110**

was cooking for dinner that I realized how much pain she was in. The boys helped me tuck her in and then we left her to rest — I was tempted to lie down beside her, but I took the boys out to the park instead and played I Spy . . . I snapped after the forty-seventh word. I could take it no more. They should use it as a form of torture in wars: it works.

# CHAPTER
# FOURTEEN

The next couple of weeks passed in a blur of driving the boys to school, picking them up, cleaning the house, making them lunch and dinner and pinning Fiona to the bed to rest. As each day passed she grew stronger, and by the time she was due to start her chemotherapy she was feeling much better, which was a pity in a way: just when she felt herself again she had to face intense treatment. Although she was trying to be positive, I could see she was dreading it. Every time I thought about it I felt sick for her.

Fiona had decided not to postpone the treatment and was just hoping it wouldn't cause permanent infertility. When Dad had found out she was thinking about delaying it he had gone mental. I don't ever remember seeing him so angry. He ranted and raged at her, telling her she was selfish for even thinking about it.

"You've two fine boys here who need their mother. Get some sense, girl. You can't put off getting better for some ridiculous egg collection — you're not a bloody hen. Be grateful for the two children you have and start that chemotherapy as soon as possible. You're to focus on one thing only, getting better, and if I have to drag you there by the scruff of your neck, you'll be starting that treatment next week, and I don't want to hear another bloody word about it. *Do you understand?*"

Fiona was shocked. Dad never shouted at her. He'd never had reason to. He'd roared at me and Derek on a regular basis, but Fiona was always so good and kind and responsible that he'd never had to raise his voice to her. When he had stormed out of the house to go for a walk and calm down, Fiona had looked at me wide-eyed.

"I know," I said. "He seems to think he's Marlon Brando in *The Godfather*." I wanted to make light of it because it was obvious that Dad was terrified Fiona was going to die, and his outburst had made me nervous. He had first-hand experience of losing someone from this disease: did he think Fiona was going to end up like Mum?

"What have you done to the old man?" asked Derek, arriving in. "I asked him to lend me a few quid and he pinned me up against the wall and told me I was a waste of space and it was time I grew up. It's practically child abuse."

"Derek, you're twenty-six," I reminded him. "It'd be adult abuse."

"I might have to write a song about it — 'My fatha shouted me out, and called me a useless lout, I'm damaged from the shout . . .'"

"You've used 'shout' twice in three lines," said Fiona, and we dissolved with laughter.

"It's all just a joke to you. Well, when I'm living in a far-out crib, we'll see who's laughing then," said the sensitive artist with high expectations.

"Come on, Derek, we're only joking," said Fiona the peace-maker, as he flounced out of the room to finish his bestselling rap-song about how his father had abused him by supporting him financially for twenty-six years.

At last the day of Fiona's first chemotherapy session came round. She had organized it to take place when the boys were at school. As usual, Mark couldn't be there because of work. This time I didn't bite my tongue. Two days before we had had a huge argument when he told me he wouldn't be going with Fiona.

"What do you mean you can't go? Do you not understand what's going on here? Your wife is about to undergo a horrific bout of treatment. What the hell could be more important than being at her side?"

"Of course I'd like to be there, but I only have a few weeks left to produce this paper and Fiona is one hundred per cent behind me. I will be here to look after her every evening, as I always am. I should be able to take her to the next session. I just can't be with her at this one. You came home to help, so can you please just help and stop nagging me?"

"Nagging you? Oh, Mark, I haven't even got warmed up."

"Fiona is the one whose opinion matters and she's fully supportive. I'll have more time to be with her after this competition, when she really needs me."

"In the mean time, good old Kate will pick up the pieces. Don't worry, I'll hold your wife's hand. You go off and do your sums."

Fiona and I drove to the hospital in silence. She was too terrified to speak and I couldn't think of anything comforting to say. She was now facing six months of chemotherapy — eight sessions, one every three to four weeks, followed by radiotherapy five days a week for five weeks. The oncologist had said her chances of full recovery were very good and it would all be over in seven and a half months' time. Fiona was a fighter, I reminded myself. She'd survive this. It was February so, all going well, she'd be completely finished her treatment by September or October and then she could put it behind her. We all could.

When we arrived at the treatment centre, a friendly nurse called June showed us into a large, sunny room with six big comfortable chairs and several smaller ones for visitors. This was where the chemotherapy would be administered. But, first of all, Fiona had to go for a series of blood tests.

A couple of hours later she was given the go-ahead to start the chemotherapy. She lay back in one of the chairs in the treatment room and waited for her drugs to be made up. I had bought stacks of magazines to distract her, which I placed on her lap.

There were four other patients in the room: two men, one in his fifties, who was completely bald, and a young guy, who looked about twenty-five and had a full head of hair. Two women sat on Fiona's side of the room. One looked to be in her mid-sixties, had thinning hair and a very grey pallor; the other was younger — mid-forties, I reckoned — and completely bald. She was wearing bright red lipstick and a funky, multicoloured hat lay at her side.

The older man was working, his briefcase perched on his lap. The young guy was lying back, eyes closed, listening to music. The older woman was knitting and the other lady, who was sitting closest to us, was reading a book and laughing out loud every now and then. Fiona caught her eye and smiled.

She winked. "First time?"

"Is it that obvious?"

"You have that look of terror. It's not so bad, honestly. I'm Anne."

"I'm Fiona. So, uhm, how long does it take before your hair falls out?"

I winced and hoped that Anne would say something comforting, like, "Never."

"I was bald as a badger after a week, but everyone's different. Some people don't lose it at all. You could be lucky."

"I feel about as lucky as a turkey on Christmas Day," Fiona said, letting her guard down for once.

I laughed a little too enthusiastically, as Anne smiled at Fiona and said, "Good girl. A sense of humour will help you more than anything to get through this."

The oncology nurse came back in and inserted a needle into a vein in Fiona's arm. She attached the needle to a tube, which would deliver the chemotherapy from a plastic bag into Fiona's bloodstream. Fiona was

116

told to sit back and relax and wait until all the liquid had gone into her vein — it would take a couple of hours. I went off to get coffee and muffins, but Fiona was too scared to eat, so I polished them off — I hadn't eaten a muffin in five years: too many calories. So, for someone who had been constantly hungry for five years, they tasted heavenly.

After a few minutes of flicking through magazines, Fiona said, "I can't concentrate. I keep thinking they're injecting poison into my blood and it's going to make me worse."

"It's going to make you better, Fiona, I swear it is," I said, willing her to believe me.

She smiled at me. "I'm sorry, Kate."

"For what?"

"Dragging you home from London and turning you into a child-minder and nurse."

"I always quite fancied myself as a nurse," I said, grinning. "I think the uniform would look great on me. Besides, I've enjoyed spending time with the boys."

"Really? They can be a handful at times."

"True, but I feel that I'm actually getting to know them now, and it's really nice."

"Do you think you'll ever settle down?"

"Well, considering that my last boyfriend turned out to be married, I don't see myself in a white frock any time soon. I seem to have the worst taste in men."

"Sam was great," said Fiona.

"Yeah, he was one of the good ones."

"Do you ever regret breaking up with him and moving to London?"

"No. I had to go away and find out who I was and spread my wings, but I've certainly never met anyone I liked as much. Still, I'm only thirty, plenty of time for all that," I said, smiling at my sister. It was nice, chatting like this, like friends. Our conversations had always been about flight times, presents for Dad and Derek, how my career was going and how the boys were doing.

"Fiona?"

"Yes?"

"Does it bother you that Mark is always so busy?"

She sighed and took on her older-sister tone: "He told me you gave him a hard time about not being able to come today. He feels bad enough as it is. You have to understand, Kate, this prize he's working towards is something that no Irishman has ever dared to go for. It's incredibly prestigious in the world of mathematics. It's like an actor winning an Oscar. It's a really big deal, and if he wins, he'll be considered one of the leading mathematicians in Europe. I know it might seem selfish, but I am one hundred per cent behind him, so please don't make him feel bad."

We were back to square one — the little sister being scolded by the big one. My loathing for Mark was even greater now that he'd ruined my "moment" with Fiona.

She immersed herself in a magazine while I leant back in my chair and thought about Sam and the last time we had met, seven years ago, the year after I'd moved to London. We were at a mutual friend's wedding and we were both alone, but Sam had gone out of his way to annoy me by flirting with every girl there. It shouldn't have bothered me: I was dating a cute Australian guy at the time, but seeing Sam again unsettled me more than I'd expected. He looked gorgeous in his tuxedo and he was very pleased with himself, having just landed a job as staff writer on the *Irish Independent*. I was still making tea at Lifechange, waiting for my break. When we finally met face to face, sparks flew.

"Hey, how are you?" he asked.

"Great, thanks. Fantastic, actually. Things are going really well," I said, never one for understatement.

"Good for you. So, you're enjoying the cattle market over there?"

"Yeah, well, I've always liked a challenge. Some people are afraid of success, but not me."

"No, definitely not you. Have you got a job in television? I don't recall having seen you on the screen."

"Yes actually, I'm a researcher on the Lifechange morning show. That's where everyone starts. I should be in front of the camera within the next six months," I lied. "And I'm going out with Jason, an Australian news reporter, so I'm meeting all the right people," I said, as my nose began to compete with Pinocchio's. Jason was the manager at Bar Oz, the pub round the corner from work.

"Well, it sounds great, Kate. So it was worth it, then?" He was staring at me and I felt as if his eyes could see right through me. God, I missed those eyes.

"I think so," I mumbled, thrown by the tingling sensation in my stomach. "By the way, congratulations on your new job. Tara told me. You must be really pleased."

"Well, for a small-town hick like me, working for the *Independent* is a dream come true — but I'm sure for a big-city girl like you it seems a bit sad."

"No, it doesn't," I said quietly. "It's great. You deserve it."

Sam looked at me the way he used to, when he had actually liked me — even loved me. It was a look that had always made me feel ten feet tall. My heart skipped a beat. I could see he still had feelings for me. "I miss you," I said, reaching out for his hand before I could stop myself.

"Don't do that," he said, pulling it back. "You decided to go to London. You ended our relationship because of your career. You said you didn't want any ties to Dublin when you left. It was your choice, not mine, so don't come back here a year later and tell me you miss me."

"I thought it was the right thing to do. I needed to be focused," I said, as a lump formed in my throat.

"And now you've changed your mind? What does that mean? 'I miss you and I fancy sex tonight?' Or 'I miss you and realize I made a mistake — I was wrong, stupid, selfish'?"

"It meant nothing. It was a stupid, momentary lapse. It won't happen again. Thanks for reminding me why I made the right decision. Have a nice life," I said, running off, partly to hide my tears and partly because I didn't trust myself not to beg him to get back with me. I really missed him. London was lonely and a lot harder to crack than I had imagined it would be. Damn. Why had I said that? Now he presumed I regretted my decision to move to London and, despite everything, I didn't. I had felt suffocated in Dublin. I needed to explore new places, have new experiences and follow my dreams. To hell with him, I thought. I'll prove him wrong. He'll be sorry when he sees me presenting my own show and earning great money.

And that was the last time we saw each other.

# CHAPTER
# FIFTEEN

After dropping Fiona home, tucking her up in bed and placing her anti-nausea tablets beside her, I went to collect the boys from school. I was planning to do a quick sprint to the supermarket to buy her all the comfort food I could think of, then get back to check on her.

But nothing was quick or straightforward with the twins. It was my first trip to the supermarket with them and I had no idea what a minefield it would be. They jumped around like gorillas in the shop, pushing and shoving each other until Jack fell over and hit his head on the floor. He howled the place down and it took a good five minutes and some bribery — in the form of a chocolate bar — to get him to stop crying. Then Bobby insisted on having one too, so for a while there was peace . . . Until they'd finished the chocolate and started grabbing everything they could reach and pulling it down from the shelves. When Jack dropped a large carton of Ribena, which spilt everywhere, I lost my cool. Most of the contents had ended up over me — which didn't really matter as I was in my uniform of sweatshirt and jeans — but the floor was covered with sticky liquid. I pushed back my Ribena-soaked hair, pulled a tissue out of my pocket and bent down to try to wipe it up. By the time I turned round the boys were running down the aisle. I tore after them, shouting, like a fishwife, "Jack, Bobby, get back here before I smack you. *Jack! Bobby!*"

I managed to tackle Jack to the floor and, holding him under one arm, went after Bobby, who had run in a full circle and ended up slipping on the spilt Ribena. Thankfully he was unhurt and thought that rolling around in the purple mess was great fun. Jack wriggled out of my arm and joined in. As my temperature rose a hundred degrees, I grabbed Jack and flung him into the trolley. "You are a very bold boy. Now, stay there or, I promise you, I will smack you very hard."

"Mean Kate. Mummy says no smacking," said Jack.

I grabbed Bobby, and as I tried to put him into the trolley, he kicked me. "I hate you," he said.

"Well, I hate you too," I bellowed.

"Kate? Is that you?" an all-too-familiar voice asked.

Oh, God, come on, give me a break. Not now, not shouting at my nephews, not looking like a dog, covered with Ribena. Please don't do this to me. I'm a good person — how can you be so cruel?

I decided to keep walking and ignore it. Maybe if I pretended I wasn't me, he'd think he'd made a mistake. A hand reached out to take my arm.

"Kate, my God, it *is* you! Hi — how are you?" asked Sam, trying and failing to hide his shock.

I looked like hell and I knew it. I turned about ten shades of red. "Hi, yep, it's me. Underneath all this gunk. How's it going?" I said, glancing up, and immediately regretting it. His eyes were just as green and heart-stopping as I remembered. God, he was gorgeous. Sure, he'd aged a bit, but the wrinkles round his eyes were attractive. I cursed myself for not making an effort this morning. A month ago I wouldn't have been seen dead without makeup and nice clothes. Now I looked like a homeless person.

"Good, thanks. I met Tara a few weeks ago and she told me you were home. I'm so sorry to hear about Fiona. How's she feeling?"

"Well, she had her first chemo session today so it's hard for her," I said, trying to pull my matted fringe down over my face.

"Are you home for a while?"

"Yep. I'm looking after the boys and helping out. I dunno how long I'll be here, probably about six months."

"What about your job?"

"Oh, that. Well, I've been replaced so I'll have to find something else," I said, trying not to sound as devastated as I felt.

"I'm sorry, I know how much that job meant to you."

"Well, Fiona's more important," I said, glad I had finally proven I wasn't a heartless bitch who abandoned everything for her career.

"Of course. I'm sure she's glad to have you around."

I nodded. I was afraid I was going to cry. It was all too much — Fiona, the kids, my job, Sam and — to be shallow and honest — the fact that I looked like shit.

"Can I call you while you're home?" he asked.

"Pity call, because I've no job, am back living with my dad, and my sister has cancer?"

"No," said Sam, smiling. "Friend call. If it makes you feel any better my wife left me for her boss so I'm a sad case too."

"Bitch."

"Thanks for the support."

"I always thought she was a loser," I said, smirking.

"You should have given me a heads up."

"We weren't exactly pen-pals at the time."

"How's your love life?" he asked.

"Oh, they're queuing round the block. I'm a real catch. Thirty, jobless, homeless, penniless and looking like a freak."

"I dunno, there's a 9½ Weeks element to being covered with liquid."

"It's Ribena, not hot chocolate, and there are children present. You need to get out more," I said, laughing.

"So, how about one loser calls another?"

"I guess that'd be OK," I said, trying to give him a flirty look via my Ribena-stained face.

"Great. It's a non-pity non-date."

"Sounds too good to be true," I said.

"OK, I'll see you soon. 'Bye, guys, be good for your auntie Kate," he said to the twins, then ruffled their hair and walked away.

I watched him go, admiring his bum. He'd always had a great backside.

"Hey, Kate," he said, turning around and catching me.

"What?" I said, blushing at being caught out ogling.

"It was good to see you," he said, and winked.

I turned round to hide the grin that was threatening to swallow my face and to balance my shaking legs against the trolley.

"Auntie Kate," said a little voice.

"Yes?"

"Do you really hate me?"

"Oh, Bobby, of course not," I said, kissing his sticky cheek. "I'm so sorry, I deserve a slap for saying something so mean. Here, slap my hand."

Jack joined in, and while they were slapping me black and blue, all I could do was smile.

When we got back to the house, I could hear Fiona retching in the bathroom. I sat the boys down to do their afternoon sums and ran up to her. She was lying on the bathroom floor, looking green.

"Are you OK?"

"It came over me all of a sudden. I was fine until about ten minutes ago."

"Have you taken your anti-nausea tablets?"

"Every time I try to swallow one it makes me gag."

"Here, let me help you. Maybe if you tilt your head this way," I said, gently leaning her back against me. She managed to swallow one without throwing up. I helped her back into bed, where she curled up in the foetal position.

"You're all sticky," she said, noticing my hair and clothes.

"Ribena accident."

She smiled. "Welcome to my world. And you used to wonder why I didn't make more of an effort to dress well."

I nodded. "I apologize. I had no idea of the mess kids cause. I'm constantly covered with mush or spilt drinks."

"I'll be down in a minute to help with dinner."

"Fiona, just put your feet up and leave dinner to me. Is there anything you think you could face eating?"

"Not now, maybe later."

"I bought enough food for an army, so there's plenty of choice."

"You seem very chirpy."

I blushed.

"What? Tell me — distract me with whatever it is."

"I bumped into Sam at the supermarket," I said, omitting to tell her that it was directly after I'd told her five-year-old child that I hated him.

"No! What happened?"

"He asked if he could call me."

"Wow! That's great."

"Relax, it's not a date. We're going to meet up for a drink as mates."

"For a casual drink with a friend, you've got some glow," said Fiona, grinning.

"You shush and go to sleep," I said, coming over all matron-like to hide my embarrassment.

Later that afternoon, Dad and Derek called over to see how Fiona was feeling. Dad strolled in, followed by Derek, who was carrying a large bunch of grapes.

"Fiona hates grapes," I said.

"No, *you* hate grapes," said Derek.

"No, you dope, I like them, Fiona hates them."

"Bollox."

Dad rolled his eyes, "Have you met my son Albert — Albert Einstein?"

"Have you met Billy Connolly?" drawled Derek.

"Albert Einstein was born in Germany," Bobby piped up.

"You're right. He was," said Mark, arriving back early for once.

"Ah, here's Florence Nightingale himself," muttered Dad.

"And in Einstein's early days in Berlin, he postulated that the correct interpretation of the special theory of relativity must also furnish a theory of gravitation, and in 1916, he published his paper on the general theory of relativity," continued Mark.

"And you think you pulled the short straw with me as a father," Dad whispered to Derek.

"I'd rather boil my head in hot wax than have to listen to that every day," muttered Derek.

"I couldn't have put it better myself," said Dad.

"How is she?" Mark asked me.

"I'm fine, thanks," said Fiona, coming in with Jack hanging off her arm. She looked much better after her nap.

"Get away out of that," said Dad to Jack. "Don't be hanging on to your mother. Go over to your father and let him tell you some mind-numbing — sorry, I meant mind-*blowing* facts about Albert Einstein."

I busied myself with the kettle so I wouldn't laugh.

"It's great you still have hair," said Derek, to Fiona. "I thought you might be bald after today. Roxanne's cousin had chemo and all her hair fell out — like, I mean, all of it. She had nothing *anywhere*."

"I think Fiona understands what you're saying, Derek. You don't have to spell it out," I said.

"It probably will fall out over the next few sessions, so I should really get it cut short," said Fiona, running her hands through her lovely hair.

"Short hair is really in now. All the chicks on MTV have short hair," lied Derek.

"You've got great cheekbones so it'll suit you," I added.

"Sure she'd be gorgeous bald an' all," said Dad.

"Hey, I forgot to tell you. Roxanne fixed my tattoo and she didn't charge me," said Derek.

"Sure aren't you paying her with sex on demand?" said Dad.

"Dad, the twins," said Fiona, frowning.

"Sorry, boys," said Dad, with a grin.

"So, like, do you want to see it or what?" asked Derek.

Fiona and I nodded.

"Now, lads," said Dad, to the twins, "your uncle Derek is going to demonstrate what a Latin scholar his lovely girlfriend is. Watch carefully."

Derek turned round and pulled down his trousers. Roxanne had created "Carpe Derek" out of "Carpe Deim". You could see the I and the M underneath the R and the E.

"Well, son, you've really outdone yourself this time," said Dad. "I'm speechless."

"Cool, huh?" said Derek. "So, like, it now says, 'Seize the Derek.' Awesome!"

# CHAPTER
# SIXTEEN

Sam didn't call the next day or the day after or even the day after that. I kept getting the twins to call my mobile from the landline to see if it was working — it was. Eventually I met up with Tara for a moan.

"It's not like it was a date or anything, but he said he'd call so why hasn't he?"

"It's only been five days. I'm sure he will," she said, trying to reassure me in her best-friend way.

"But why would he wait? It's not as if he needs to play it cool. We're just meeting up as friends."

"So you keep saying," she said, smiling. "Look, maybe he's tied up with work. Maybe he had to go away on an assignment to cover some big sports event."

"I bet you he said he'd ring because I looked so awful and stressed out that he felt sorry for me and was trying to be nice."

"I'm sure you looked fine."

"Tara — I had no makeup on, I hadn't washed my hair in four days and my jeans are so tight on me now that I look like a heifer — not to mention that I was covered with Ribena and shouting at poor Bobby. I could see he was shocked by my appearance. I really have let myself go. How is anyone with kids supposed to look good? It's impossible! All your clothes get ruined and I'd rather have an extra half-hour in bed than wash my hair, so it's permanently stuck to my head."

"How do you feel about children now?"

"Oh, God, I'm never having any. They're too much work. You literally have to give up your life. It's non-stop. No wonder Fiona always looks tired. Don't get me wrong, it's nice to spend time with them and get to know them and they can be really cute — but most of the time it's hard slog. You wash, cook, clean, collect, and then do it all over again. I can't wait to get back to my life in London."

"Yeah, but Fiona loves being a mum, doesn't she?"

I nodded. "Yes, she does, but she was always maternal. Not like you and me! God, I'm so dying for a night out on the town. Let's get smashed. Come on, I need to blow off steam and it'll distract me from obsessing about Sam not calling."

Tara looked down at the glass of wine she had barely touched. "Actually, Kate, I've got some news. I'm pregnant."

What? Tara pregnant? Oh, God, me and my big mouth. I knew it was ridiculous but I was totally shocked. Sure, she was happily married and the next natural step was a baby, but Tara was far too young to have kids. We were only thirty — almost thirty-one, to be precise. It was too early for her to give up her life — maybe when she was thirty-five, but not now. What about going out and having fun? What about being young and carefree? When did life get so serious and responsible and tied down?

"Oh, wow! Was it a surprise?"

"No," she said, a little defensively. "We'd been trying for a few months. We're thrilled — we really want children."

"I'm sorry, I just can't imagine you as a mother," I said, laughing.

"Why not?" she said, glaring at me.

"Well, you know, you like to go out and have fun and you love your sleep and you never seemed that into kids."

"Well, it's different when it's your own. Besides, I'd never have thought you'd be able to look after twins and you're managing."

"Yeah, but that's because I hand them back every night and I know it's only for a few months."

"Look, Kate, I'm thrilled about my pregnancy. I spent my twenties partying and sleeping all day, and I'm ready for the next stage in my life. I don't care if I don't get to go out all the time and I really don't care if I have dribble on my clothes. Those things don't bother me any more. I've moved on. I'm dying to have kids."

Her face was flushed. She was clearly furious with me.

"So you're happy never to go clubbing again or lounge in bed on Saturday morning reading, or go away for a weekend at the drop of a hat?"

"Yes, I am. Who cares about those things any more? Come on, we're in our thirties. It's time to grow up and move on with our lives. It's a bit shallow and juvenile to sacrifice marriage and kids because you want to go out and party."

"I disagree. I don't want to get old and settled. I still want to have fun. I don't feel thirty, I feel twenty-five," I said, annoyed at her implication that it was childish to want to have a good time. Since when was it a crime to enjoy yourself?

"Look, Kate, I guess I've moved on and you haven't. It's probably because you're living the single life in London and I'm in a settled situation here. You were always more restless than me, always looking for distractions and new experiences. We're just different. But I'd like you to be happy for me."

"I'm sorry, Tara, and of course I'm happy for you. It's great news. Just don't ask me to babysit," I said, faking a smile but I was thrown by what she'd said.

Was I going to end up like one of those sad women you see in nightclubs, squeezed into a leopard-print mini-dress with four inches of makeup on, trying to compete with girls twenty years younger? Would I be getting Botox every six months to hide the wrinkles that gave away my age? Was I going to be sad old Auntie Kate, who lived in London on her own, married to her career? And, let's face it, the business I was in was a young person's game.

But, on the other hand, I didn't want what Fiona had. I felt sorry for her: she had no life of her own. Her kids were too young to appreciate everything she did for them and her husband was never there. The twins would disappear at eighteen and she'd have sacrificed all those years for what? Raising kids who were good at sums? It wasn't what I wanted. I couldn't imagine myself settled with kids. I'd hate it. I liked spontaneity and sleep, shopping and travelling. I suppose I was selfish, but I wasn't hurting anyone so why should I feel bad about it? Why did I feel like a freak all of a sudden? I twisted and turned all night, mulling it over in my head.

The next morning I was none the wiser, just even more exhausted. Sod it, I was for the single life and I wasn't going to feel guilty about it.

Two weeks after her chemotherapy session, Fiona began to feel much better, which was great for her and not so great for me. She took it upon herself to teach me how to cook for children. We did a new recipe every day. Day three was risotto. I'd always thought that risotto was something trained chefs made. It looked long and complicated — and I was right. Instead of using a stock cube, like most normal people, to make vegetable stock, Fiona insisted on boiling real vegetables in water for hours.

"Why bother?" I asked. "It's just mucky water. Why not take the quick and easy option?"

"That's the whole point, Kate. The easy option is not the most nutritious one. Stock cubes contain a lot of salt and children shouldn't be eating any at all."

I decided not to mention that I'd been pouring salt over the twins' mashed potatoes. "Oh, come on, Fiona, a little bit of salt isn't going to kill them and it'll knock hours off cooking this meal," I said, stifling a yawn.

"Taking the easy way isn't right. You need to do things properly in life to achieve the best results. People who cut corners are only fooling themselves. If you're going to bother cooking dinner, do it properly, or you might as well feed your kids junk food," she said.

I was fed up. My best friend thought I was juvenile and my sister thought I was a lazy cow who cut corners at the expense of her children's health. Not to mention the fact that Sam still hadn't rung and I lurched from feeling furious to upset to pretending not to care. I knew that if I didn't get out of the house I'd take out my grumpiness on Fiona and, with her chemo coming up, I really didn't want to do that, so I told her I had to go and went home to Dad's to sulk.

His car was in the driveway, but I didn't feel like talking to anyone so I crept upstairs to my room. I was opening my bedroom door when I heard noises coming from his bedroom. It sounded as if he was having a panic-attack. I charged through the door, ready to perform CPR.

"Jesus Christ," he roared. "Whatever happened to knocking?"

"Argggggh!" I screamed, as my father's hairy, naked backside greeted me. Underneath him lay a woman who looked about forty and they were mid-action. I couldn't believe that I had walked in on my father shagging. Widowed sixty-two-year-olds aren't supposed to have sex.

"What are you doing home?" he shouted, very red in the face, although whether that was from exertion or shame, I'm not sure.

I should have walked out but I was rooted to the spot and there was something oddly familiar about the woman . . . Oh, my God! It was Mrs Jones, my old gym teacher.

"OUT!" yelled Dad.

I turned on my heels and fled downstairs. I could hear music from the TV room, so I went in to tell Derek about the scene I'd just witnessed.

"Derek, you're not going to believe —" I said, stopping mid-sentence as two panting faces looked up at me from the couch. Jesus, was I the only person in this house not getting any action?

I backed out of the room and went to pour myself a large glass of wine. I hadn't had sex in months, and here were my father and brother hard at it. It was official: I was a crotchety old dried-up maiden aunt at the grand old age of thirty and three-quarters.

Before I had the chance to wallow completely in self-pity and my lifetime membership of the Shelf, Dad arrived downstairs in his dressing-gown followed by Mrs Jones, his new — lover, friend, fuck-buddy?

"Hello, Kate, nice to see you again," said the brazen hussy, not looking at all put out that I'd just caught her naked, shagging my father. Mind you, she'd never liked me very much. Gym was not my forte — to be fair, I didn't have a forte. I was not blessed with bendy limbs — I couldn't get close to the splits. To be bendy when you're young guarantees you cool status. I couldn't even twist my tongue into a sausage roll, not to mind do a decent cartwheel. As a result, Mrs Jones and I hadn't been the best of pals. She openly favoured double-jointed elasticated girls and scorned us normal ladies.

"Hi, Mrs Jones, I see you're as fit as ever," I said, smirking. This was my house, my father, and it was her knickers that had been down — I was damned if I was going to be the one to feel embarrassed.

"Yes, thanks," said the old slapper, without batting an eyelid. Then she turned to Dad, kissed him — in front of me! — and headed out the door. The cheek of her.

"Sheryl's in training for the marathon," said Dad, as proudly as if he were running it himself.

"I see — and does her training include much horizontal jogging?"

"Don't you give me any lip, young lady."

"Dad, I don't think you're in a position to take the moral high ground here. I just caught you with your pants down riding my gym teacher. How long has this been going on?"

"About six months."

"Did you fancy her when we were in school?"

"I always thought she was fit-looking."

"Jesus, did you try and chat her up at the parent-teacher meetings?"

"I'd never be so unprofessional," he said, sounding genuinely insulted. "Besides, she was married."

"Where's her husband now? Should we expect the door to be kicked in any minute?"

"He died of a heart-attack a few years back."

"You'd better watch out — she seems to wear men out."

"I'm well able for her," said Dad, flexing non-existent muscles.

"How long were you dating before you had sex?"

"None of your business."

"Are you using protection?"

"I'm warning you, Kate."

"OK. What age is the lovely Sheryl?"

"Forty-eight."

"Do you love her?"

"She's a very nice lady."

"Do you always have sex with women you find 'nice'?"

"It depends what they look like."

"Jesus, Dad!"

"A man can't live on bread alone," he said.

How had I missed all this? How had I not known that my father was dating? I was in London, not Timbuc-bloody-too.

"Do Fiona and Derek know?"

He shrugged. "Derek's met her, but sure it all goes over his head and Fiona knows I'm seeing her."

"Why did no one tell me?"

"Probably because you never asked."

He had a point there, but were children supposed to ask their parents how their sex lives were? Wasn't that a little too modern? I'm all for communication but you can have too much information . . . and what I had just witnessed was *way* too much information.

"Do you think it's going to last?"

"Who knows? We're having fun so we'll have to wait and see."

Bloody men! They're all the same, no matter what age they are — noncommittal to the end.

"Well, I hope you're not leading that poor woman up the garden path," I said, suddenly finding myself defending Sheryl Jones, who had never been very nice to me.

"She knows the score."

"Which is that you want the company, the sex, the fun but not the commitment?"

"No need to be dramatic. She knows I'm not looking for a wife."

"Does she want to get married?"

"Don't all women?"

"No — well, maybe eventually. I dunno, I give up on men," I said, and slugged back some wine.

My phone beeped.

I glanced down. I had a new text message. It was from Sam: *Sry not in touch sooner — bloody work! Friday, Blues wine bar 8?*

# CHAPTER
# SEVENTEEN

The Friday of my non-date with Sam was the day of Fiona's second chemotherapy session. I was glad to have the drink to look forward to, because I was dreading the day for Fiona. I'd been looking at the Internet and it seemed pretty common for patients' hair to fall out after the second or third treatment.

The day before her chemo, I booked her an appointment with a local hairdresser and cut out a picture of Sharon Stone with short hair to bring along, so she wouldn't end up with a pudding bowl. Fiona insisted I didn't tell them why she was getting her hair cut — she didn't want people feeling sorry for her. Besides, she was feeling much better and she didn't want to focus on her illness.

While her locks were being chopped off I told her about finding Dad and Mrs Jones in a compromising position.

"Oh, God, Kate! What did you do?"

"When I started breathing again, I ran out as fast as I could. How could you not have told me he was seeing someone?"

"I suppose I presumed you knew. It's been going on for a while now."

"But it's Mrs Jones! She's a cow! Don't you remember her from school?"

Fiona looked a bit vague. "No — what did she teach?"

"Gymnastics. Come on, you must remember her. She was like a sergeant bloody major, ordering everyone about and flinging girls on and off the beam and trying to twist our bodies into unnatural shapes."

"I didn't do gym — it clashed with special maths."

I had forgotten that Fiona and the other mathematical super-brains — all three of them — had done a special brainiac class. Compared to maths, gym was a walk in the park, as far as I was concerned. Give me a forward roll over a theorem any day.

"Well, take it from me, she's not a very sweet person and I don't want Dad to end up with her."

"I didn't have the impression they were getting married," said Fiona. "He's obviously just after her body." She grinned.

"Fiona, if you'd *seen* them! It was gross. I can't get the image of Dad's wrinkly bum out of my head. Old people shouldn't have sex without bolting their doors. I'm traumatized!"

"Good old Dad. At least he's still up to it. Sex is becoming a distant memory for me," she murmured.

"What do you mean?" I asked.

"Oh, nothing," said Fiona. "You know how it is, couples with young kids . . ." She tailed off.

142

"Well, you couldn't be getting less action than I am," I said.

"I wouldn't bet on it." She turned back to her magazine.

Clearly Mark was underperforming in the bedroom as well as in every other aspect of his marriage. I wondered if his uselessness was grounds for annulment, and wished Fiona could be swept off her feet by a tall dark handsome stranger with big strong arms who'd carry her to and from chemotherapy and tell her how wonderful and beautiful she was and ravish her every night . . .

"Kate?" Fiona's voice interrupted my match-making.

The hairdresser had finished drying her hair.

"Oh, wow! You look fantastic," I lied. Her beautiful curly dark hair lay strewn around her on the floor and she was left with very tightly cut curls that stuck up in clumps all over her head, nothing like Sharon Stone's cool crop in the picture I'd shown the stylist.

Fiona looked at herself in the mirror and tried to pat down a stray curl. "I look like a poodle," she said, as her eyes filled.

"You do not," I snapped. "You look gorgeous. Mark's a very lucky guy."

She stood up and wiped away a tear. As she turned towards the door, I picked up a stray curl from the floor and popped it into my bag. I don't know why — good luck, superstition, in the hope that when her hair grew back we could laugh about the shorn curls . . . I'm not sure, but it was strangely comforting, as if I had a piece of Fiona that no one could take away.

When we collected the twins from school, they stared at their mum in silence. Fiona had always had long hair.

"Where's your hair?" asked Jack, walking round to see if it was hidden behind her.

"I cut it off today," said Fiona, putting on her cheeriest smile.

"Why?" asked Jack. "You look like a boy now," he added, lip quivering.

Jesus, kids could be brutal sometimes.

"No, she doesn't," I said, frowning at him. "She looks beautiful."

"Boys," said Fiona, crouching so she could talk to them directly, eye to eye, "the medicine that the doctor is giving me to make me better might make my hair fall out, so if I look a bit strange, don't worry, I'm still your mummy. I'll just have funny hair for a while."

"But why does the medicine make your hair fall out?" asked Jack, very worried.

"Because it's strong medicine that I need to take to fight the bad cells. But my hair will grow back, sweetheart," said Fiona, as her own lip began to tremble.

"But I thought the doctor took out all the bad cells already," said Bobby.

"Well, yes, he did, but the medicine is to make sure that no bad cells come back so that I don't get sick again."

"Are they fighting each other?" asked Bobby.

144

"Well, yes, I suppose they are."

"Inside your tummy?" asked Jack.

"Yes."

"Cool," said Bobby.

"Can you feel them punching each other?" asked Jack.

"No, sweetheart, it's not violent."

"But how —"

"OK, boys, that's enough questions," I interrupted, before it turned into *Mastermind*. "Come on, into the car. Give your mum a break."

Mark was working late — again — so I helped Fiona bathe the twins and put them to bed. At prayer time, Bobby piped up, "God bless Mummy and Daddy and Teddy and Uncle Derek and Granddad and Auntie Kate, and please make Mummy's hair come back so she looks like an angel again."

I could see Fiona from the corner of my eye, struggling not to cry.

The next morning Mark took Fiona to hospital and I took the boys to school. Mark was going to stay with her while she had her blood tests and I'd join her when the drugs were being administered. I'd called Derek to tell him to pop in and give Fiona some moral support and I'd asked Casanova to tear himself away from horizontal gym lessons with my old teacher and drop by too.

Dad arrived first, laden with flowers, chocolates and newspapers.

"If it isn't the Don Juan of Dublin," I said.

"Hi, Dad," said Fiona. "I hear you've been working out lately."

Ignoring us, and determined to change the subject, Dad asked, "How many times has Meryl Streep been nominated for an Oscar?"

Fiona looked at him blankly — she'd have preferred a chess question.

"Thirteen nominations in twenty-six years," I answered. "Don't try to change the subject."

Luckily for Dad, Derek chose that moment to stroll through the door, Roxanne in tow.

"Ah, the lovely Roxanne, said Dad, thrilled to be off the hook.

"Yo, sis, this is Roxanne, Roxanne, my sister Fiona," said Derek.

"'Sup?" said Roxanne plonking herself beside Fiona. Her extremely low-rise jeans exposed ninety per cent of her G-string to the room.

Dad didn't know where to look. Now he knew how I'd felt when I saw his arse.

"Roxanne's cousin had cancer so she totally knows all about it. Any questions, just ask her," said Derek.

"Isn't that marvellous?" said Dad. "An expert in the field of tattooism, a Latin scholar and now a cancer specialist. I must say I'm impressed."

Roxanne twisted her nose-ring. "Some people just have what it takes."

"How's business?" asked Dad.

"*Insane*. I barely have time to eat. Everyone wants a tattoo."

"I can see why. They really are very attractive," said Dad. "Lookit, Fiona, have you seen Roxanne's lovely snake?" he asked, as Fiona gazed in horror at Roxanne's stomach.

"You seem keen. Come down any time. I'll give you a discount cos of Derek being your son and all."

"What do you think I should get?" said Dad, stirring it.

Roxanne looked him up and down. "For oldies, it's best to get something where the skin isn't so wrinkly. Maybe a skull on your forearm."

"Or you could get 'Sheryl for ever'." I giggled.

"I might go for something subtle like Derek has," said Dad.

"Roxanne said to avoid wrinkly areas, and after my recent exposure to your backside, we can safely say it isn't a runner." I sniggered.

"It's up to you. I've tattooed every part of clients' bodies so nothing would shock me."

"That I can believe," said Dad, rolling his eyes.

"How is your cousin now?" Fiona asked, changing the subject and getting back to the reason Roxanne had graced us with her presence.

"Actually, she's, like, totally fucked. It came back and they said she'll be lucky to get six months."

We glared at Derek, who had gone white. "Roxanne! You told me your cousin was fine."

"Her boobs are fine, but she just found out that the cancer turned up in her liver or some shit, so it's *bon voyage* for her."

I leant over and whispered in Derek's ear, "Get your fuck-buddy out of here before I strangle her."

"What cheery news. I must say, Derek, it was a stroke of genius bringing Roxanne to cheer Fiona up," snapped Dad, as Derek dragged the girl out the door.

He came straight back in, looking very sheepish. "Jeez, Fiona, I'm really sorry. She told me her cousin was fine — except when her hair fell out, but it grew back. I'm a knob, I should have checked the details. Are you freaked out now?"

Fiona shook her head. "It's OK. People die every day of cancer. It's a reality I have to face."

"But lots of people get better," I added.

"You'll be fine, pet. Nothing's going to take you away from us," said Dad, putting his arm round her protectively.

"I feel terrible, Fiona," said Derek, miserably.

"Forget about it. It's not your fault your friend's a moron," said Fiona, smiling.

"I've written a song for you," said Derek. "I'm going to showcase it at the gig I'm doing in two weeks. You all have to come. It's going to be awesome."

The door opened. "Yo, Derek, I'm late," called Roxanne.

"Yo, Roxie," said Derek. He stood up and rapped: "It was fun while we lasted but now that you casted a shadow over my sista, I'm not gonna miss ya, so go to hell, you frickin cow, cos believe me when I tell you I ain't interested now."

"Good on you," I said.

"Well done, son," said Dad.

"You're well rid of her," said Fiona.

"Get a move on," snapped Roxanne, as our hero shuffled out after her.

# CHAPTER
# EIGHTEEN

By the time we got back from the hospital, Fiona was feeling awful. I left her to go and pick the boys up from their friend Zach's house, where they had spent the afternoon. Zach's mother was mightily relieved to see me. Judging from the state of the house, the twins had spent the rainy afternoon trashing the place. I thanked her profusely and drove them home.

Before we got out of the car, I turned to face them. "Now, boys, Mummy's feeling sick today because she was in hospital getting more of that nasty medicine, so you have to be very quiet and gentle. OK?"

Their little faces fell. Their mum was sick again and they were scared.

"But she'll be much better tomorrow and Daddy'll be home soon to tuck you in and read you a story."

Mark had promised to be back by six. I needed a few hours to get ready for my date and he needed to spend some time with his sick wife and kids.

We went in and the boys climbed the stairs to see their mum, who was in bed, trying not to throw up. I let them stay for a few minutes, then took them down to give them their dinner.

At six o'clock the twins were fed, the kitchen had been cleaned, I had laid their pyjamas on their beds and had two warm towels ready for their bath. I slung on my coat and looked out the window for Mark's car.

At six thirty, nine chewed fingernails later and having snapped at the boys when they'd asked me why I was staring out the window, I called him, but his mobile was switched off. I left a terse message, took off my coat and gave the boys their bath.

Seven o'clock: still no sign. Fiona was asleep in bed while I was turning into the Incredible Hulk. I had never known anger like it.

I rang Mark's phone again and spat out a message that left nothing to the imagination.

Seven thirty: the boys were in bed and I tried to read them a story.

"Why is your voice all funny?" asked Bobby, referring to the strangling sound my throat made as I tried desperately to keep my boiling rage under control.

"This story's boring. Read something else," grumbled Jack.

"I want a glass of milk," said Bobby, and began to get out of bed.

"Get back into that bloody bed and do not move," I growled, pinning him down as he stared up at me. "You've had milk. Now you will go to sleep, and I'm warning you both, don't mess with me tonight. I am in a very, very bad mood."

"But you haven't finished the story," whined Jack. "I want my mummy."

"Well, she's not available right now and your father is a total wanker so you're stuck with me."

"What's a wanker?" asked Bobby.

"What a lovely scene to come home to," said Mark, walking through the door. "Don't mind me. Carry on."

I blushed. Granted I was furious with him, but I was ashamed at having slated him to his own children.

"Daddy will be with you in a minute. I just have to talk to him downstairs," I said, and frogmarched him into the kitchen. I closed the door: I didn't want Fiona or the kids to hear what I had to say.

"How could you be so selfish? The one time in seven weeks I ask you to be home early because I'm going out and you can't even be bothered to do that. I'm not some slave, Mark. I'm doing this for Fiona and the boys. I've given up everything to help out, but your life hasn't skipped a beat. You just carry on as normal. Well, news flash, Mark. I quit. You're on your own. I won't be here tomorrow."

"Yes, you will," said Mark, "because you're not doing it for me, you're doing it for Fiona. You owe her years of sacrifice and you know it. The only reason you came back is because you feel guilty about having disappeared to London, leaving her to look after Derek and your father. I'm not neglecting my family. I'm working. Who do you think pays for Fiona's treatment, the boys' schooling and this house?"

"Don't use your job as an excuse. You're late every day because of that stupid project. You don't have to enter that competition. It won't make any difference to Fiona's life — but it'll make a big difference to Mark

Kennedy's already inflated ego. You're doing this for yourself and the reflected glory that winning will give you. I hope it's worth it, Mark."

"You went to London and ignored your family for eight years so don't lecture me about ambition and ego."

"I came back when it mattered. You're running away now at the most crucial time in Fiona's life."

"Where have I run off to? The office. I'm here every night, as always. Nothing has changed."

"You're emotionally detached."

"Oh, please spare me your cheesy psychobabble. If you want to talk about behaviour, I really don't think telling two five-year-olds that their father is a wanker is very helpful."

The kitchen clock chimed eight. I had to get out of there. I needed a stiff drink. I needed to see someone outside my family. I needed Sam. "Much as I'd love to stay and chat, I have to try to salvage the only night out I've had in almost two months."

With that I stormed out the door and drove home like a maniac to get changed. I sent Sam a text explaining I was running late and to order me a double vodka. Then I got changed — fifteen times. Nothing fitted. I couldn't understand it. I knew I'd put on a few pounds but I'd been wearing the same clothes all the time so I hadn't noticed just how much weight had crept on. Clearly my metabolism was messed up after all those years of starving myself and now I was eating normally — with the odd packet of chocolate biscuits for dinner — I'd whacked on the weight.

Eventually I squeezed myself into a black skirt and polo neck and tried to disguise my protruding stomach by tying a scarf round my waist. I threw on some makeup and tied up my hair — I had no time to wash it — then looked at myself in the mirror. Not good. Where the hell was the old Kate? I looked older than thirty-one, stressed and chubby. As I was contemplating cancelling the date, my phone buzzed: *Where the hell r u? Am half pissed already.*

I hopped into the car and prayed silently that the bar would be dimly lit and that Sam wouldn't take one look at me and run for the hills.

When I got there, he was sitting at the bar, reading the paper. He smiled when he saw me and didn't seem repulsed. Things were looking up.

"About bloody time," he said, handing me a double vodka and Diet Coke.

"I'm sorry. Mark arrived home late and we got into this huge row and it was all a bit of a nightmare," I said, and suddenly began to cry. Once I'd started I couldn't stop. I sobbed and sniffled in between gulping my drink. "God . . . sorry . . . just tired and emotional . . . long day." I tried to wipe my nose with a beer mat.

Sam handed me a tissue. "You've been through a lot."

"Thanks," I said, blowing my nose. "I'm just worn out."

"Well, you do look wrecked," Sam said, as I welled up again. Did he have to rub it in? I knew I looked like shit, but couldn't he have lied and told me I looked fantastic?

Don't men get it? We're not complicated: we just want to be lied to. When your friend arrives out wearing a hideous dress and asks you what you think, you lie. She's out, for God's sake, it's too late for her to get changed. Telling her she looks like a bag of hammers isn't going to help. Does my bum look big in this? *No!* Jesus, it's not rocket science.

"Hey, there, come on, it's not that bad. Fiona'll be OK," said Sam, as I covered my face with the tissue, ashamed that I was crying because he'd told me I looked tired and because now my makeup was streaked and I knew I looked even worse. Maybe Mark was right: I was selfish and shallow.

"How's her chemo going?"

"She had the second session today," I said, pulling myself together. "It's making her sick, but she recovered well after the first dose. I'm worried her hair will fall out this time and that that might push her over the edge. She's pretending to cope well and that it doesn't bother her, but it's taking its toll and the fact that her husband is a tosser doesn't help."

"Your relationship with Mark hasn't improved over the years, then?" asked Sam.

"You can safely say it's at an all-time low."

"Maybe he's finding it hard to deal with. She's his wife and the mother of his kids, after all."

"Exactly, and that's why he should be a rock to her and not spend all his time at the bloody office avoiding his responsibilities. I'm like the father in the bloody family. He's never there."

"Some guys fall apart when their wives get sick."

"Why are you defending him?"

"I just think it must be hard for him — you know, frightening."

"What about me?"

"You have another life in London. He doesn't. If Fiona dies he has no wife and no mother for the boys."

"What about me, losing a sister?"

"Of course that'd be awful, but still worse for Mark. He has more to lose."

"I'm beginning to wonder if she'd be better off without him."

"Really?"

"Oh, don't mind me. I'm blowing off steam. Besides, I'm biased because I blame him for dragging me back. It does bother me that he isn't more involved, though. He should be."

"I always thought they were well suited," said Sam.

"I used to think so too, because they were both into maths and chess, but I don't know any more. His big ego has smothered his nicer side. Anyway, enough about Mark. Tell me about that cow you married," I said.

Sam groaned. "The lovely Nikki had an affair with her perma-tanned, sports-car driving, filthy-rich boss. When I found out, she said she was sorry but she wanted a big house, nice car and holidays in the Caribbean."

"Bitch! Was she always like that?"

"When I first met her she was the receptionist at her company and thought my job and apartment were the high life. But then she got promoted and started earning good money and saw the life the senior partners in the ad agency were living and decided she wanted more. She knew that, as a journalist, I was never going to give her a life of luxury, so she aimed high and shagged the CEO."

"What a ruthless cow. You're better off without her."

"Yes. Ambition can be a curse," he said, looking directly at me.

I shrank back in my chair. He wasn't only referring to the ladder-climbing Nikki. I decided to concentrate on her infidelity: I wanted to avoid the ambition conversation at all costs.

"I don't understand people having affairs. Why bother getting married?" I said, pushing my own affair, last year, with a married man to the back of my mind. In fairness, at the beginning I hadn't known he had a wife, but when I found out I had continued to see him for a few weeks.

"You get married because you're in love."

"Were you?" I said, hoping he'd say no. I wanted him to say that he'd only ever been really in love once, a long time ago, and then we'd stare into each other's eyes and he would take me home and ravish me. Of course, I'd have to hold my stomach in all night but, oh, God, it'd be worth it.

"Of course I was," he said, looking at me as if I was thick.

"Well, sometimes people get pressured into marriage."

"She didn't pressure me. I wanted to get married, have kids, the whole nine yards."

"Are you over it now?" I asked, giving him my sexiest vodka-hazed smile. I was feeling rather light-headed.

"Not really. Maybe when the divorce comes through I'll be able to move on. But it'll take a while. I'm a slow healer," he said, staring into his pint.

"Maybe I can help you out there," I purred, putting my hand on his knee.

His head snapped up. "Oh, uhm, Kate, I don't think so. I hope you didn't get the wrong idea. It's great to see you and all that, but I'm actually with someone at the moment."

"What happened to the slow healing?" I asked, shocked into sobriety.

"I'm trying to get on with my life."

I was mortified. I had made a total fool of myself. How could I have misjudged the situation so completely? I had to save face. "Good for you," I said, lurching from sexy siren to chief cheerleader. "And who is the girl? A gorgeous young one with big boobs, I hope."

Sam looked a little taken aback at my sudden turn-around. "Oh, she's, uhm, a girl from work."

"Young?"

"Twenty-one."

I hated her already. "Foxy?"

"Not bad."

"Good in the sack?" I said, morphing into one of the lads.

"Fine," he said, looking bemused.

"Give a good blow-job?"

"Jesus, Kate."

**158**

"Just kidding," I said, slapping him on the back. "Right, excellent stuff. Well, I'll be off, leave you to meet up with your young one for the Friday-night shag. Good to see you and — yeah — see you around . . . or something. Cheerio," I said, and rushed out the door before I started crying again.

# CHAPTER
# NINETEEN

I woke the next morning to Derek banging on my bedroom door. I peeled my face from the pillow and shouted at him to go away.

"Yo, Mark's on the phone."

"Tell him to fuck off."

"He sounds kinda freaked."

"Tough."

"He said Fiona's locked herself in the bathroom and won't come out."

While I had no intention of helping Mark, Fiona was a different matter. Ungluing my eyes, I shuffled over and unlocked the door. Derek handed me the phone. "Yes?" I grunted.

"Kate, I need you to come over. Fiona won't come out of the bathroom and I can hear her crying in there."

"So deal with it. She's your wife."

"She won't talk to me and the boys are getting upset. Maybe she'll talk to you. She sounds very distressed."

"She has cancer. Of course she's upset. Welcome to reality, Mark."

"Can you save the jibes for later and please come over?"

I was tempted to leave him alone to deal with his family issues himself, but I could hear Bobby howling in the background and I was worried about Fiona. "I'll be over in ten minutes," I said, and hung up.

I washed my mascara-streaked face and threw on my jeans and sweatshirt. On the five-minute drive to Fiona's I almost crashed the car twice as I remembered the holy show I'd made of myself the night before. How could I have misread the situation so badly? I couldn't believe I'd made such an obvious pass at Sam. Oh, God, it was toe-curling humiliation. Could my life possibly get any sadder? Jobless, chubby, penniless — and now I was a social reject.

When I got to the house, the twins ran up to me. "Mummy's crying and she won't come out," they said in unison.

"Don't worry, she's probably a bit sick from the nasty medicine," I said. "Now, you go and brush your teeth and wash your hands while I talk to your mum. OK?" I ushered them into the main bathroom and went to find Mark.

He was crouched on the bedroom floor, talking to Fiona through the keyhole of the *en suite*. Teddy was sitting beside him, scratching the door with his paw and whimpering. For once, Mark seemed pleased to see me — well, relieved, at least.

"Thanks for coming. She won't talk to me," he said.

"Go and take the boys to the park or something. I'll call you later."

I knelt outside the door and tapped lightly. "Fiona, it's me. Are you OK?"

I could hear her crying but she didn't say anything.

"Do you feel awful? Are you having a panic-attack? Because freaking out right now would be extremely normal."

Silence.

I lay down and put my eye to the bottom of the door. She was holding a clump of hair. "Oh, Fiona, is your hair falling out? Is that it? You poor thing, is it bad? Can I come in and look? I'll get some scissors and we'll fix it up. Come on, there's nothing we can't sort out."

She started sobbing.

"If it makes you feel any better I made a pass at Sam last night, and after he'd ricocheted off his seat in revulsion, he told me he was seeing a young one from the office. My face is still bright red from the shame of it. Come on, open up and let me hide in there with you. I'm a danger to myself."

The lock clicked and my sister's blotchy face peered out. "Has Mark gone?"

"Yes."

She sighed and pulled the door back, putting the other hand over her head. Clumps of hair lay on the floor.

"It started falling out in the shower and then I combed it — and *voilà!*" she said, taking her hand down to reveal a large bald patch on the right side of her head. She looked so sad and vulnerable I reached out to comfort her, but she stepped back. Clearly I was a leper at the moment. No man or woman wanted me anywhere near them.

"What am I going to do? I look like a freak. I don't recognize myself. What have I become? Look at me!" she wailed.

"Come on, don't say that. OK, losing your hair is rotten, but you're still you, still gorgeous. We can fix this. You just need to shave it off. We'll go out and buy amazing hats and bandannas and wigs. It'll be fun."

"Fun? I'm a bald thirty-four-year-old mother of two, with lopsided breasts whose husband hasn't gone near her in almost a year. Mark's going to run a mile when he sees my bald head. I know he doesn't find me attractive any more and I don't blame him. I'm hideous!"

"Don't you dare say that! Now, listen to me," I said, grabbing her by the shoulders and shaking her, "you're the most amazing person I know. I've looked up to you my whole life. You're an incredible wife, mother, sister and daughter. Your hair — or lack of it — does not make you any less beautiful. Now, put some clothes on. We're going shopping."

While Fiona got dressed I called Derek and asked him to get Gonzo to come over with his head-shaver.

"Dude," said Derek, when he saw Fiona, "you can't be going around like that. You look like someone's attacked you with blunt scissors."

"I'm well aware of how appalling I look, thanks, Derek."

"I think you need a number two," said Gonzo. "It'll be cool. You'll look like Sigourney Weaver in *Alien* — hot!"

"Or Demi Moore in *GI Jane*," I added, as Fiona did her best to smile.

Gonzo plugged in his razor. "Don't sweat it, Fiona, I'm good at this. Plenty practice," he said, pointing to his own tightly shaved head.

"Well, I can't look worse than I already do, so go ahead," she said, trying not to cry.

Gonzo shaved her head gently and carefully and turned her round to admire his handiwork.

"Good job, bro," said Derek, relieved to see that his sister was now more of a punk than an old woman with thinning hair.

Fiona took a deep breath and looked into the mirror. "It's not as bad as I thought. I still look like hell, but I'm glad it's all off," she said gulping back tears.

"Any time you need a top-up, just let me know," said the newly appointed Vidal Sassoon.

I looked at Fiona's bald head. There was something incredibly lonely and sad about it. It was as if her cancer was now a badge. Without her hair, everyone would know she was sick. When she walked down the street, people would stare. She'd never be able to say, "I'm great thanks, how are you?" to anyone she met. It was as if she had an I HAVE CANCER sticker plastered across her forehead. She looked sick too. It was so much easier to pretend everything was going to be OK when she looked like her old self. But the image staring back at us was that of a sick person. A cancer victim.

"Well, I'll be off," said Gonzo.

"*Wait!*" I shouted. "Do me."

"What?" he asked, confused.

"Shave my hair off too."

"No way," said Fiona.

"It's my hair, my decision, and I want it off," I said.

"Awesome idea, me too," said Derek.

"I will not allow you to do this," said Fiona.

"It's got nothing to do with you, so sit down and be quiet," I said, already in GI Jane mode. I grabbed the kitchen scissors and chopped off my ponytail as Fiona stared at me. It felt fantastic. I was getting a huge adrenaline rush from doing this for her.

Gonzo set to, and half an hour later, Derek and I were as bald as coots.

"You look hot," whispered Gonzo, into my ear and proceeded to nibble it.

For once I didn't swat him away or insult him. I knew what it was like to be rejected. Instead I tried to pull my head away gently, but then he shoved his tongue into my ear so I thumped him.

"Newsflash, Gonzo. Women hate having a tongue rammed down their ear," I snapped.

Gonzo and Derek looked at each other. "Really?" Gonzo asked, put out. "I thought chicks really dug it."

"Well, this one doesn't," I said. Even in my current male-famine, it did nothing for me.

Derek looked at Fiona. She shook her head. "Sorry, guys, I'm not a fan of tongue-in-ear either."

Gonzo slouched out of the house to his car.

As Derek began to follow him, Fiona stopped him. Looking down at the floor, she said, "You both know I'm not very good at the whole emotions thing, but what you just did means . . . means . . ." She broke down.

Derek patted her shoulder. "I get it that you're grateful. It's no biggie. Gotta fly cos I need to get some lyrics down for my gig next week. *Adios, muchachas.*"

It was just me and Fiona, and suddenly I felt awkward. I didn't know what to say and I could see she was struggling. She wanted to say so much, but it was too overwhelming.

"Kate, I —"

"Hey," I said, "I know, and you're welcome, and it's really no big deal. Now, come on, let's get this mess cleared up."

Mark called to see how Fiona was. I told him about the hair-shaving and said I'd pick the boys up from the park and take them off for lunch so he could go home to his wife. I pulled the mirror down in the car to look at my hairless self for the first time. The person gazing back at me was a total stranger. Oh, God, what had I done? I looked like a freak. It was terrifying. I panicked. Would I ever look nice again? How long would my hair take to grow back? How long before I could go out in public without people staring at me and crossing the road to avoid me? I was a cross between a skinhead and a cancer patient. My hair had always been my best feature. Why, oh, why had I been so impulsive? I suppressed the urge to wail.

I had done the right thing. It had meant a lot to Fiona. After all, what was the big deal? It wasn't as if I had a job that required me to look good or a boyfriend

I wanted to seduce. Gulping back the sobs that were threatening to escape, I tried not to think about the fact that my hair would take years to grow back and that no man would ever fancy me again.

"Where's your hair?" asked Bobby, wide-eyed.

"In the bin," I said, as casually as I could. I wondered if I could take it out of the bin and bring it to a shop to have it stuck back on. They could do wonders with hair, these days. "I decided to shave it off. What do you think?"

"You look scary," said Jack, giggling nervously. "Like an alien."

"Well, boys, Mummy's hair is the same and so is Uncle Derek's."

"Why?" asked Bobby.

"Because we wanted to look like Kojak."

"Who's that?" asked Bobby.

"Bob the Builder's dad," I said, pulling it out of thin air. I was getting good at this.

"Bob doesn't have a dad," said Jack. "He has Scoop the Digger, Dizzy the Cement Mixer and . . ."

"Pilchard the Cat and Wendy and JJ!" shouted Bobby.

"And Roley the steam-roller, but no dad," added Jack.

"Maybe that's because Bob's dad, Kojak, lives in America."

"Oh," said the twins.

"Where does Bob live?" asked Bobby.

"In England," I said.

"Is that where you used to live?" asked Jack.

"Yes, you clever boy, it is."

"But you live with Granddad now," said Bobby, not wanting to be shown up by his brother.

"Exactly," I said.

"Can I touch it?" asked Jack, reaching up to feel the scalp formerly occupied by my lovely hair.

"Sure." I knelt down so the boys could feel it. They squealed with delight as they rubbed my fuzzy head.

"Cool," said Jack. "I want to be bald."

"When you're grown-up you can."

"I want to now," whined Jack. "I want to be like Bob the Builder and Mummy and Uncle Derek and Dojak."

"Me too, me too," said Bobby, slapping my head.

"First of all you have to let your hair grow and then when it's finished growing, when you're eighteen and you have a good job like Bob the Builder, you can have it cut off. But not now. Besides, I don't think Mrs Foley would let you go to school with no hair."

"Is Daddy bald too?" asked Jack.

"No, sweetheart, but I think we should ask him to cut his hair off tonight when he comes home," I said, grinning at the idea of Professor Kennedy shaving his head.

# CHAPTER
# TWENTY

Later that evening I was rummaging around in the kitchen drawers, looking for a tea-towel that could pass as a bandanna — I was thinking Yasser Arafat meets Mother Teresa — when I heard, "Take what you want. I don't want any trouble. Just help yourself to the goods and go."

I turned to find Dad wielding a golf club. "Jesus, Dad!"

"Kate?" he said, staring at my shorn scalp in horror. Subtlety was never his strong point.

"What are you doing with the golf club?"

"I thought a skinhead was robbing the place. What in God's name have you done to your hair?"

"Fiona's fell out after the chemo so she had to shave her head, and Derek and I joined in as a gesture of solidarity."

"Oh, Katie," said Dad, coming over to hug me, "your beautiful hair."

"What the hell? It'll grow back," I said, stifling a sob.

"I've never been more proud of you," said Dad, getting a bit weepy himself. We were all turning into emotional wrecks.

"What were you planning on doing with the golf club?"

"Battering you round the head for daring to rob my house."

"Good thing I turned round. My chances of meeting a guy are pretty slim at this point, I think a facial scar would stamp out the last glimmer of hope."

"Sure any man'd be lucky to have you."

"Would you be going out with Sheryl if she was bald?"

"Can't you wear a wig or something till it grows?" he side-stepped.

"That bad, huh?"

"No, you look grand, but a lad might find it a bit . . . ah . . . butch. He might mistake you for a girl who likes motorbikes and prefers other girls, if you get my drift."

"You know, Dad, telling me I look like a lesbian really isn't doing anything for my confidence. Couldn't you lie?"

"What good would that do you? Lads like hair, so here's a few quid to get yourself a nice long wig and sure they'll be queuing up," he said. "Take Fiona with you and buy one each. You can swap them."

Derek strolled in. "'Sup?"

"Dad's forking out for wigs. Want one?"

"No way. Roxanne thinks the shaved look's hot. She was all over me this afternoon. I'm never growing it back."

"And the beauty of it is that if she changes her mind — which she seems prone to doing — she can always tattoo some hair on to you," said Dad, chuckling.

**170**

"How's Fiona doing?" Derek asked me.

"Better. She was relieved that the boys took it well. They want to shave their own heads and Mark's now."

"What did Mark say?" asked Dad.

"Oh, you know Mark. Mr Sacrifice himself. He said he'd love to join in, but he didn't think the dean would approve."

Derek and Dad rolled their eyes.

Shortly after the shaving of our heads, Derek and Gonzo — a.k.a. Rap-sodie — were playing their gig in a pub in town. Mark volunteered gallantly to babysit so he could avoid having to go. I picked up Fiona and we headed off, wearing colourful head scarves. Courtesy of Dad, we had each purchased a wig. I had gone for a fun platinum blonde one but Fiona had been much more practical and opted for one that was closer to her own dark curly hair. Neither of us felt totally comfortable in them: they *felt* fake and, after a while, they made your head itch, and Derek's gig was in a basement so it was bound to be hot and uncomfortable. So we opted for scarves and looked like two charladies instead.

Dad was waiting for us when we arrived, sticking out like a sore thumb in the dingy room, surrounded by yoof in saggy-arsed jeans and hoodies. He had invited Sheryl along — which I thought was a really bad idea — and, judging by the grumpy face on him, he regretted it now. "Thank God you've arrived," he muttered. "Jesus, will you look at the state of the crowd? They're like a gang of car-jackers."

"Dad!" I scolded. "You can't go around saying things like that. It's not politically correct."

"I don't give a fiddler's about political correctness. Why do young lads today have to go around with their trousers half-way down their arses and their faces covered with hoods? They need a good kick up the backside and an honest day's work to sort them out."

"Keep your voice down," I hissed. "They're Derek's friends and fans."

"And we don't want to get stabbed," said Sheryl, fearfully. Clearly she didn't get out much — too busy shagging sixty-two-year-olds into early graves.

"It's not Hell's Kitchen, Sheryl," I said.

"Dublin's one of the most dangerous cities in Europe now," she retorted. "People get stabbed and shot here every day. The police are far too tolerant. They should lock up all those criminals and throw away the key," added our liberal-minded marathon runner.

"A bunch of wasters is what they are," said Dad, glancing at the motley crew. "That brother of yours had better smarten up his act. I'm having no more of this music rubbish. He's coming to work for me full-time and that's the end of it."

"You have to admire him for chasing his dream," said Fiona.

"Not when it involves spending most of the last three years watching MTV while fat fellas in vests and big gold chains roar at each other. I've had enough," Dad fumed, warming to his theme.

"He's very talented," Fiona said, continuing her defence of Derek. "Some of his songs are really good."

172

"*Pffff*! Any fool can shout —"

"I can't understand this rap stuff at all. Why are they so angry all the time?" asked Sheryl.

"Too much time on their hands," ranted Dad. "In my day fellas were out ploughing fields from dusk till dawn. They'd no time to be moaning about everything. That's what's wrong with the world today, too much bloody complaining and not enough hard work."

"Shush, he's coming over," I said, as Derek and Gonzo strutted to the table.

"Dig the head decoration," said Gonzo, pointing to my scarf but, thankfully, refraining from licking it.

"Thanks. Are you nervous?" I asked.

"Bricking it," said Derek.

"No," said Gonzo.

"Nice crowd," said Dad. "The future leaders of the country."

"Yes, great turn-out," I cut across him.

"Mostly mates but the guy from *Hot Press* is here," said Derek, chewing his lip nervously.

Dad, Sheryl and Fiona stared blankly at him. "It's a music magazine. It helped launch U2," I said, exaggerating slightly.

"We've gotta go, bro, we're on in five," said Gonzo, and hustled Derek towards the stage.

"Good luck," said Fiona. Then, turning to me, she asked, "Is the magazine really that influential?"

"Well, if he gets a good write-up it'll help open doors."

"Will it get him a six-figure recording deal so he can stop sponging off me?" asked Dad.

"You're too generous, Bill, that's your problem," smarmed the elastic woman.

"You never know, stranger things have happened," I said, ignoring Sheryl, just as she had ignored me for years in gym class. Immature, I know, but it felt great.

"It's hardly likely, though, is it?" she retorted.

"Every artist starts out doing small gigs," I snapped. How dare she insult my brother? Only family members were allowed that privilege.

"We live in hope," said Dad, trying to defuse the tension.

"You've great optimism, Bill. It's very endearing," said Sheryl, squeezing his thigh. The cheek of her, molesting my father in front of me! I turned away in disgust.

"Yo, dogs, zip it," roared Gonzo, into the microphone. The crowd hushed. "We're Rap-sodie and we're gonna blow you away with our lyrics tonight. My man MC D-Rek here got it goin' on. N-joy."

"I take it MC D-Rek is my son, Derek John O'Brien," said Dad rolling his eyes.

"Shush," I said, suddenly feeling very nervous for Derek.

He came forward, microphone in hand (shaking slightly) and introduced the first song. It was about losing your virginity in a hedge. Dad squirmed in his seat while Sheryl — who was in no position to take the moral high ground on sex — tut-tutted.

The crowd swayed and whooped every time Derek said "fuck" or "pussy" — which was frequently.

**174**

The song ended after five graphic verses, during which the former virgin contracted herpes from the ho' he'd slept with.

"If Father Brendan could see him now," said Dad, shaking his head. "Fifteen years of Yeats, Shakespeare and Dickens, and this is how he chooses to express himself."

"You did your best, Bill. That's all you can do."

"Have you children yourself, Sheryl?" Fiona asked.

"No, I don't, and I can't say I'm sorry. It seems like a life sentence. You never stop worrying, do you, Bill?"

Dad shrugged. Even he drew the line at slagging off his children in front of their faces.

"And how are you doing, Fiona?" Sheryl asked, laying a hand on Fiona's arm and tilting her head in a lame attempt to be sympathetic. "I hear you lost all your hair. You're very brave to be out and about."

"I like getting out. It helps me forget about it for a while," said Fiona, pointedly.

"Good for you, although I'd say the bald head is a constant reminder."

"Not if people stopped referring to it," I murmured.

Before Sheryl could reply, Derek announced that he was going to sing a new song. "I wrote this last night and I'm dedicating it to my sister Fiona, who inspired it. Yo listen up,

" 'So my big sista found out she got da big C,
We is all scared coz of what it might mean,
We don't know nothin' all we can do is try
To keep it together an' not start to cry.

175

We gonna help her thro this difficult stage
And it ain't hard, man, coz she bein' so brave
But then last week after the chemotherapy
We is in the house and we hear a squeal
She freakin' big coz when she wakes up
Her hair's fallen out and dude that suck
Coz the bald look, man, it ain't so hot.
So my other sista Kate went and got
My man Gonzo here to shave our heads too
Coz we don't want our sista feeling so blue.
She need to know that we always be
Supportin' her and showin' our solidarity.
So now we all is bald because of our sista
But we don't care coz we wanna be with her
Coz we is a family dat stick together
In times of trouble now and for eva.'"

Fiona and I stood and cheered. Eminem wouldn't exactly be shaking in his boots, but it was a good effort and had come from the heart. Derek looked chuffed at our enthusiasm. Even Dad clapped.

"That was brilliant," said Fiona.

"Well, at least it was clean and no one contracted venereal disease," said Dad, and we laughed. Even Sheryl managed to crack a smile.

A couple more songs followed. One about "my bitch who went off with my bro'" though we weren't sure if it was his imaginary brother or just his friend bro'. Another dealt with feuding gangs and drive-by shootings, and there was a long one about racism.

"He's a lively imagination, I'll say that for him," said Dad. "The closest that boy ever got to a drive-by shooting was getting hit by bird shit on his tricycle."

# CHAPTER
# TWENTY-ONE

A few days later when I went to pick the twins up from school they were both in the bold corner. "What's going on?" I asked Mrs Foley. "What heinous crime did they commit this time?"

"They were seen kicking Nigel in the shins," said the old witch. "If this continues, I'm going to have to seriously consider their position here at the school. We cannot allow unruly behaviour to upset the other children. The twins seem to have lost the run of themselves recently," she said, staring at me. Clearly I was an Unfit child-minder, with a capital U.

"Mrs Foley, do you understand how ill their mother is?" I asked, as if she was one of her pupils. "Are you aware of what chemotherapy entails? Do you realize how traumatic it is for children to see their mother go through physical and emotional hell? Because I'd be glad to bring in some breast-cancer information leaflets to help you get a grasp on what the boys are dealing with."

She was furious at being spoken down to. "That won't be necessary. Lots of the children here have difficulties at home and my school is the one place they can come to get away from it all. They need routine, discipline and consistency. It makes them feel safe and shelters them from upheavals at home."

I was a bit taken aback. She had a point there. They loved school and seemed to be thriving. Knowing Fiona, I'm sure it was the best school in Dublin. Still, I thought that a little extra understanding and a bending of the rules under exceptional circumstances would be all right.

"Did you find out why they kicked Whatshisname?" I asked.

"Apparently *Nigel Boyd* said something about Mrs Kennedy's hair loss. He asked them why she had no hair or some such and they reacted with violence, which, as I said, is unacceptable."

"Well, maybe *Nigel Boyd* needs to be told to keep his gob shut," I retorted.

"Nigel is a gentle boy and an only child. He's traumatized by the incident."

I decided not to tell her what I thought Nigel needed to toughen him up, and went over to the boys. "OK, guys, it's time to go home." Two little tearstained faces turned towards me. I threw my arms round the boys and they let me hug them — which was rare as they normally squirmed when I showed them affection. "Hey, it's OK, don't mind Mrs Foley. I think you're the best boys in Ireland."

"Mrs Foley said we were the boldest."

"Well, Mrs Foley's wrong. What did that Nigel boy say to you anyway?" I asked, as we were walking to the car.

"He said Mummy looked like a scary monster and that she was going to die from the bad cancer," said Bobby.

"He said *what*?" I hissed. "Where is he? Which one is Nigel? Point him out to me now."

"There," said Jack, pointing to a pasty kid with glasses, who was standing just inside the schoolroom.

"Stay here and don't move," I said. I strode back in, leant down to Nigel's ear and whispered, "Listen here, nerd boy, if you ever say anything about Jack and Bobby's mother again I will pull your hair out so you will look like a freak and no one will ever play with you again. Do you understand?"

Nigel gaped at me.

"Everything all right, Nigel?" asked Mrs Foley, from across the room, as I put my arm round Nigel's shoulders.

"Fine, thanks." I smiled. "Just checking that Nigel here has recovered after his traumatic day." Turning back to him, I whispered, "Don't even think about telling anyone what I just said to you."

With that, I left the schoolhouse and walked out to the boys, feeling pleased with myself. I was the defender, the tigress protecting her cubs. No one messed with Kate O'Brien's family.

"*Daaaaaaaaaaaaaaaaaaaaaad!*" I heard behind me, as Nigel sprinted past and threw himself into the arms of his father. "That nasty woman said she was going to pull my hair out," he whined, pointing at me.

Nigel's father — who was surprisingly attractive and non-nerdy — grabbed his son's hand and strode over. "Is this true?"

"No," I lied.

"Yes, you did," said Specky-four-eyes, landing me in it. "You said you were going to make me into a freak."

The cute father glared at me. He was obviously going to believe his only child over a chubby, sweatshirt-wearing woman in a dodgy platinum wig.

"Did you say that, Auntie Kate?" asked Jack, plainly thrilled.

"I think there's been a misunderstanding," I said, coming over all formal. "Nigel upset the twins this morning by saying something nasty about their mother — my sister — I'm not married myself." Well, you never know, he might be divorced and at this stage I was getting desperate, although if it meant having Nigel as a stepson Mr Boyd would have to be sensational in bed.

Mr Boyd looked at his son. "What did you say, Nigel?"

Nerd-boy might be good at chucking insults around but he was no liar. "I said she looks like a scary monster," he admitted.

"Why would you say something so unkind?"

"Because she has no hair. She's all baldy."

I decided to fill the handsome father in. "My sister's having chemotherapy at the moment and her hair's fallen out."

"I'm sorry to hear that."

"It's been tough for the boys so they reacted badly, kicked Nigel and ended up in the bold corner. When we were leaving I just said to your son here that it wasn't nice to call people names because they were bald," I said, bending the truth. This man was never going to ask me on a date if he thought I'd threatened to rip his five-year-old's hair out with my bare hands.

"Nigel, I'm very disappointed," said my future husband. "The twins' mummy is sick and you should be extra nice to them and not say nasty things. Your mummy's going to be very cross when we get home and I tell her what you did."

Typical. Just my luck. Mrs bloody Boyd was alive and well and happily married to Mr Boyd. And I bet she had hair, was thin, wore nice clothes and fed nutritious homemade meals to her family.

"But she was mean to me," said Nigel, who was going home with bruised shins and threats ringing in his ears.

"Say you're sorry to the boys," said his father.

Nigel mumbled an apology to Jack and Bobby.

"Now, lads, you tell Nigel you're sorry for kicking him," I said, trying to match like with like.

"Sorry, Nigel," they said.

"Right. Glad that's all sorted. 'Bye now," said Mr Boyd, and disappeared into his cool sports car, leaving me destitute.

I felt a tug on my arm. "Did you really tell Nigel you were going to pull his hair out?" asked Bobby.

I bent down and the two boys huddled up to me. "Yes, I did, but don't tell Mummy because if you do I'll end up in the bold corner for a very long time."

"You're cool," said Jack.

"Really cool," added Bobby.

I smiled. Maybe older guys wouldn't touch me with a barge-pole, but at least my two mini-men thought I rocked.

That evening I called over to Tara. I'd warned her about my shorn head — I didn't want her going into early labour when she saw me.

"Oh, my God," she said, as her hand flew to her mouth.

"I know it ain't pretty," I said ruefully.

"No, it's . . . just . . . different, that's all," she lied.

"It's OK. I know I look like hell but it was worth it to see Fiona's face."

"I'd say she was really touched," said Tara, recovering from her shock. "It was a lovely thing to do."

"I just hope her eyebrows and eyelashes don't fall out. I'm not sure I can go that far."

"I think you've shown enough kinship." Tara smiled. "Come on, tell me what happened with Sam. I want proper details," she said, as she put on the kettle.

I shrugged. "Nothing to tell. As I said on the phone, I made a pass at him, he said he was seeing someone else and I fled."

Tara made a pot of tea.

"Any biccies?" I asked.

"You never eat rubbish," she said, surprised.

"Well, let's face it, no one's going to come near me in this state so I might as well stuff my face."

"Stop that, you're still gorgeous," said Tara, handing me a plate of chocolate-chip cookies, which I began to wolf down.

"I know you, Kate," she mused. "There's no way you would have made a pass at Sam unless you were sure he was interested."

"I dunno. My head's all over the place at the moment. The *old* me would never have made a show of herself like that. I did think Sam was keen, we were getting on so well, and I thought he was looking at me the way he used to . . . but I was completely wrong. I don't actually know who I am any more. I feel like I've lost my identity. I don't have a job or an apartment, I never go out and I just seem to be stumbling along at the moment. I can't believe how much my life has changed," I said, staring into my cup.

"It must be really hard, but what you're doing for Fiona and the twins is amazing. You'll never regret it and they'll always be grateful. And, yes, you have changed but, if you don't mind my saying so, it's for the better."

"How'd you mean?"

"You're a bit softer," said Tara, treading carefully. "You've got more patience and compassion. You're a warmer, more cuddly person."

"I'm cuddly, all right," I said, reaching for another biscuit.

"Seriously, Kate, the little weight you've put on suits you. You were far too thin and obsessive about your figure."

I bristled. "I had to be thin for TV."

184

"I know, but being hungry all the time was making you tense. You're more relaxed, less regimented about everything. You always seemed restless before, as if you wanted to be somewhere else all the time. Now you're calmer and, in a way, happier."

"I'm not, though." I sighed. "I feel lost. I had a purpose with my job. I wasn't changing anyone's life, but doing the best show I could was important to me. Now all I do is look after the twins and clean. It's fine, but it's not going to get me anywhere. I'm thirty and I need to focus on my career. Sadly I don't have a handsome millionaire to take care of me, and I don't fancy living with Dad and Derek for ever. The longer I stay away from London and presenting, the harder it's going to be to get back in. I'm scared. I don't know how to do anything else. I've no other skills and I don't think taking a long sabbatical to wipe the twins' noses and arses is going to convince the head of ITV to hire me."

"Have you been in touch with your producer?"

"Yes, but she said that there was nothing she could do for me until I had a definite date of return, and right now I don't have one. Fiona's got her fourth chemo session coming up, then another four to go and then the radiation, so it'll be at least another four or five months."

"Well, I think you're brilliant and I bet you end up with a better job — and the fling Sam's having with that young one won't last. She's just his rebound person."

"I need to find someone new. Lunging at my ex-boyfriend after eight years is a bit sad."

"Did he look good?"

"Amazing." I groaned. "Anyway, what about you? I see your bump's coming along nicely. How're you feeling?"

"Fine, thanks," said Tara, placing a hand protectively on her swollen stomach. "It's great actually. The baby's started to kick, which makes it all so much more real."

I studied her flushed face. She looked so happy and settled: she was exactly where she wanted to be in life. She had achieved what she had dreamt of: a lovely husband and now a baby. I felt very empty as her joy and contentment washed over me. The old me would have been far too busy jetting off to some foreign capital to interview a sexy film star to feel lonely, but the new me felt it acutely. What did I want from my life? What did I need to make me feel as fulfilled as my friend? Would I ever find it? Or was I doomed to spend the rest of my life alone, going on holidays with other sad, lonely people? Travelling by coach from town to town to visit places of historical interest and staying in run-down hotels where the rooms smelt of boiled cabbage and everyone got tipsy on sherry and sang songs like "It's A Long Way To Tipperary", spitting out pieces of mashed turnip when they got to the "Tip" in "Tipperary".

I had to take control of my life: throwing myself at past loves was not a good idea, and ignoring my appearance wouldn't help either. I would cut out all junk food, except maybe the odd bar of chocolate, and walk to and from Fiona's house . . . as long as it wasn't raining. Sighing, I popped another biscuit into my mouth. After all, as Scarlett O'Hara said, tomorrow was another day.

# CHAPTER
# TWENTY-TWO

After Fiona's fourth chemotherapy session she got mouth sores. As if she didn't have enough to deal with, eating became increasingly difficult and she began to lose weight.

I was really worried about her and did my best to build her up with tasty blended food so she could fight the cancer. But no matter how nice the ingredients, mushed food is just not appetizing. Unfortunately it tends to look like vomit. The only thing Fiona seemed to enjoy were the fruit smoothies I made in the morning. I put as many superfruits into them as I could. In my days of starvation in London when I was really hungry, I'd allow myself as a treat to buy a superfruit smoothie from the deli around the corner. I bought kiwis, strawberries and blueberries in bulk and tried to get Fiona to drink the home-made smoothies. Most of the time she'd manage one, and on the days when she didn't feel up to it, the twins hoovered them down. They loved them.

I also cross-referenced food and cancer on the Internet and discovered that breast-cancer survivors favoured certain herbs and supplements, so I read up on them to figure out which would be safe to put into Fiona's smoothies.

Ginger was supposed to help with nausea, and echinacea, in small doses, to fight colds and flu. Ginkgo improved the memory (Fiona certainly didn't need that: she had the memory of an elephant), the blood circulation, and might block a chemical that caused tumour growth. Ginseng was thought to fight disease, which was obviously a bonus. And then some weird thing called St John's wort was listed as easing depression. Of all the names, wouldn't you think they'd have come up with something a bit nicer-sounding to aid depression? I decided to stick with small amounts of ginger and ginseng for the moment — I was no herbalist and I didn't want to give her an overdose and have her bouncing off the walls.

She was definitely getting weaker with each dose of chemo and it was taking her longer to recover. The awful thing was that by the time she was feeling well again she'd have to go back for another blast. Although she tried to keep her spirits up for the boys, I could see it was really wearing her down.

I read up on alternative therapies for cancer patients and found out that visualization was supposed to help. Some people even claimed they had cured themselves by relaxing deeply and imagining their white blood cells battling the cancer cells. You could visualize the white blood cells as anything — maybe Fiona could pretend they were the knights on the chessboard, and the bad cells could be the opposition's pawns or something. It couldn't do any harm.

I booked us into a visualization class and only broke the news to Fiona when we were sitting outside the meeting place. I knew she'd never have agreed to it otherwise.

Her head whipped around. "I thought you said we were going to the cinema."

"Well, in a way we are. It's a cinema inside your head."

"I don't want to sit around with a bunch of bald sick people talking about cancer," she snapped.

"You won't have to talk at all. It's not therapy, it's visualization so it's silent. Besides, it's supposed to be brilliant at helping patients cope, and destressing and all that."

"I'm not going in."

"Come on, Fiona, give it a try. If you hate it we'll leave."

"I'm not a group person, you know that. I like to deal with things on my own, in my own way."

"Maybe it's time you tried something else."

"No."

"Jesus, Fiona, just get out of the bloody car and give it five minutes," I said, losing my temper. She looked shocked. I'd been tiptoeing around her for months but now I wanted her to help herself. "Stop trying to pretend you can do this on your own. Not talking about it won't make it go away. You have cancer. Accept help." I got out of the car and marched towards the door.

"Don't tell me how to deal with my disease," she shouted after me. "You don't know what it's like to wake up every day thinking you might die, and be terrified of not seeing your kids grow up. It's hell, Kate. It's a living hell. Don't assume you know what's best for me because you haven't got a clue. Shaving your head doesn't make you a cancer patient. If I choose not to talk about it then you should respect that. This is the way I always deal with things — alone. I've never been a talker and I've got through a lot of problems without your help, so don't you dare try to bully me into doing something I don't want to do."

"Well, maybe it's time you accepted help. Maybe all that dealing-with-stuff-on-your-own is bullshit, and maybe it's the reason you seem stressed all the time. I'm not just talking about now, I'm talking about before as well. Let people help you, Fiona! Stop trying to protect everyone! Scream, shout, cry about the injustice of it. It's *not* fair. You shouldn't have cancer. It's shit. Let out your anger. Stop being such a control freak."

"Fuck you!" she screamed, clearly taking my advice. "Swanning back here with your Florence Nightingale cape on! You have no idea what my life is like. You didn't have your childhood taken away when Mum died — I *did*. I'm the one who had to run the house while Dad buried his head in the sand. Your life didn't change, but mine was turned upside-down."

"She was my mother too!" I yelled. "You seem to forget that I suffered just like you did."

"You didn't get up to soothe Derek in the middle of the night. You didn't make the school lunches, wash the uniforms, cook dinner, give up your youth. While you were out having fun with your friends I was running a home with a broken heart."

"You didn't have to do it all, Fiona. You could have asked Dad for help."

"He needed me to be strong."

"He thought you were all right because you never let him see how upset you were."

"I was a child, for God's sake."

"He's not a mind-reader — although I agree he should have helped you. It was wrong of him to leave so much up to you." What had he been thinking? Fiona was only a little girl and shouldn't have had to take on so much responsibility. But I knew he regretted it because since she'd got older he was always trying to make it up to her. He told anyone who'd listen how wonderful she had been when Mum died. He had paid for a very lavish wedding, been nice to Mark, even though he thought he was a prat, and doted on the twins.

She shrugged. "He didn't mean to lean on me, it just happened that way."

"You were twelve. You should have been out having fun."

"Like you," she said.

"Am I supposed to feel guilty for being a normal kid?"

"Don't you think I'd have liked that too?"

"You were never normal. I mean, you were always superbright and into maths and chess and things most kids find boring. You were different," I said, as Fiona's face darkened. "In a brilliant, more mature, clever way," I added, in a lame attempt to soften her up.

192

"Being bright doesn't mean you don't want to play Spin the Bottle and giggle with your friends about boys."

"I thought you found all that silly and childish."

"I was pretending, so I wouldn't look like a total reject."

I looked at my sister. All this time I'd had no idea she'd wanted to be a silly teenager like everyone else. I'd always assumed she was too mature and clever for that carry-on. But she'd been lonely and miserable the whole time.

"I really thought you preferred playing chess."

"I did like playing chess. I loved it. It was a link to Mum and it ended up giving me a social life. At least I met people at chess competitions. A lot of them were devoid of personality, but at least it got me out. That was why I liked Mark so much when I first met him. He was so much fun."

Mark . . . *fun?* I tried to remember back to the first few times I'd met him. He'd never struck me as fun, but I suppose that was because most of his stories and jokes went over my head. I did remember him and Fiona laughing a lot, as Derek and I watched them blankly.

"I know Mark hasn't been much fun in the last few years but that's because his career has taken off and he has so little spare time now," said Fiona, reading my mind.

"Doesn't that bother you?"

"I mind him not being around, but I've been so busy with my teaching and the twins that I haven't really had much chance to think about it."

"It must be hard not getting any time together."

She sighed. "Yes, it is. I miss the nights we used to spend drinking wine, talking about prime-number sequences and formulas for computing *pi* and analysing the Reimann hypothesis. You know," she said ruefully, "the last time we had sex was after a passionate debate about Fermat's Last Theorem, which carried on into the bedroom."

Fiona really needed to revise her view of normal. No one I knew got aroused by theorems. "Well, it's good to hear that the passion's still alive," I said.

"It's a while ago now," she said quietly.

"Well, sure you'll be fighting fit and ready for action after this treatment's over. The two of you'll be at it like rabbits," I said lamely.

"I hope so, Kate," she said, looking directly at me. "I really hope so."

"Come on," I said. "I'll take you home."

"No," she said firmly. "I'll give it a go."

We found ourselves in a small room with four other cancer patients. Lily, the facilitator, asked us to introduce ourselves. Two of them were very despondent while the others were angry. It was pretty grim.

Fiona was by far the calmest when she spoke. "I'm a married mother of twin boys. I've got breast cancer and I'm half-way through my chemotherapy. I'm finding it increasingly difficult to be upbeat as I'm feeling worse after each session. But my boys keep me going. They give me a reason to get up in the morning. My sister

**194**

brought me here today. She's been helping me and I don't know what I'd do without her."

I squeezed my hands together and willed myself not to cry.

"And what about you?" Lily asked me.

"Well, I'm here because I wanted Fiona to try something that didn't involve poisonous drugs and I thought that maybe she'd find it helpful."

"Are you looking to get anything for yourself by using visualization?" Lily wondered.

"A nice man would be good."

"We'll see what we can do," said Lily.

She asked us to close our eyes and led us through some exercises designed to hone our senses and help us discover which of the five we found most evocative. We were told to imagine the taste of a lemon, the sound of bells, the feeling of silk against our bodies, the sight of a field of sunflowers and the smell of a rose. It was quite nice, and I found it easier to get into than I'd thought I would. When I peeked at Fiona her eyes were closed and she was smiling.

Lily asked one of the angry ladies to describe what she had visualized. "A guy with a hammer and a nail," she said. "The hammer represents my white blood cells and the nail is the cancer cells."

"Excellent," said Lily. "Now, each of you has to come up with your own image, but good versus evil tends to be the most effective. We've had cowboys and Indians, cops and robbers, a dog chasing a rabbit, a calm sea suddenly infested with a shark . . . Whatever works for you, run with it."

"I can't do it today," groaned one of the sad ladies. "I'm too depressed. I lost my eyelashes, eyebrows and pubic hair this time. It's not fair. I feel like a freak."

"Think of the money you'll save on waxing," said Lily. "Besides, the Brazilian is all in. You're at the height of fashion."

Everyone laughed, then began to compare notes on how bad their post-chemotherapy symptoms were. I felt totally out of place. I didn't belong here. I wasn't sick. I was an intruder on these brave women's lives. I sat quietly, trying desperately to blend into the wall, and listened as they discussed vomiting, hair loss, mouth sores, hot flashes, tactless families and friends, the isolation of being sick . . .

As they found humour in the darkest places, I was delighted to see Fiona joining in. She wasn't exactly leading the charge, but she was throwing in a comment here and there.

I decided to focus on my visualization. I imagined Fiona's cancer cells as the young girl Sam was sleeping with. Naturally *I* represented the white blood cells. When we bumped into each other, the young cancer cells, wearing a frumpy yellow dress, were no match for me, looking sensational in a backless ivory gown. Sam cast Cancer aside when he saw me, the resplendent white-blood-cell queen, and we headed off to bed where I had no trouble visualizing the feel of satin sheets on my skin as we rekindled our passion.

When it was time to go Fiona had to drag me out of my trance.

196

# CHAPTER
# TWENTY-THREE

Mark continued to spend all his time at the university, working on his world-shattering paper for the competition. When he told me he couldn't go with Fiona to the fifth chemo session, I exploded. "What do you mean 'can't'? There's no such word as 'can't'. You'll just have to reschedule your really important meeting and take your sick wife to hospital. It's called prioritizing, Mark. You might want to look up the word in the dictionary. It's on the same page as 'prat'."

Sweeping his hair back from his forehead — which I think he just did to wind me up as I had none to sweep — he sighed.

"Look, Kate, if I could rearrange the meeting of course I would, but Professor de la Toit is flying in from Paris that morning to help me with the final stage of the paper. I need his expertise to work through a glitch in the findings."

"Can't you let him figure it out while you sit with Fiona, then meet up with him later when I take over as usual?"

"He's only here for five hours and I need to work with him on this."

"Isn't that cheating? Getting someone else to finish your homework for you?"

"It's called collaboration, Kate. It's near 'common sense' in the dictionary."

"Would that be close to 'cold-hearted'?"

"Having a conversation with you is impossible."

"If Fiona dies, will you be glad you spent all this precious time on some pathetic ego-trip?"

"Fiona's going to be fine," snapped Mark. "Don't you dare use my wife's illness as leverage against me."

"That's rich coming from the man who called me in London and blackmailed me into coming back. I've given up everything to help and your life hasn't skipped a beat. In fact, you've more free time now I'm here to chauffeur your family around and cook dinner and clean up."

"I'll be in my office if you need me," he said, and left the room.

"Need you for what exactly?" I shouted, to the back of his hairy head.

When I got home my blood was still boiling. Derek was in the kitchen with Roxanne, both shovelling bacon sandwiches down their throats as some rap artist screamed insults from the stereo. I switched off the noise, grabbed a bottle of wine from the fridge, filled a glass to the brim and began to glug.

"Mark?" Derek asked, between bites.

I nodded.

"What this time?"

"Can't take her to chemo."

"Again?"

"Yep."

"Coz he's got prize shit going on?"

"What do you think?"

"That dude is always busy when she needs him," said Derek, getting as riled as he was capable of.

"He's fucking someone else," said Roxanne, as casually as if she'd commented on the weather.

"Excuse me?" I said, as some wine spilt down my chin.

Roxanne shrugged. "'Sobvious. He's having an affair. Probably a student. All this bullshit about his work is a smokescreen."

"What the hell would you know?" She was beginning to get on my nerves. First, she'd upset Fiona by telling her about her cousin who was dying of cancer, and now she was accusing Mark of having an affair. He couldn't be, could he? He was too much of a nerd. Nerds didn't have affairs.

"Yo, sis, relax," said Derek, defending his fuck-buddy. "Maybe Roxie's right. It'd explain why he's never around and why he's always working late and shit."

"Come on, Derek, this is Mark we're talking about. The only thing he's interested in is maths."

"And himself," added Derek. "And dudes who are into themselves have affairs."

"But he's only interested in himself from a career point of view," I said. "I've never even heard Mark say a girl is good-looking. He doesn't notice women."

"All dudes notice fine women," said Derek, with authority.

"Not Mark," I said.

"There's one way to find out," said our resident tattooist. Derek and I stared at her. "I'll make a pass at him and we'll see what happens."

I laughed, "If Mark was going to cheat on Fiona, believe me, it wouldn't be with you."

Roxanne stared at me. "Give me two hours and you'll eat your words," she said, grabbed her car keys and headed out the door.

Two hours later the doorbell rang. I answered it and there stood the girl formerly known as Roxanne. Her dreadlocks were pinned back into a neat ponytail and she was wearing a grey wool dress that showed off her fantastic figure while hiding all her tattoos. Her makeup was subtle and she had sexy-secretary glasses on. She looked amazing.

"Wow," I said.

"Told ya." She grinned.

"I'm impressed," I admitted.

"You look like a total android," said Derek, from behind me.

"Duh, this is what maths freaks look like," said the new student.

"Now what?" I asked, unsure what we were planning to do.

"I go to college and try to get the leg over," said Roxanne.

We sat down to come up with a more detailed plan. I knew Mark was staying late because he had a tutorial or some such, and I wasn't sure if Roxanne would be able to barge in. These things tended to be closed to tattooist seducers.

"No worries, leave it to Roxie. She could talk her way into the White House," said Derek, proudly.

Were we all mad? Plotting to seduce Fiona's husband? Maybe Roxanne was the wrong person for the job. After all, she was a bit of a live wire — God knows what she'd do if he did make a pass at her.

"OK, look, guys, whatever happens, Mark mustn't suspect a set-up. If he ever finds out we organized this, we're dead and Fiona will never forgive us. So, no matter what happens, you cannot tell him who you are. If he does make a pass at you, just —"

"Tell him he's a dirty old man and knee him in the balls," said Derek.

"No," I said firmly. "There is to be no drama. Just walk away. This is a very delicate matter. He's our sister's husband and let's not forget that," I said, looking Roxanne in the eye. "No violence or shouting. OK?"

She nodded. "Don't sweat it, Kate. I'll sort him."

I was a bit nervous about what "sorting him" might mean. I hoped she wasn't going to maim him. I didn't want to hurt him, just to find out if he was a love-rat, and then we could think of ways to harm him.

A car tooted outside. I looked at Derek.

"Gonzo," he said. "Volunteered to be our getaway driver."

"Jesus, Derek, it's not a bloody bank robbery and it's supposed to be low-key. I'll drive."

"Too late now," said Derek, as Gonzo walked into the kitchen in a balaclava and army combats.

"Your chariot awaits," he announced.

We piled into the back of his Fiesta and I got Roxanne to help me with my wig. Mark had never seen me with it on, and although I planned to stay well out of sight, at least this way he might not recognize me if he caught a glimpse of me.

When we got to the university, Gonzo insisted on driving around in circles until he found the perfect parking spot — behind the rubbish bins at the back of the dining-hall. "I'll keep the engine running so we can make a speedy escape," he said, in a dodgy American accent.

"Do me a favour and take off that ridiculous face mask. You're only going to draw attention to yourself," I said, as we clambered out of the car.

"For you, Princess, anything," he said, and peeled it off to reveal a face blackened with charcoal.

"What exactly did you think we were doing here tonight?" I asked.

"My man Derek said it was a covert mission of a delicate nature, so I came prepared." Gonzo waved a Swiss Army knife in the air. Was he planning to attack Mark with a miniature nail file?

Sighing, I said, "Do me a favour, stay in the car and don't talk to anyone. OK?"

Derek, Roxanne and I headed for the maths department, and when we got close, I asked a studious-looking guy where Professor Kennedy's office was. He gave us directions, taking time to check out Roxanne via his thick glasses. She gave him a dazzling smile, and he tripped as he went to walk away. This girl was a pro. I could pick up some tips.

When we got near to Mark's office, Derek and I hid behind a pillar and I gave Roxanne some last-minute instructions while she rearranged her cleavage so that it would give Pamela Anderson a run for her money.

"Remember, no violence and no admitting who you are. Just keep calm and be flirty without throwing yourself at him."

"Kate," she said, placing a hand on my arm, "I don't need instructions from you. I *know* what I'm doing."

There was no time to be insulted, although I was. I pushed her out from behind the pillar and off she strutted, high heels clicking on the concrete.

Mark's office window was directly in front of the pillar, so with a little manoeuvring, we could see inside. Derek had got Roxanne to call his mobile and leave her phone on, tucked inside her bag, so we could hear everything — that pair had clearly missed their vocation as private detectives.

Mark was perched on his desk, surrounded by six students. Four guys and two girls. One of the girls was very stern-looking but the other was attractive and wearing an extremely short skirt. They looked up as Roxanne walked in.

"Can I help you?" Mark asked.

"Are you Professor Kennedy?" she asked breathlessly.

"Yes." He smiled.

"I'm Denise Brown, a friend of the dean's. He said it'd be OK if I sat in on your class. I'm thinking of taking maths next year," said the vixen.

"Oh, I see," said Mark, surprised. "Well, this is actually a tutorial in which we'll be discussing the relationship between mass and velocity, but if you don't think it'll put you off maths for life, you're welcome to stay. However, you might be better to come to one of the more general lectures."

"Oh, no, I'd just love to hear about the velocity," gushed Roxanne, as two of the boys shifted uncomfortably in their seats.

"Trying to hide their hard-ons," whispered Derek, knowledgeably.

I looked at Mark: he wasn't shifting at all. She wasn't affecting him the way she was the younger students.

"OK. Grab a seat here and we'll get going," said the professor.

Roxanne sat down opposite him, hiking up her dress to reveal a little more leg.

"Does mass change with velocity?" asked Mark. "There is sometimes confusion surrounding the subject of *mass* in relativity. This is because there are two separate uses of the term. Sometimes people say 'mass' when they mean 'relativistic mass', $m_r$, but at other times they say 'mass' when they mean 'invariant mass', $m_o$. These two meanings are not the same. The invariant mass of a particle is independent of its velocity, $v$, whereas relativistic mass increases with velocity and tends to infinity as the velocity approaches the speed of light, $c$. They can be defined as follows:

$$m_r = E \,/\, c^2$$
$$m_o = \mathrm{sqrt}\,(E^2 \,/\, c^4 - p^2 \,/\, c^2),$$

where $E$ is energy, $p$ is momentum and $c$ is the speed of light in a vacuum. The velocity-dependent relation between the two is,

$$m_r = m_o \,/\, \mathrm{sqrt}\,(1 - v^2 \,/\, c^2) \ldots "$$

We watched as Roxanne stifled a yawn while the other students scribbled furiously, hanging on Mark's every word. Bored stupid, our actress dropped her pen, and bent slowly to pick it up, giving Mark a full view of her considerable cleavage. But he didn't skip a beat. On and on he droned about velocity and mass . . . until finally it was over.

"I hope that wasn't too much to take in," Mark said to Roxanne, as she seductively smoothed down her dress. The guys stared at her while the girls rolled their eyes.

"Oh, no, professor, I loved every second of it. I'd heard you were a genius in the field of mathematics. Now I know you are," she whispered, moving closer to him.

Mark smiled. "Thank you. What exactly is your relationship with the dean?"

"I'm his little cousin," said Roxanne, fluttering her eyelids. She was giving it everything but Mark wasn't biting.

"I see. Well, it was nice to meet you. OK, class, I'll see you tomorrow bright and early at the nine o'clock on prime numbers," he said, turning his back on Roxanne to go and sit at his desk.

As the others trailed out the door, Roxanne gave it one last shot. "Don't you feel thirsty after all that talking?" she purred. "Can I buy you a drink for allowing me to sit in on it?"

He looked up and smiled at her. "No, thanks, I've a lot of work to do. But I'm sure some of the younger boys would be very keen to take you up on the offer."

"Are you kidding me? Those nerds? Not on your life," said Roxanne, as the tattooed lady raised her snake head.

"Well, I'm sure you'll find they're very nice young men."

"I've always preferred men to boys," she said, leaning forward and placing her hand over his.

He pulled away. "It's time you went home."

"This is the best offer you'll ever get, old man," she snapped.

"I'm not interested, thank you. Now, I really must get back to work," said Mark, and steered her out the door.

"Are you blind, gay or impotent?" she shouted, as the door shut in her face.

"Grab her before she causes a scene!" I hissed, and Derek sprinted out, his hoodie hiding his face. He pulled Roxanne behind the pillar.

"The guy is a fucking faggot," said Roxanne. "There's your answer."

As we were turning to go, the student in the short skirt came back down the empty path and knocked on Mark's door. He answered it and smiled when he saw her. "I forgot to give you this," she said. "It's the research I did for your competition paper. I hope it helps."

"Thank you, Jessica. I've no doubt it will."

"I was going to grab a coffee now, if you'd like to join me," she said, flicking her hair.

"I'm afraid I have a meeting to go to."

"Oh, well, next time." She giggled.

"Certainly," said Mark.

He closed his door and the leggy maths student strutted off. I nudged Derek. "Go after her and pump her for information."

He caught up with her and introduced himself as a fan of Mark's. "Hey, I saw you talking to Professor Kennedy. He's, like, my total hero. I'm hoping to get into his class next year," said Derek.

"Are you a freshman?" Jessica asked, looking surprised.

"Mature student," said Derek. "I travelled for a couple of years after school, hung out with some maths guys in, uh, China and stuff, so now I'm totally into it."

"Did you meet Professor Hung?" asked Jessica, looking excited.

"Yeah, totally. He's a really cool guy," lied Derek.

"Wow, you lucky sod," said the cute blonde.

"Well, you're pretty lucky too, hanging with Mar — Professor Kennedy," said Derek, catching himself.

"Oh, yes, he's amazing, so inspirational. I love his classes."

"And does he ever hang out with you guys after class? In China, I used to drink jasmine tea with my man Hung all the time," said Derek, getting into the swing of it.

"Not normally because he's so busy ... but sometimes," said Jessica, grinning, "he makes an exception."

"Like with you?"

She nodded, looking proud of her "special" status.

"Do you hook up a lot?"

"Not really. He's so busy with the Goldwin Prize he has no time."

"Doesn't he have a wife and kids and stuff?" said Derek, trying to sound casual.

"Oh, yes! He talks about Mrs Kennedy and the twins all the time. She's a mathematician too — isn't that so romantic?" she gushed.

Derek snorted. "Whatever floats your boat."

"Professor Kennedy says that his wife is really gifted. Apparently her family is not very cerebrally inclined, and the fact that she did so well, despite very little support, defies logic."

"What?" said Derek, outraged at the suggestion that we hadn't been supportive.

"I know. Isn't it awful? Some people just don't understand genius. It's hard being super-bright, and I can sympathize," sighed Jessica. "My family thinks I'm a freak."

208

"Yeah, well, maybe that's cos you are," snapped Derek, "and you can tell that arrogant —"

"*Sketch*," shouted Roxanne, as Mark appeared at his office door.

Derek pulled up his hoodie and legged it.

I watched as Mark asked Jessica who the road-runner was and she said some strange groupie had been hanging around outside his office, asking about him and his family. Mark sighed and said it was part of the job. They headed off in the same direction, and we went back to meet Gonzo in the slowest getaway car in existence. It took him six goes to get the engine started.

"Not cerebrally inclined," said Derek, staring at me. "Who the hell does he think he is? Stephen fuckin' what's-his-face, the guy in the wheelchair who writes all those maths books?"

"Halkins?" I ventured.

"Hawking," said Gonzo, with authority, as we stared at him. "I've read *A Brief History of Time*. It's good shit. The dude is funny."

"You need to get out more," said Derek.

"Anyway, at least it looks like we were wrong about Mark cheating," I said, trying to move on from the fact that our brother-in-law was going around telling everyone that our family was a few sandwiches short of a picnic. The nerve of him!

"Of course he isn't cheating? Hello! The guy's a roaring queen," said the spurned tattooist. "His eyes didn't even dilate when I bent down to pick up the pen. He's just into spending time with that maths geek because she does research and shit for him. Your sister is safe, her husband isn't cheating on her. He's either gay or asexual."

"Stephen Hawking had an affair," announced Gonzo.

"What?" I asked impatiently.

"He left his wife and did a runner with his nurse."

"He's completely paralysed — he can't run anywhere with anyone," I reminded him.

"If there's a will there's a way," said Gonzo, as the car kangarooed out of the car park. We would have been faster in Stephen Hawking's wheelchair.

As we were driving out I caught a glimpse of Mark holding the door of a building open for an attractive woman in a trench-coat. They were laughing.

"Stop the car!" I shouted.

Gonzo slammed on the brakes and we skidded to a halt.

"What's going on?" asked Derek.

Clearly they hadn't seen Mark so I decided to be discreet. I wanted to check this out alone. "Nothing. I just need some air. I'm going to go for a walk around the campus and I'll grab a cab home."

"I'll come with you," Gonzo said, handing the keys to Roxanne.

"No," I said firmly. "I need some space. I'll catch up with you all later." With that I hopped out and walked briskly towards the building I'd seen Mark go into.

I waited until they had driven off and opened the door slowly. Expecting to find Mark in a clinch with the woman in the trench-coat, I was shocked to see that I was in a small library and about ten people were sitting down, drinking tea and coffee from Styrofoam cups.

A lady stood up and welcomed everyone to the meeting. Then she turned to Mark and asked him how things were going.

"Not very well. I had to tell my sister-in-law, Kate, that I couldn't take Fiona to her next chemo session and she flipped. She thinks I'm a completely selfish git. All we seem to do is argue. She can't see things from my point of view and I suppose, if I'm being honest, I'm not very good at seeing things from hers. We can't seem to get on. Maybe it's because we're both struggling to deal with Fiona's cancer in different ways. To be honest, I don't know how we'd cope without her — she's been a life-saver," he said. I could hardly believe my ears. Was Mark actually *praising* me? Did he *really* appreciate me coming back instead of thinking it was my duty? Why couldn't he say any of this to my face? . . . Had I ever given him the opportunity to say it? I was transfixed.

"I'm finding the cancer even harder to deal with, now Fiona's bald," Mark continued, his voice beginning to shake. "I don't recognize the woman who used to be my wife. She looks like a cancer victim now. I can't see Fiona. I just see bald head and illness. It terrifies me to see her like this. I don't know what to say or do. Suddenly her dying seems like a reality. I can't deal with it. I can't bring up the boys alone. I need Fiona — she's the core of our family. She *is* the family. I wish I could do something. Fix it. Make it go away. But I just stand by and watch her suffer. I'm immersing myself in work because it's the only time I switch off. I feel selfish for not being there more, but I dread going home. I don't —"

"Excuse me, is this the relatives-of-cancer meeting?" said a voice behind me.

I nodded and legged it before Mark had a chance to turn around.

I felt stupid for having assumed he was having an affair. For all his flaws, I knew Mark loved Fiona, but he had been behaving so selfishly . . .

I knew what he meant when he said he felt helpless and how he wanted to fix her, but running away to the office wasn't helping. He needed to come home, deal with the reality of cancer and be more supportive. The more time you spent with Fiona, the less scary it was. He had to get a grip and spend more time with his sick wife and less time moaning about it in self-help meetings.

# CHAPTER
# TWENTY-FOUR

Over the next few weeks I watched Mark for any signs of improvement, but he was, as usual, busy. Clearly the meetings weren't making him understand that he needed to be at home more.

He was due to present the paper the following week, and was like an excited kid at the prospect. One day I asked him casually if he was a fan of alternative medicine and self-help groups. He looked at me blankly. "Not really, no. I hope you're not planning on taking Fiona to some dodgy healer with false promises of miracle cures. It's the last thing she needs."

I walked out of the room before I strangled him. The self-help group was clearly just that: self-help. No help for the poor sods who had to live with you.

In the meantime — possibly to keep me off the streets doing bad *Cagney and Lacey* imitations — Tara had called and told me about an upcoming school reunion. It was our thirteenth and everyone was meeting in a restaurant in town to catch up. We had gone to an all-girls convent school, so these gatherings tended to be competitive in every way — clothes, careers, husbands, diamonds, figures . . . You name it, they noticed.

For our tenth school reunion I had flown in late from London after covering a film première in the freezing cold and lashing rain. With some careful embellishment I had made it all sound very glamorous. I had also spent two months' wages on a gorgeous designer dress so I'd look the part of a successful TV presenter when I made my entrance.

In I strutted, half-way through the meal, brimming with confidence, loudly greeting everyone like long-lost friends. I pitied the girls who had never left the backwater of Dublin — girls who had sensible, pensionable jobs in the bank or the civil service and married the boy next door. How dull, I thought, how incredibly insular . . . How could they stand to be stuck in the same rut for ten years? While they told me about their children, I cut across them with stories of jetting to Rome to interview Brad Pitt (a bare-faced lie, but who would know?) and my wild social life, partying with other media stars in London.

Some of my former schoolmates had seemed impressed, some bored and others sceptical. But I didn't care. I had created the person I wanted to be — glamorous, adventurous, successful and, best of all, away from Ireland. Who cared if I really lived in a cramped studio flat, earned almost no money and spent my days interviewing D-celebs or making tea for the presenters whose jobs I coveted? They'd never know. I could talk the talk better than anyone I knew.

But this year's reunion was going to be a different story. I didn't want to go. I didn't want to expose myself and my current pathetic status to anyone, let

214

alone a group of women I'd lorded it over three years ago. I told Tara there was no way I was going.

"Come on," she pleaded, over coffee. "It'll be good for you to get out and meet people again. You're spending far too much time cooped up with two five-year-olds. It's making you do crazy things, like stalk your brother-in-law." Tara had disapproved of my attempts to catch Mark out. She said there was no way he would be doing the dirt on Fiona, especially not now in her time of need. Tara always saw the best in people: it was one of her endearing qualities. I expected the worst, and was usually proven right . . .

"Seriously, Kate, you need to be with people your own age," she continued. "We'll have a few drinks — well, you can have a few drinks, I'll be on water — and have a laugh."

"They'll be laughing at me. I'll be the biggest loser there."

"No, they won't. They'll be sympathetic and admire you."

"I doubt it, and I've only myself to blame. I spent the whole of the ten-year reunion boasting about how amazing my life was."

"It *was* amazing, and it will be again when Fiona's better."

"It wasn't really that great. It only took off when I got my own show last year. Even then the effort of competing with younger, more ambitious, more beautiful women was wearing me down. It's dog eat dog out there. Still, it's a lot better than spending your days covered with snot and jam or holding a bucket for your sister to vomit into." I sighed.

"Just come along to it and if it's awful we'll leave," begged Tara.

I shook my head. "I can't do it. It's too humiliating. Sorry."

Tara admitted defeat and told me to call her if I changed my mind.

I went home feeling like an all-time failure. As I was bashing about in the kitchen making myself an enormous comfort sandwich, my phone rang.

"Hello?"

"Hi, is that Kate O'Brien?"

"Yes."

"Peter Kildare here. I'm a producer at TV3. I hear you're in town for the next few months and I wondered if you'd be interested in helping us out with a bit of presenting."

"Sure, absolutely, I'd love to," I said, not having the slightest inclination to play hard to get or pretend I needed to check my busy schedule. All the old tricks were out the window.

"Great. We're covering *Party in the Park* at the end of the month so it'll be an all-day affair. Our female presenter broke her leg water-skiing."

"Sounds great. Not the broken-leg bit, the job," I added, not wanting him to think I was a cut-throat wench who wished ill on others, although I was jumping up and down and silently thanking God for her accident.

"It'll be live, but it should be a piece of cake to someone with your experience. Why don't you pop into the studio tomorrow and we'll run through the list of bands playing and the schedule?"

"I'd love to."

"OK, see you then."

"Peter?"

"Yes?"

"How did you know I was back in Dublin?"

"I bumped into your pal Sam Taylor a couple of weeks ago and he said you were going to be in town for a while and would probably be up for occasional work. He filled me in on your experience in London, so I thought I'd give you a call."

"Well, I'm glad you did. Thanks."

We hung up and it was then that I realized my hands were shaking. "Yippee!" I screeched. A job, a real job, something I was good at, where I had to use my brain and think on my feet. Oh, the joy of doing something for myself. And, best of all, Sam had been thinking of me — in between shagging the young one in his office. Still, it felt good to know he was looking out for me.

I sent him a text — after agonizing over the wording for a good half an hour. I wanted to sound grateful but not overly so — grateful but breezy. I didn't want him to get the impression that, because he'd mentioned my name, I might lunge at him again. Eventually I sent: *Just got call re TV3 job. Txs for mentioning me 2 Peter. Prciate it. Kate.*

I dumped my sandwich in the bin and opted for some crackers and a pint of water. I needed to starve myself for the next week so I wouldn't look like a frump on TV. Then it hit me. My hair! Shit! I couldn't go on TV in a dodgy platinum wig. I'd have to go and buy a new one, a nice one that looked like my own chocolate-brown hair. I'd go into the shop first thing in the morning after I'd dropped the twins to school and have it for my meeting with Peter.

I called Tara to tell her my good news and she asked if I'd come to the reunion now. What the hell? I thought. I could do with a night out. I wanted to celebrate my job. I wanted to shout it from the rooftops. Kate O'Brien is back!

Dad walked in as I was introducing the next band, using the wooden spoon as my microphone.

"Hi." I grinned.

He looked around suspiciously.

"What?" I asked.

"You seem happy," he said.

"And?"

"You haven't in a while."

"Haven't I?" I asked, surprised. Sure I hadn't been a bundle of joy, but I'd thought I was hiding it well.

"You've had a face on you that could curdle milk."

"Well, maybe I haven't had much to smile about until now."

"Did you meet a lad?" he asked eagerly.

"No, I got a job," I said, beaming.

"Oh," he said, sounding disappointed. "No boyfriend, then?"

"No," I said, annoyed that he was ruining my buzz. "I'm really excited about this job. It'll be great to work again."

"Ah, you put far too much emphasis on that old job. What you need is to meet a nice lad who'll look after you."

"Like Mark?"

"You'd never end up with a gobshite like him," said Dad, giving me a vote of confidence.

"I've kissed a lot of frogs," I admitted.

"I don't want to hear about that."

"I didn't say I'd slept with them all."

"Jesus, will you stop? Just go out and find yourself a nice, sensible boy and get hitched so I can sleep in peace."

"Why? Are you worried I'll be living with you for ever? Am I cramping your style?"

"Every father wants to see his girls settled and not end up old maids."

"Thanks a lot."

"Well, you're not getting any younger."

"I've got loads of time. Where's the fire? I haven't met anyone I really liked yet."

"Maybe you're too choosy."

"Am I supposed to compromise and marry some tosser?"

"Life's all about compromise."

"You didn't compromise with Mum. You said it was love at first sight."

"True, but we were lucky. Most people grow on each other over time."

"Like weeds?"

"There's no need to be smart. I'm just saying don't turn a lad down because he might not be the best-looking fella around."

"Marry an ugly guy and he'll grow on me?"

"Stranger things have happened."

"Do you have anyone in mind?"

"Well, I know Derek's pal is keen on you."

"I sincerely hope you're not referring to Gonzo."

Dad shrugged.

"Jesus, Dad, how desperate do you think I am?"

"I'm not suggesting you go out with *him*. All I'm saying is, don't rule out a fella for not looking like George Best."

"I'm glad we don't have arranged marriages here or you'd sell me off to Quasimodo."

"There's no need to fly off the handle. I'm only telling you to keep an open mind. You should have stayed with that fella Sam. He'd have looked after you."

"Yeah, well, he's got someone else."

"The good ones always get snapped up. He was mad about you before you ran off to London."

"I went to pursue a career in media."

"And sure where did that get you?"

"It got me my own TV show, Dad. Which, by the way, is a really big deal."

"Didn't find you a husband, though, did it?"

"I don't want a bloody husband. I can look after myself."

"What about children?"

220

"What about them? I don't want any. I'm not ready for all that."

"Life passes by very quickly, Kate. Don't miss out on the good things."

"I was happy," I snapped. "I had a great life before I had to give it all up."

"You never seemed that happy to me. You were always stressed out."

"I like stress," I muttered.

"All I'm saying is that sometimes the best things in life are to be found on your own front doorstep. The grass isn't always greener elsewhere."

"And sometimes, Dad, it is. A lot greener. I like being independent."

"I just want you to be happy, pet," he said, patting my arm.

"Dad?"

"Yes, Kate?"

"Can I borrow some money?"

Two nights later, as I waited for Tara to pick me up for the reunion, I began to regret my decision. The wig I had bought with Dad's money wouldn't be ready until the next day so I was wearing a white scarf on my head, which made me look even more washed out than I was. I still couldn't fit into most of my clothes so I had put on a green wrap dress that didn't really suit me, but it was the only vaguely dressy thing that fitted so I had to wear it. I felt marginally better when I saw Tara, who was wearing a tent-like maternity top over stretchy trousers.

The minute we walked into the restaurant I knew it had been a mistake to come. The first group of girls we bumped into looked fantastic. Their hair was shiny, thick and beautiful, and their clothes fitted properly. Hilary Dunne was in the middle of them. She was the girl who had always intimidated everyone in the class. The "super-cool bitch". Good-looking, confident and sporty, she had ruled the roost in our year. She and I had never got on — mainly because I was jealous of her and she thought me far too uncool to hang out with. I had particularly enjoyed chatting to her at the last reunion and rubbing my "fabulous" career in her face.

After school she had tried to make it as a model and failed. While she was still young and beautiful she had married an older man with oodles of cash and become a lady of leisure, which you could tell she was bored with. At the ten-year reunion, as I had spun my stories of glitzy parties and Hollywood-star encounters, she had tried to put me down in front of a group of our classmates.

"I heard Brad Pitt hates being interviewed."

I gave her my most dazzling smile and said, "Have you met him?"

"Of course not," she snapped.

"Oh, right. Well, he's actually really charming and only dislikes being interviewed by presenters who ask him about his private life. He also told me he has a thing for Irish women," I lied, while Hilary smouldered.

"So when is this amazing interview going to be on?" she asked.

Without skipping a beat — I was getting good at this — I said, "It's due to be aired over the next week. Probably Thursday in conjunction with his new movie's première, which I'm also covering."

That there was no interview to air was irrelevant. I hadn't seen these people in ten years and I probably wouldn't for another ten. Besides, I was enjoying winding her up.

"It sounds almost too good to be true. I'll have to stay in and watch you flirting with him."

"I hope you can squeeze it in between tennis and coffee," I said, walking off before she could throw her drink over me.

And now, three years later, here I was. Looking awful and feeling deeply insecure.

"Well, look who it is," said Hilary, coming up to us. "It's our TV star. I didn't expect you to be here, Kate. How did you find time between recording your show? Or has that stunning blonde girl taken over? What happened?"

"Hi, Hilary, good to see you," said Tara, cutting in before I could say anything.

"Hi — my God, I hope you're pregnant," said Hilary, pointing at Tara's belly.

The other girls tittered as Tara glowered. "Yes, I am pregnant, and it's wonderful. I love my new shape."

"Rather you than me," said Hilary, glancing down at her washboard stomach. "How anyone would want kids is beyond me. They're far too much admin. So, anyway, what happened to your show, Kate?"

"I've taken leave of absence," I said, gripping my wine glass in an effort to remain calm.

"So you weren't replaced?" she asked.

"No, I've got some time off."

"Why would you do that? You'd only just got the job."

"I felt like a change of scenery."

"I see you've also gone for a change of image. What's with the short hair and scarf? Is that some new trend in London?"

"Kate came home for personal reasons," said Tara, glaring at Hilary in a lame attempt to get her to shut up.

"Oh, I get it. Your boyfriend dumped you and you cut off your hair. Why do women always do that when they break up with men? It's such a mistake. Why cut off your best asset?"

I plastered a smile on my face and said nothing.

"Never mind, plenty more fish in the sea. Are you staying in Dublin?"

"If you must know, I took time off to come home because my sister has cancer and I wanted to be here for her. I'm also dealing with the 'admin' of looking after her twin boys — which, by the way, is very rewarding. You should try it some time. As for boyfriends — I didn't have one to dump me. And I shaved my hair off the same day my sister's fell out. I think that answers all your questions, but if you have any more I'll be at the bar."

I walked away, followed closely by Tara. "You totally cut her down to size," she said. "You were amazing."

I turned to her, with tears in my eyes. "Then how come I feel so utterly miserable?" I asked, and downed the wine in one gulp.

# CHAPTER
# TWENTY-FIVE

Miraculously, Mark managed to take Fiona to her sixth chemo session. He was obviously feeling guilty about his upcoming trip to Berlin for four days to present his paper for the Goldwin Prize. She seemed pleased that he was making an effort, even though she was really sick and spent hours throwing up after the treatment.

Each session made her weaker and I hated to see my sister so ill. I got the boys to make a "Best Mummy in the World" poster to hang at the end of her bed to cheer her up. But they insisted that Teddy deliver it to her, so it was a soggy saliva-y mess by the time he had scampered up the stairs to the bedroom. Still, Fiona oohed and aahed and said it was the most beautiful poster she'd ever seen and I duly pinned it to the wall.

I had told both Fiona and Mark about my upcoming job, Fiona because I knew she'd be pleased for me, and Mark to make sure he was on hand to help out with the twins. He was flying out to Berlin the following day, so it was all falling neatly into place. Until two days before . . .

Bobby came home from school with a bad cold, which Fiona picked up immediately. Because her immune

226

system was so battered by the chemotherapy, she was susceptible to every sniffle going. Overnight, her cold got a lot worse and she spiked a fever. Mark called the doctor, who said she'd have to be admitted to hospital for a day or two so they could make sure she had enough fluids and bring her temperature down. He assured us it was nothing to worry about, just a bad cold, but due to her low white blood cell count, she couldn't fight it on her own.

The next day, the day of my job, I brought the twins to school while Mark went into hospital to check on Fiona. He called to tell me that the doctor had said she was improving, but he wanted to keep her in for another day. We could bring her home tomorrow.

"OK, great. I'll try to pop in to her before I head off," I said, relieved to hear she was on the mend. "Now, don't forget to pick the twins up at twelve. I'm just going back to make their lunch and then I'll get ready for work."

"Actually, Kate, there's been a bit of a hitch," Mark said.

"What?"

"I've had a call from the co-researcher in Berlin and I need to fly over this afternoon. We've had a small crisis on the paper that needs to be ironed out. If we don't sort it out today we'll lose our chance of winning. I'm sorry, Kate, but I have to go."

Was he actually saying these words? Had he lost his mind? He was going nowhere.

"Mark," I said, trying to remain calm, "you can't go anywhere today. I have a job I told you about ten days ago and we agreed that you'd look after your children and wife for the afternoon. You'll have to do your work via the phone and email."

"I can't, Kate. This needs to be worked out in a laboratory — it's a very complex and detailed problem. Can you get your dad to help?"

"He's in London on a dirty weekend with Sheryl. You're the only person who can do this. You can't go, end of story."

"I have to go. I'm booked on the two o'clock flight. I have no choice. A year's work depends on this. My *future* depends on it."

"What about *my* future? What about *my* life?" I shouted. "If you don't collect your kids from school, they'll be left on the side of the street because I won't be there to pick up the pieces. I'm not available today. I told you that, so you'll just have to sort it out yourself. Goodbye," I said, slamming down the phone.

No way — *no bloody way* — was I giving up this job. It was the only thing keeping me sane, my little beacon of light in a few very dark months. To hell with Mark and his stupid competition. He'd have to fly over first thing in the morning as planned.

I got back to the house, made chicken soup and cheesy bread, the way the boys liked, and set it out. All Mark had to do was make sure they ate it. Even he should be able to manage that. I cleaned the house, and just as I was about to leave, Fiona rang. "I wanted to wish you luck," she said.

"Thanks. Are you feeling better?" I asked.

"Much, thanks. Are you nervous?"

228

"Very nervous and very excited. I can't wait to get there and soak it all up. I love live TV — it's such an adrenaline rush."

"I'll be watching you from here. By the way, is Mark on his way to pick up the boys?"

"Yes," I said. I hadn't heard from him so I was taking that as a good sign.

"OK, great. Well, break a leg," she said.

"Thanks."

As I was driving back to Dad's to get changed my phone rang. It was the boys' school.

"Hello?"

"Ms O'Brien, it's Mrs Foley here."

"Hi."

"Are you on your way to pick up the twins?"

"Isn't their father there?"

"If he were here, Ms O'Brien, I'd hardly be calling you, now, would I?" said the old witch.

"Well, he should be there because *he*'s collecting them today."

"I just spoke to Professor Kennedy. He's at the airport, so I believe it's *you* who should be picking the twins up."

"He's where?"

"At the airport. Now, really, Ms O'Brien, the school closes at twelve, midday, and it's now a quarter past. This is unacceptable. The boys are quite upset."

DAMNBOLLOXWANKERSONOFABITCH . . .

"I'm on my way."

I swung the car round, causing havoc on the road, and drove like a maniac to the school. I felt as if my head was going to explode. I didn't know this level of anger existed. My message minder beeped. It was Mark — the coward had called directly into my voicemail. He hadn't even had the decency to speak to me in person.

"I'm really sorry, Kate, I know I've landed you in it, but this is out of my control. I have to sort out this glitch or the paper is useless. I've called Derek, who said he might be able to help out."

I threw the phone across the car.

When I arrived at the school, the twins were staring forlornly out the window with a cross Mrs Foley tut-tutting behind them. They looked very pleased to see me. Clearly they'd thought they'd been abandoned. It was bad enough having a bald, sick mother in hospital, but to have a useless fecker for a father was really scraping the bottom of the barrel.

I bundled them into the car, trying to pretend everything was fine, then proceeded to drive to the airport in record time. Many was the corner I took on two wheels, many was the red light I broke. I was a woman possessed. The boys giggled in the back. They were having their very own private rollercoaster ride. I flung the car on to the kerb outside Departures, grabbed the boys and ran in. The place was full of happy travellers and I couldn't see Mark anywhere. Luckily Jack spotted him in the security queue.

"There's Daddy!" he shouted, and ran over to his fugitive father, who looked shocked to see us.

"Hi," I said. "Going somewhere?"

230

Mark took in my dangerously red face. "Hello, Kate."

"Here are your children. I'm off to work," I said, and stormed away, leaving the twins with their father.

"Wait!" Mark shouted, but I kept walking. He caught up with me and grabbed my arm. "I have to get that plane."

"It's not my problem," I said, walking towards the exit door.

Mark followed me, dragging the twins with him. "You have to do me this one last favour, Kate. After this competition is over I promise I'll be much more hands-on. But I have to go now."

"*Fuck you* and your stupid bloody paper!" I shouted, as people queuing spun round to see what was going on.

"There's no need to cause a scene."

"If it's the only way to get through to you I'll cause the biggest scene you've ever witnessed."

Mark looked at his watch. "Kate, listen to me, I have to get that flight. Fiona understands the importance of this. Please bear with me on this one. Once this is over you can work as many days as you like. I'm sorry but I have to go now."

"Don't even think about it!" I lunged at him as he tried to walk away.

Meanwhile Bobby tugged at my leg. "Jack just did a pee-pee," he said, and I turned to see Jack, in tears, standing in a puddle of urine.

"Oh, Jack, pet," I said, bending down to him.

"I'm sorry, Auntie Kate. The shouting made me scared."

I looked at Mark. "Go on — go. You're no use here, anyway."

He bent down to kiss the boys. "It's OK, Jack. Kate and Daddy are being silly. It'll all be fine now. No more shouting, I promise, but I have to get on the plane. Be good for your auntie, and give Mummy a big kiss for me. I'll see you very soon." Then, to me, he said, "Kate, I really am sorry about this, but I have no choice."

"Every decision you make is a choice," I replied, and went to look for a bathroom where I could clean Jack up.

When we got back into the car, my phone was ringing. It was Derek. "So, like, Mark said there was some emergency with the twins and I needed to look after the little dudes or something," he said, stifling a yawn.

"Have you just woken up?"

"Yeah, it was a late one last night. So, what's the story?"

"I've got to be at *Party in the Park* in an hour. I need you to keep an eye on the boys. I'll be working until about eight, so you'll have to put them to bed and give them dinner and a bath and all that."

"Yeah, cool, whatever. Just leave me some instructions."

"Derek," I snapped, "I haven't got time to write instructions. Just feed them, play with them, bathe them and put them to bed. It's not rocket science."

"OK, chill, I'll sort it."

"I'll pick you up in twenty minutes and drop you all back to the house. I've made lunch, so all you need to do is dinner."

"Cool, whatever."

I hung up with a sinking feeling in my stomach. Derek wasn't the most responsible twenty-six-and-a-half-year-old. Would he be able to cope with the boys? They were pretty full on. Still, he was an intelligent young man ... "Boys, your uncle Derek is going to look after you today. It's his first time in charge, so you need to tell him what to do. OK?"

"I'm hungry," whimpered Jack.

"Me too," said Bobby.

"I've made your favourite cheesy bread for lunch."

"I don't want cheesy bread. I want ice-cream," said the emotional Jack.

"I want Mummy to put me to bed," said Bobby.

"I want Mummy to give me my bath," sobbed Jack.

"I want Mummy to come home," said Bobby, crying now.

I turned around. "Come on, guys, I know it's hard, but Mummy'll be back tomorrow and then she can give you your baths. She'll be better then."

"All better from the bad sickness?" asked Jack.

"Will she not have to have the nasty medicine any more that makes her hair fall out?" said Bobby, perking up at the thought that his mother was going to be back to normal.

Damn, I shouldn't have said "better": now they had their hopes up.

"Well, what I meant was that tomorrow she'll be better from the cold. But she still has to have the strong medicine to fight the bad sickness."

"When will she be all better?" asked Jack.

"Soon, sweetheart. Very soon."

"Next week?" asked Bobby.

"Not exactly next week, but a few weeks after that," I said. She had about three months of treatment to go, but to a five-year-old three months was a lifetime, so I opted for a more short-term answer.

Jack kicked the seat. "I want Mummy to be better now."

"So do I," I said, "but we have to be patient. I promise you it will be worth the wait. You'll see, she'll be back to her old self soon. It'll be great. But for now we have to be very kind to Mummy and give her lots of hugs and kisses and not be grouchy. OK?"

The two little heads nodded. They'd walk on fire if it meant their mother's cancer would go away.

When I picked up Derek, Gonzo was lurking in the background. Both were equally hung-over. They climbed into the back of the car and we set off for Fiona's house.

"You smell yucky," Jack said to Gonzo.

"Oh, yeah? Well, you smell of piss," said Gonzo.

"Shut up," I hissed. "He's only a kid."

"He peed in his pants," giggled Bobby, as Jack punched him.

"That's cool," said Gonzo. "Sometimes you just gotta go."

234

"Kate said 'fuck' to Daddy in the airport," Bobby snitched.

"Did she really?" said Derek, grinning at me. "I don't blame her."

"It was bold of me and I'm sorry, so we won't mention it again," I said, trying to do some damage control. I didn't want them telling Fiona about my fishwife behaviour in the airport.

"And what did your dad say?" asked Derek, stirring it up.

"Derek . . ." I warned.

"He said, 'Jesus'," said Jack.

"That's enough, boys. Let's forget about the airport," I said firmly, as I parked the car.

I showed Derek and Gonzo where everything was, laid out fresh towels and pyjamas on the bed, then hugged the twins and told them I'd be back in time to kiss them goodnight.

God knows what kind of babysitters the two rappers would turn in to. I had a pit in my stomach as I drove away leaving the twins in their care.

# CHAPTER
# TWENTY-SIX

Two hours later, I was standing backstage in a football stadium as *Party in the Park* was about to begin. I had my new wig on, makeup professionally applied, clothes provided by a stylist, and I felt good about myself for the first time in ages. In fact, I felt wonderful. I looked like me again. The adrenaline rush of doing a live show was indescribable. My heart was thumping in my chest and my palms were sweaty — I felt completely exhilarated.

The director counted down and we were live on air. Everything becomes a blur when you're doing live TV. Nothing else going on in your life matters. You're completely in the moment. Time stands still. The world outside the show was irrelevant to me. I had only one thought — what I was going to say next. It was incredibly liberating.

I interviewed the opening act before they went on, as the crowd went wild in anticipation. They were a group of four teenage boys from Kerry, who had just had a UK number one with their second single and they were as hyped and excited as I was. We fed off each other, and a few minutes later, when they ran on to the stage, I knew I'd done a good job. We'd opened the day with a bang. Enthusiasm is infectious and makes for great TV. I was on fire.

The next five hours were a whirlwind of interviews, commentaries, filling in the gaps while bands set up, and going into the crowd to talk to the excited fans. I also bantered to and fro with my co-host, Barry, an ambitious young guy who was a rising star on Irish TV. He was good-looking, confident and smart. He'd go a long way.

By the end of the show we had built up a good rapport and were joking and laughing like old friends. When we were finally off-air, Barry quizzed me about working in London. I saw his eyes light up when I told him I'd presented my own show. I failed to mention it was on a channel with low viewing figures and even smaller budgets. It felt good to be admired again. I liked being looked up to for what I had achieved instead of being given out to for not knowing that Bob the Builder's stupid blue cat was called Pilchard.

"That's amazing," said Barry. "It's my dream to have my own show. London's where it's at. This is all fine," he said, gesticulating around him, "but I want more. If you make it in London, you've really made it."

I smiled to myself. It was like looking into a mirror. I'd felt exactly the same way when I'd emigrated. London was the Mecca for ambitious television presenters from Ireland. "Well, if you do go over, let me know and I'll put you in touch with my old producers," I said. "They may not be able to help, but it'll open a few doors."

"Brilliant, thanks. I'm planning to move over next year when I'll have two years' experience under my belt. I don't want to leave it any later — you need to be young in this game. If you haven't made it by the time you're twenty-six, forget it, you're a has-been," he said, as I squirmed in my seat. "So how come you're back here?" he asked, clearly horrified that anyone would leave London to return to Dublin.

"I'm just on a break to help my sister, who's sick. I should be back in London within three months," I said. And after the day I'd had I couldn't *wait* to get back. I'd forgotten how much I loved my job. The feeling of doing something that I was good at was a high. A few blissful hours that didn't involve having to think about anyone or anything but me. I'd needed this for my sanity. I wanted to be Kate O'Brien the individual again, not Auntie Kate, sister Kate, daughter Kate or general-dogsbody Kate. Granted I wasn't sure how things would go when I got back to London, but I was hoping that Donna would find me something to tide me over while I looked for a new presenting job. I was no spring chicken, but I had experience on my side and there was always Botox.

"No one who hasn't experienced it can understand the high of this job," said Barry, as we smiled knowingly at each other.

"Well done, guys," said Peter Kildare, coming over with a tray of drinks. "That was fantastic. You're a total pro, Kate. I'm impressed."

"Thanks," I said, beaming at him. "I enjoyed it. If anything else comes up, let me know."

"I certainly will. I owe Sam a pint for recommending you."

He wasn't the only one who owed Sam. I did too. I was disappointed when he had responded to my thank-you text with a curt *"You're welcome"*. It hadn't left much of an opening for conversation. He was probably far too busy having wild sex with the young one from the office.

"Now, what'll you have?" asked Peter. "Beer, wine?"

"Beer, thanks. What time is it?" I asked absent-mindedly.

"Half eight."

"*What?* Shit! Sorry, I've got to kiss the twins goodnight," I said, promptly ruining any kudos I had built up with Barry.

I rang Derek but there was no answer. I called Gonzo's mobile — no answer. No one was picking up the home phone. I put my foot on the accelerator and tried not to think of worst-case scenarios. There was probably a simple explanation — maybe Derek was reading them a story about an inventor that was so engrossing no one had heard the phone . . . and pigs will fly.

When I got to the house, it was in chaos. The kitchen was like a bombsite. Pizza boxes lay strewn on the floor and green peppers were stuck to the cupboard doors. I ran upstairs to the twins' room. No one there. Maybe they'd been kidnapped by an axe-murderer. Stifling a sob, as I imagined the worst, I saw the light on in Fiona's room and heard the low thud of music. I opened the door slowly and there before me lay a sight to behold.

Derek and Gonzo were passed out on the bed in their boxer shorts — not a pretty sight. Bobby was curled up under Gonzo's armpit — God love him, I'd say the smell was only rancid — and Jack was sprawled across Derek's chest. Both twins had wet hair and were butt naked. I was so relieved to see them in one piece that I didn't care about the mess.

The TV was on in the background and some overweight rapper with gold teeth and saggy jeans was growling about the injustice of life. Wet towels lay on the floor beside soggy footprints. I felt a nudge and turned to see a drenched Teddy, looking very forlorn and fed up. Evidently he'd been given a bath too. I picked up a towel and rubbed him down. He looked directly at me and I swear I could almost hear him pleading with me never to leave him alone with these four men again. I patted his head and promised to give him a juicy bone in the morning.

Then I lifted Jack up and put him into his own bed, snuggling him up under his duvet. He opened a sleepy eye and smiled at me. I kissed him, then went to rescue his brother. As I carried him to bed, Bobby woke briefly and mumbled, "I'm glad you're back, Auntie Kate. I missed you," and fell back into a deep sleep as I cuddled him.

After I'd tucked him in, I went to wake the two sleeping beauties.

"Whassat?" said Derek, as I shook him.

"What the hell happened here tonight?" I asked. "The place is a state and the boys aren't even in their pyjamas. Why are you in your underwear?"

"Kate," said Derek, "you have no idea what we've been through. Those two little dudes are too much. We tried to give them a bath but they soaked us. Tell her, Gonzo," he said, as his bandmate woke up and rubbed sleep out of his eyes.

"Total nightmare. I'm so never having kids. I'm wiped out."

"Welcome to my world," I said, smiling.

"How does Fiona do this every day?" wondered Derek.

"What about me? I've been doing it for months," I said, put out that he wasn't acknowledging my hard work.

"Yeah, but it's only temporary. She's a lifer," he said. "Man, you'd need some serious speed to get you through parenthood."

"What did you give them for dinner?" I asked.

"Domino's Pizza."

"Derek!"

"What? It shut them up for a whole ten minutes. It was worth it. I ordered the one with peppers on it so they'd get, like, some vegetable intake."

"Judging by the kitchen, the peppers didn't go down too well. Come on, get up and help me clean up the

241

mess. Fiona's home tomorrow and the place is a dump."

"I'm too tired, Kate, I need some chill-out time."

"Get off your lazy arse now," I scolded, and pulled him off the bed.

"I'll help you," said Gonzo, rubbing his puny white body against me. "Do you want to start by helping me get dressed?" he whispered, blowing stale drink and pizza fumes up my nose.

I pushed him away. "Seriously, Gonzo, you have to get laid soon. It's not healthy."

"But it's you I want," he said, winking at me. "I'm prepared to wait for perfection."

"It's never going to happen. So unless you want it to fall off from lack of activity, you need to look elsewhere," I said.

"Some day, Princess, you'll regret spurning me." He sighed as he put on his damp trousers.

"Don't hold your breath," I retorted. "No, actually, for the time being, do. It stinks."

After blitzing the house, I let the two musicians go home and sat down to have a celebratory drink alone. I ached to dissect my exciting day with someone. I called Tara, but her phone was switched off. I didn't want to try Fiona because she was probably sleeping, and Dad thought my job was pointless, and Sam clearly didn't want to hear from me. I sighed and snuggled into the couch, replaying the day in my head.

Two glasses of wine and a lot of self-praise later my phone rang. It was Sam.

"Hi," I said, trying not to sound absolutely thrilled to hear from him.

"Hey, there, I wanted to tell you how great you were today."

"Really?"

"You were brilliant."

I basked in the praise. "God, Sam, it felt so good to be working again. I'm still on a high. Thanks again for putting Peter in touch with me. I owe you."

"Well, actually I've a favour to ask you."

"Oh, yeah?"

"Are you free next Friday?"

"Uhm, I think so," I said, forcing myself not to scream *yes*.

"I have this sports-awards dinner thing and I need someone to come with me, so if you're at a loose end and you fancy a free meal . . ." He tailed off.

"What about your girlfriend?"

"Gone."

"To school?"

"Funny. No, we decided that it wasn't going anywhere."

"Sorry to hear that," I said, whooping silently.

"To be honest she was wearing me out."

Jesus, I didn't want to hear this. I had no desire to listen to tales of his seven-hour sex marathons. I said nothing.

"She wanted to go clubbing every night. I'm too old. I can't dance to the music, I don't like blue drinks with umbrellas in them and the last time I checked, 50 Cent was currency, which apparently makes me a sad old git."

I giggled. "Serves you right for thinking you could keep up with a teenager."

"She was twenty-one."

"Practically a granny."

"Well, my short-lived stint as a sugar-daddy is well and truly over."

"Come on, you're not at the pipe-and-slippers stage yet."

"Sounds good to me. By the way, who is 50 Cent?"

"Probably the biggest star in the music industry at the moment."

Sam groaned. "Oh, God, I *am* a sad git."

"What was the last concert you went to?"

"Simple Minds in 1985."

"There's no hope for you."

"Will you take pity on an old man and come to the awards with me?"

"It might be bad for my street cred."

"You owe me for today, remember?"

"Bribery?"

"I'm desperate."

"Charming!"

"I can be."

"Sometimes."

"Will you?"

"What the hell?"

"Thanks."

"You're welcome."

"Kate?"

244

"Yeah?"

"You looked sensational today."

Before I could think of anything to say he'd hung up. The smile on my face would have melted ice.

# CHAPTER
# TWENTY-SEVEN

Fiona came out of hospital the next day, looking much better. The twins were thrilled to see her.

"Let's go out for tea tonight," she suggested.

"Great idea. Where do you want to go?" I said, presuming she'd choose the Green Olive health-food restaurant.

"TGI Friday's," she said.

The twins and I were flabbergasted.

"Really?" said Bobby.

"Yes, pet," she said, kissing him. "You've been such good boys and I'm so proud of you that I think you deserve a proper treat. So, TGI Friday's it is."

I smiled at her as the twins jumped up and down. This was a big step for Fiona: she had never before allowed the boys to eat non-organic food.

"You can have anything on the menu except nachos. They're just too awful," she said.

"OK," said the boys.

"Oh, and those greasy potato skins are out too, and I'm not sure about —"

"Fiona!" I interrupted. "Don't ruin it."

I could see she was on the verge of telling me about the nasty additives to be found in non-organic foods, but when she looked at the boys' disappointed faces, she stopped herself. "Kate's right. You can have anything you want. Just this once."

"Hurrah," said Jack, and hurried to put on his coat before his mother changed her mind again.

We were having a lovely time, eating greasy food and laughing at the twins' excitement, when Fiona's phone rang. "Oh, no . . . Oh, God . . . How awful, poor you . . . All that hard work . . . Never mind, it's still an amazing achievement . . . Sorry . . . See you in a few days . . . Don't be too hard on yourself . . . 'Bye." She hung up, looking miserable.

"What's up?" I asked

"Mark came third. He didn't win the prize or the money. He sounded gutted."

Typical, I thought. Just when Fiona was relaxing and enjoying herself for the first time in months, he'd had to ruin it.

"Third's pretty good, though, isn't it?" I said, trying to be positive.

"Absolutely, but for him it's the same as coming last. It was all or nothing for Mark. Poor thing, he's devastated. All that work . . ." She fished about for a hanky to wipe her tears before the twins — who were running around, high as kites on additives — noticed.

"Come on, Fiona, it's not the end of the world. He did really well to be second runner-up in a worldwide competition. He'll be fine in a few days."

"I don't know, Kate. He really thought he was going to win. Mark's very ambitious. This is a big knock-back for him. He said the dean was disappointed too. Oh, God, it's such a pity, I was praying he'd win."

Jesus, I thought. You should be saving your prayers for yourself. Praying that the cancer will go away and you live to see your kids grow up. What the hell was she wasting good prayers on Mark's poxy competition for?

"Fiona," I said sternly, "forget about Mark. Your priority is to get better. Stressing about your husband's career is not helping you. The doctor said that stress can aggravate the cancer. You have to focus on yourself and your health."

"I'm sick of being sick." She sighed. "It's a relief to focus on something else."

"Fine, focus on something positive, then, like how well the boys are coping and how their personalities are developing in such a fantastic way. Look at how cute and clever they are, and how mature they've been in handling your sickness."

Fiona looked at me and grinned. "Careful, Kate, you almost sound besotted. They've worked their magic on you."

I felt embarrassed, I don't know why, but it had been strange admitting how wonderful I thought the boys were. Maybe it was because they weren't mine. They'd always belong to Fiona and Mark, and I was just temporary. They'd never love me the way they adored their mother. Was I getting too involved? As if he had read my thoughts, Bobby fell over and banged his head on a chair. He started to bawl and came running over for comfort. Instinctively both Fiona and I opened our arms to comfort him. He ran by me into his mother's arms.

It was the day of my date with Sam and I was trying on my outfit for Fiona. I had eaten nothing but milkshakes for four days so I could fit into my killer red dress with the plunging back. It hadn't been hard to starve myself as I was so jittery with nerves that I could barely sit still. I couldn't wait to see Sam again and I was determined to look the best I possibly could.

Fiona was saying all the right things and I felt really good about myself. I went to put my wig on to show her the finished product, but I couldn't find it where I had left it, hanging on the coat rack out of reach of little hands.

Then I heard giggling from the bathroom. When I went in to see what was going on, I found the twins and Teddy in a tug-of-war. Teddy had my wig in his mouth as the twins, squealing with laughter, tried to pull it out. Chunks of long brown hair were strewn about the floor.

"He thinks it's another dog," said Jack, giggling, as I stared in horror at my silky hair.

"Look," said Bobby, and put Fiona's wig over his hand. He shook it in Teddy's face, making barking sounds. Teddy dropped mine and attacked Fiona's.

"Oh, boys!" said Fiona, pushing past my paralysed body to rescue the wigs.

She held mine up and stared at the big bald patch on the left-hand side. The right side was merely drowned in dog dribble.

"You know these aren't for playing with," Fiona said, in an attempt to reason with the twins. "Mummy and Auntie Kate need them until their hair grows back. It's naughty to let Teddy bite them."

She glanced at me and shook my wig, then tried to brush some strands from right to left. "Maybe we could put a bow on it to hide this bit."

I couldn't believe it. My big night was ruined. "Thanks a lot, boys," I said. I turned on my heels and stormed out.

"Come on, Kate," Fiona called after me, "they didn't mean it. It was an accident."

"Fiona, the wig is fucked, as is my bloody date," I said.

I cried the whole way home. How could I go to a black-tie ball with clumpy, fuzzy hair. I needed that wig. I felt naked without it. I'd have to call Sam and cancel. There was no way I was going to turn up looking like a dog, while all the other stunning women with sleek, shiny cascading hair swished about.

I slammed the front door and threw myself on the couch for a self-indulgent sob.

"Jesus, you nearly took that door off its hinges," Dad said, coming in to see what was going on.

"Stupid boys . . . wig . . . ruined . . . disaster . . . Not going . . . Ugly pig."

"Well, I've no idea what you're mumbling, but Fiona called and said there'd been an incident with a wig and you were upset. I take it you've no hair for tonight, which I can see is not ideal. But we can sort it out. Come on, Katie, stop crying — you'll ruin your dress."

I looked down. I had forgotten I was still in the red dress, which was now covered in tears. I began to howl again.

"Kate!" Dad snapped. "Feeling sorry for yourself won't help and you don't want to be going out with a big red face on you and puffy eyes. Now, dry up and let's see what we can do about this hair situation."

"There's nothing to do!" I shouted. "You can't fix it — and I'm not going out looking like a freak! I have to call Sam and cancel." I reached into my bag to fish out my phone.

But Dad was too quick for me: he grabbed it and tucked it into his pocket. "Stop being such a bloody drama queen. There must be something you can do with a bit of hairspray or a scarf or something. Sheryl might have a hat you could borrow."

"*Sheryl* is the last person in the world I want to see right now," I roared. "The only fashion she knows anything about is tracksuits."

"Shush, will you? She's on her way over. After Fiona called I rang her," said Dad, as the doorbell sounded.

In came Sheryl, looking annoyed. She must have heard me slagging off her clothes — although as I'd spent eight years in school seeing her in a tracksuit every day, it hadn't been that insulting. Even now she was wearing jeans with runners and a zip-up sports top. The woman couldn't help it: she loved sporty clothes. Which was fine, but I was going to a black-tie dinner and I didn't fancy wearing a baseball cap.

Sheryl placed a bag of hats and scarves on the couch beside me and turning to Dad said, "I'll talk to you later, Bill. I can see you have your hands full here."

"Ah, don't mind Kate. She's just emotional," said Dad, following her out while I riffled through the bag. The scarves all had sporty themes — a bright yellow one was covered with horses and horseshoes, a green one with tennis players and rackets, and a red one with golfers and golfballs. They would have looked good on the Queen. The hats were worse — a big black felt one that looked like a spaceship, a cream boater and a purple thing that resembled a swimming-cap, covered with flowers.

Having spent ten minutes trying to placate Sheryl in the hall, Dad came back in. "She wouldn't stay. Very upset she is," he said, wagging a finger at me. "Said she couldn't come into such a hostile environment. She said she'd collect her things tomorrow. These are all her favourites and not a tracksuit among them. You can apologize to her when you've calmed down."

I put on the purple swimming-cap. "How can I possibly go out like this?"

"There must be something nicer in there," he said, rummaging through the bag. He thrust the red scarf into my hand. "There now, a nice red scarf to match your dress."

I put it on — all you could see were big white golfballs and clubs. Despite himself, Dad began to laugh.

"This isn't funny!" I snapped. "This is my life! I can't go. I'll have to call Sam."

252

My phone beeped. I went to grab it from Dad's pocket and opened the message. *Hey gorgeous, pick u up at 7.30.*

Dad was reading it over my shoulder. "You can't back out now," he said. "It's seven already and you can't let the lad down. Now, take that stupid thing off your head. Go and put on one of your own scarves, smile and you'll be fine. No lad wants to look at a grumpy face. You need to encourage them, not scare them off."

I had half an hour to do some serious work on my blotchy face, dry the wet patches on my dress and find something non-Sherylesque to cover my head.

When the taxi pulled up to the house at exactly seven thirty, I watched Sam get out and come to ring the doorbell. I heard Dad welcome him warmly. He had always liked Sam. They had bonded from the beginning over sport. When Sam had begun to write his column, Dad had always read it and, most of the time, agreed with his point of view.

At the top of the stairs, I took a deep breath, fixed the chiffon scarf round my head — it wasn't ideal, but it didn't look too bad — and walked down, knees shaking like a teenager's on a first date.

Sam looked amazing in his tuxedo, which made me feel even more self-conscious. Eventually they paused in their heated debate about the sorry state of the Irish soccer team and smiled at me, although I could see Sam was a bit puzzled by the scarf — he had always loved my hair long and down.

As we were leaving, Dad leant over to kiss me and whispered in my ear, "You look as glamorous as Grace Kelly in that scarf."

"Thanks," I said.

"What picture did she win the Oscar for?"

"*The Country Girl*," I replied.

"That's my Katie," said Dad, beaming. "Enjoy yourself and remember to smile. It'll distract from the hair."

# CHAPTER
# TWENTY-EIGHT

In the taxi on the way to the awards, I felt awkward and shy. Sam chatted away and I tried to relax and enjoy myself, but I was self-conscious about the scarf and kept tugging at it. Eventually Sam stopped mid-sentence and said, "Why don't you take the scarf off? It seems to be driving you mad."

"No, I like it. It's part of my outfit," I lied.

"I've never seen you wear one before."

"Yeah, well, you haven't seen much of me in years. Besides, it's very fashionable," I added, pulling it down to make sure my head was fully covered.

Sam shrugged. "OK, but for the record, I think your hair looks great down."

"Well, I think it's nice like this." I was put out that he was making me feel worse than I already did . . . although he didn't know he was because he didn't know about the shaved head, so it was kind of a compliment.

While Sam paid the driver, I fiddled with the scarf some more, then climbed out and closed the door. The taxi drove off. I felt a tug and a wrench as my scarf, which had got stuck in the door, disappeared into the night.

"*Fuuuuuuuck!*" I screamed, putting my hands up to cover my head.

Sam started. "What the hell?" he exclaimed.

Don't cry, I urged myself. Not now.

"I decided to cut my hair off," I said, trying to sound nonchalant, although my throat felt like it was full of stones.

Sam stared at the irregular tufts, sprouting every which way. "Are you telling me a hairdresser did that?" he said, pointing to my head in horror.

He certainly knew how to make me feel like a piece of shit. "No, Gonzo did it."

"Derek's friend?" asked Sam, bemused. "Why on earth would you let him do that? He's a lunatic."

"He's grown into a very nice young man," I said, defending Gonzo for the first time ever.

"Kate," Sam said, putting his hands on my arms and making me look at him, "what's going on here? Why would you cut off your gorgeous hair?"

I tried valiantly not to cry. "Fiona's fell out after her chemo so Derek and I shaved our heads in solidarity." Then I began to cry. "I know I look like a freak, but it meant a lot to her and it'll grow back, I hope."

Sam drew me to him and hugged me. He kissed my head and whispered, "That was an incredible thing to do."

Now I was bawling and my makeup was ruined. He handed me a tissue and I wiped the remaining traces of Lancôme off my face. "I'd say I look a right state now," I hiccuped.

"You're a vision," said Sam.

**256**

"Oh, come on, you can cut the bullshit."

"OK, I've seen you look better, but every time I catch sight of your head I'll be thinking of what a great thing you did."

"Do we have to go in? Couldn't we do a runner and get smashed in a bar with dim lighting?"

Sam grinned at me. "No way. I'm showing you off tonight."

"I'm hardly a trophy at the moment. Maybe I can camouflage it with a napkin."

"Be bald and proud like Sinéad O'Connor."

"I look more like Kojak."

"Was that a wig you wore on TV?"

"Yes, but Teddy and Fiona's twins got to it."

"Teddy?"

"The twins' dog. God love him, they have him tormented — they keep shoving things up his backside."

"How's Fiona and the rest of the family?"

"Let's see. Fiona is nearly finished chemo and gets sicker after each session. She won't really talk about the cancer, and Mark is utterly useless and a selfish prick. Dad's shagging my old gym teacher and Derek still thinks he's a black man in a white man's body."

"And you?"

"I'm trying to help but I don't know if I'm making a very good job of it."

Sam put an arm round me. "It sounds like you need a drink."

"How about a vat of wine?"

"As long as I can take advantage of you when you're drunk."

"Help yourself." I grinned, perking up.

We sat up at the bar, flirting, for a blissful ten minutes before Sam suddenly went rigid.

"Bollox," he muttered.

"What's up?"

"Ex-wife."

I turned around to see Nikki Jennings walking towards us. She hadn't changed much since school — still blonde, big boobs and tan. I have to say she looked pretty great in a slinky turquoise dress that matched her eyes. "Fancy meeting you here." She laughed, bending over to kiss Sam, who recoiled. "Come on, Sammy, can't we be friends?" she asked, in a little-girl voice.

"Is he here?" Sam snapped.

"Who?"

He glared at her.

"Oh, you mean Richard," said the adulteress. "Of course he is, darling. He's one of the main sponsors tonight," she said, running a manicured hand through her hair, which got caught in the enormous ring on her finger. Elizabeth Taylor had nothing on this girl.

"Nice rock," said Sam, via gritted teeth.

"I know. Isn't it fabulous? Actually, honey, that's why I came over. I wanted to tell you before you heard it from someone else. Richard and I are engaged."

"Isn't that a little hasty? You haven't got divorced yet so technically you're still married to me," growled Sam.

"Richard said he couldn't wait," she said, admiring her ring.

The cheek of her, I fumed. How dare she come over here and lord her engagement over Sam? I tried to bite my tongue, but as usual I wasn't very good at it. "Is Richard the guy you had the affair with or is he someone new?" I asked.

Nikki swung round to face me. "Who the hell — oh, my God, Kate?"

"Yes. Hi, Nikki. Long time no see."

"What's going on with your hair?"

"Fancied a change. Long hair is so last year," I said staring at — and secretly coveting — her long locks.

"Get a mirror. So what is this? Are you guys back together?" she sneered. "God, Sam, you must be a glutton for punishment. She dumps you and eight years later you get back with her. Couldn't you find anyone new to go out with?"

"Does shagging your boss entitle you to a promotion?" I mused.

"Who are you to judge me? You dumped Sam for your career. At least I did it for love."

"I was under the impression it was more for lust and money," I retorted.

"Ladies," said Sam, "much as I'd love to sit here and listen to the reasons I got dumped twice, the dinner's about to begin."

Nikki stomped off to find Richard.

"Sorry," I said, as Sam steered me into the dining room.

"For dumping me eight years ago or for slating my ex-wife?"

"Slating Nikki," I said, avoiding the dumping comment. "Why on earth did you marry her?"

"Because she was so different from you," he said quietly, and my heart sank. I had still not been forgiven for going to London. I had my work cut out for me.

We sat down at a table with Sam's fellow journalists, who slagged him about being nominated for Sports Writer of the Year. A key piece of information he had failed to mention to me.

"Wow! That's amazing, Sam! Well done," I said.

"It's no big deal."

"Of course it is. Being recognized by your peers is a *really* big deal."

"I haven't won it. I've only been nominated."

"It's still brilliant."

"So, what's the deal with you guys?" slurred Tim, the sub-editor, knocking back his fifth glass of wine.

"Kate's an old friend," said Sam. "She lives in London, but she's back in town for a few months so we're catching up."

Old friend? I was crushed. Since the run-in with Nikki, the flirting had stopped and Sam seemed preoccupied and distant. Was it because he was upset at seeing his ex-wife flaunting her lover, or was it because she'd reminded him of why I'd left? Whether or which, the stupid cow had ruined the mood. But I was determined to get the flirting back, so I poured Sam another large glass of wine and batted my eyelids at him.

Slowly he began to loosen up, and when the dinner was coming to an end, they announced the final award of the evening — the Sports Writer of the Year award. You could have heard a pin drop. My palms were sweaty with anticipation and I prayed he'd win. Sam, on the other hand, seemed calm and composed.

"And the winner is — Sam Taylor."

Sam stood up, beaming, and the whole place erupted: he was a very popular winner. As he posed for photos holding the trophy, his editor, sitting to my right, commented on how richly deserved his win was.

"He's very talented, isn't he?" I agreed.

"I've been in this business forty years and I've never come across anyone else who writes about sport the way he does. He brings it alive. A couple of the English papers have tried to poach him, but he's stayed loyal to us, which is rare, these days."

"I had no idea he'd been offered jobs in London."

"Several times, but he turned them all down."

"Why?"

"Says he loves the passion about sport in this country and the fact that Gaelic and hurling are still amateur sports, untarnished by salaries and sponsorship deals. He has a point there. You'll not get the passion we have for sport here in many places."

"But wouldn't it be good for his career to go?" I asked.

"Depends on what you're looking for. His talent is recognized here and he comes and goes as he pleases, gets to choose which events he covers. And he has no problem getting interviews. Sure in London you've to stand in line to interview the big sports stars, and you're lucky if you get ten minutes. He's a very big fish in a small pond here. I suppose that's better than being one of a shoal over there."

"But wouldn't it be a real achievement to make it in London?"

"Why?"

"Because it's harder and there's more competition," I said.

"There's plenty competition here. Why make life hard for yourself when you've a great set-up, doing what you love and being recognized for it?"

He had a point. Why was I so impressed with success abroad? What was wrong with success at home? Why chase something elsewhere when you already have it in your lap?

While I was musing on this, Sam arrived back and everyone descended on him to congratulate him. When he broke free of a particularly long clinch with one of his female colleagues, he came over to me. I hugged him. "Well done. You so deserve it. Everyone's thrilled for you. None of the other winners got half the applause you did. I'm very proud to be your date," I said, deciding to forget that he'd referred to me earlier as an old friend.

"Would my date like a glass of champagne?" he asked, holding up one of the many bottles that had arrived at our table, post-win.

"Yes, she would."

As he was pouring, I tapped his arm. "Sam, do you recognize this song?"

He shook his head.

"It's 50 Cent. I think we should dance."

"I told you — I can't dance to this stuff. There's no rhythm."

"Maybe the problem is you don't have any rhythm."

"Or that I'm not sixteen and find it hard to dance to a guy roaring about guns and ho's."

"Derek worships him."

"Well, then, it's time to get him help."

"OK, what'll get you on the dance floor?"

" 'Baggy Trousers' by Madness."

I groaned. "I *can't* ask the DJ to play that. Give me something else."

"OK — U2's 'With or Without You'."

I looked at him. It was my favourite U2 song.

"I'd like to dance with you to that one. It brings back good memories."

I sprinted up to the DJ and begged him to play it. He refused. "Sorry, love, I was told not to do a slow set."

I leant over and grabbed his arm. "Listen to me. I haven't had sex in almost a year but my ex-boyfriend is here and if you play this song I really think my luck might change. Please don't deny me this."

"Fair enough. "I'll play it next and hopefully he'll ride you senseless."

We danced, but although I gave Sam at least twenty opportunities to snog me during the song — to the point at which I had a crick in my neck from looking up — he did nothing.

"Is it the hair?" I asked.

"No."

"Then what?"

"I just want to take things slowly. It's been a difficult year — let's see how it goes."

"How slowly?" I was desperate to know. Being this close to him with no promise of passion was killing me.

"Just relax and enjoy the music," he said, laughing.

How the hell could I relax when I was craving affection from the only man I'd ever loved? I shuffled around and prayed that "slowly" meant soon . . . Very soon.

# CHAPTER
# TWENTY-NINE

After a peck on the lips outside my house, Mr Take It Slowly told me he was off to Australia for five weeks to cover some rugby event. I waved him goodbye and resigned myself to a life on the shelf.

As I was getting undressed my phone beeped. *When I get back we might just have to speed things up!*

I went to bed smiling.

The next day was Fiona's second to last chemo session, and as Mark was too busy to take her, and the boys were now on summer holidays from school, Dad volunteered. When he arrived, with Derek in tow, Fiona was fussing over the boys' lunch menu. I was used to her at this stage and let her at it, but Dad, who was furious with Mark for being absent again and worried about being late, started to hyperventilate. "Come on, will you? Leave that to Kate," he said.

"Hang on a minute. I want to make sure they get some leafy green vegetables. They need the iron."

"They're fine, strapping fellows. Will you stop fussing? We're going to be late."

"Dad, relax. Now, boys, I want you to promise to eat the cabbage and broccoli that Kate gives you at lunch today. OK?"

"I hate boccoli," whined Bobby.

"I hate cabbage," whinged Jack.

Fiona crouched to talk to them at their eye level, something she had told me was very important. "Look, boys, if you eat your greens you'll grow up to be tall and strong like —"

"Your granddad," said Dad, seemingly oblivious to his round five-foot-five frame.

"You have a big fat belly," said Bobby.

Dad bristled. "I do not. This shirt happens to be a bit small for me."

"Anyway, please eat your greens for Auntie Kate," said Fiona, and reminded me of the renewed importance of my coming up with stimulating activities for the boys now that school was out for the summer. I nodded while Dad rolled his eyes. "At least one hour of maths. Their new exercise books are on the table in the playroom."

"Don't be locking them up on a lovely day like today doing maths," said Dad. "Let them run about outside."

"Dad," said Fiona, firmly, "can you please not interfere in my decisions?"

"Fine. I'll say nothing."

"Now, give Mummy a hug and I'll see you later."

"Are you going to be finished with the bad medicine soon?" asked Jack, hanging on to his mother's leg.

266

"Yes, sweetheart, I am. Only one more session after today, and then I have to take a different kind of medicine, which won't make me feel so sick."

"When will you be better, Mummy?" asked Bobby. "I don't want you to go."

"Get away out of that now and let your mother be. She has to go to hospital so she can get better. Don't be asking her to stay," said Dad, pulling the boys away from Fiona.

"Wait a minute, Dad, let me talk to them. It's important to explain everything to them."

"They don't need to know the details, Fiona. You'll only upset them."

"No, Dad, not knowing what's going on is upsetting. Being lied to about your mother's health is upsetting. Being told your mother's going to get better when she only has days to live is upsetting," Fiona said, getting worked up as she remembered Mum dying.

"Children need to be protected from bad news," said Dad, evenly.

"They also need the opportunity to say goodbye to their mother and not be barred from the hospital because you think it's too difficult for them," said Fiona.

"I did what I thought was best," said Dad.

In a strangled voice, Fiona asked Derek to take the boys into the playroom while she talked to Dad.

I sank deeper into my chair. This was the first time they had ever talked about Mum dying in front of me.

Fiona rounded on Dad: "You were wrong! You stole my chance to say goodbye to her."

"I didn't know she'd die so quickly."

"Well, she did, and then you put away all the photos of her and refused to talk about her. That was cruel, Dad."

"I was trying to get you to move on with your lives and not dwell on the tragedy."

"She was our mother! We needed to be allowed to grieve and talk about her," Fiona hissed.

"I was heartbroken. I didn't know what to do. I couldn't think straight for the grief."

"So were we, Dad," she shouted. "We were heartbroken too, and if I die you'd better talk to those boys about me every day of their lives. I won't be put away in a drawer. I want my memory to be kept alive."

"Jesus, will you stop that talk? You're going to be fine."

"You don't know that, Dad! I could die of this and I won't have my kids feeling too scared to ask questions about me, and I won't have their childhood taken away because their father has buried his head in the sand."

"What do you mean by that?"

"I mean that because you refused to talk about Mum, and locked yourself away with your own grief, I was left to look after Kate and Derek. You left a twelve-year-old girl to look after two kids. I had no childhood, Dad. I was too busy cooking and washing."

"I thought you liked being in charge. You were always so responsible."

"*I hated it!*" she roared, as Dad and I recoiled in shock. I had never seen her so angry. "I wanted to be kissing boys behind bicycle sheds, not ironing my brother's school uniform. I had no choice — you weren't there. If I didn't look after them, who would?"

Dad looked crestfallen. I felt sorry for them both. They had suffered equally.

"I'm sorry, pet," said Dad. "I couldn't cope without her. You're right, I did leave you on your own. I don't know what to say, just that I'm very sorry. I never meant to rob you of your childhood."

"It's OK," Fiona said, breathless from her outburst. "I know you didn't mean it. But if anything happens to me, I want the boys to be able to ask questions about me and look at photos of me and hear stories about me."

"Please don't talk like that," begged Dad.

"You have to face the possibility that I might not get better."

"You will get better, Fiona, because God can't be that cruel," said Dad, quietly.

"Dad, you have to promise me."

Dad nodded, unable to speak. Fiona went to hug him and I turned away to hide my tears.

"Yo, can you tone it down a million?" drawled Derek, poking his head round the door. "The little dudes are getting stressed out in here with all the hollering."

Fiona rushed in to comfort them.

"So, I guess Fiona's pretty pissed about her childhood," said Derek. "I have some issues myself."

"I can't wait to hear this," said Dad, sitting down.

"Is it the drive-by shootings?" I asked, concealing a grin.

"That's just it. I don't feel I'm taken seriously enough. You know? You're always taking the piss about my music."

"It's not music, Derek. It's shouting in a fake American accent about things you have no knowledge or experience of," said Dad.

"It's called an imagination," said Derek, getting about as het up as he was capable of. "My lyrics are widely respected in the underground rap scene here in Dublin."

"Is it a big scene?" Dad asked, managing to hold a straight face.

"Quite substantial, actually," said Derek. "They call me the Poet."

"Yeats was a poet, Derek," said Dad.

"Yeah, about a million years ago. I'm talking about today, like the twenty-first century."

"Seamus Heaney is a modern poet."

"Well, I never heard of him."

"He won the Nobel Prize for his poetry in 1995."

"What kind of stuff does he write?"

"Prose that requires the use of the English language and not made up, misspelt Americanized vocabulary that you have to be a gangster to understand."

"So, which is your favourite Heaney poem?" I asked Dad, and winked at Derek.

"Well, ah, I like all of them. I wouldn't say I have a particular favourite."

"OK, then, a favourite quote?"

"Ah, sure I can't remember them all now. There are so many."

"You're a chancer, Dad. You don't know any of his poems, so stop giving Derek such a hard time."

"What's going on?" Fiona asked, coming back in with the twins.

"Dad's blowing a fuse because I asked him to take my music seriously and he gave me a lecture about some, like, really famous poet called Heaney and he doesn't even know the dude's poems."

"I see what's going on here," said Dad. "It's National Pick on Your Father Day. Fine, so I'm a useless father who ruined his daughter's life and hasn't taken his son seriously. Well, Kate, what's your complaint? Come on, spit it out. What grave injustice did I do to you?"

"Well, it would be nice if you'd considered my feelings when you started shagging my least favourite teacher," I said, laughing.

Dad was in no mood for jokes. "Well, now, Missy, just wait a minute there, because Sheryl and I have broken up and it's because of my loyalty to you that we did so."

"How come?"

"She was giving out about you being ungrateful over the scarves and hats she brought over, and I said to give you a break, you hadn't had an easy time of it lately, and you'd no boy and no job. Well, she said you were the type of girl who was never satisfied and always looking for bigger and better things, and you'd never be happy and you'd no one to blame but yourself. So I told her that no one was allowed criticize my children and that you were all a credit to me and there was no harm in Kate aiming high in life. Anyway, we argued on and she said she couldn't be with someone who always put his children first, and I said that was the way I was. So she left."

"I don't know what to say. Thanks for defending me. To be honest, I think you're better off without her," I said.

"The chick was way too young for you," said Derek.

"Are you OK about it, Dad?" asked Fiona, obviously trying to make up for rubbishing his parenting skills.

"To be honest, it's a relief, she was too energetic."

"Was she looking for it night and day?" asked Derek.

"What was she looking for?" asked Jack.

"Sex," said Derek, as Fiona thumped him.

"Did she find it?" asked Bobby.

"Ask Granddad," said Derek.

"Did she?" Bobby asked Dad.

"No, Bobby, she didn't. My back couldn't take it," said Dad.

"You looked pretty agile to me when I caught you together." I giggled.

Bobby was confused. "Couldn't take what?" he asked, and Fiona said she'd explain it all later.

"Now, Fiona, can we please go to the hospital before I get accused of corrupting my grandchildren *and* ruining their lives?"

"For the record," said Derek, "I'd like to point out that you still haven't agreed to take my music seriously."

Dad sighed. "Lookit, Derek, when you start making a living from it, I'll take it seriously. In the meantime I'd like to remind you that I am bankrolling this 'career' of yours, so you have no grounds to complain. But don't forget, the funds stop on your twenty-seventh birthday so you'd want to get out from underground and let some overgrounders know about your poetic talent."

# CHAPTER
# THIRTY

The five weeks that Sam was away dragged by. With the twins at home full-time it was non-stop action. They were easily bored — I wasn't sure if this was a sign of genius minds that needed to be constantly stimulated, or attention-deficit disorder. At least fifty times a day they stood in front of me and demanded to know "what'll we do now". I became a full-time children's entertainer. We played football, climbed trees, painted, did jigsaws, read stories and sometimes, unbeknown to Fiona, watched DVDs that were not of an educational value. *Shrek 2* and *Finding Nemo* gave me a desperately needed break, so on rainy afternoons, when the boys were bouncing off the walls, I put on the movies and got twenty minutes' peace before they got bored. The downside to this was that I wanted to wring Shrek's stupid green neck — and if I heard the theme song one more time I'd shoot myself.

Every day I prayed for sunshine. I became obsessed with the weather. When the forecast was for rain, I was demented, as was Teddy — because when the boys were cooped up indoors with too much energy, he was tormented. If I turned my back for five minutes, they'd paint his tail or glue pieces of paper to his back or try to

274

ride him like a horse, except they were too heavy and he'd collapse, his four legs going in different directions. Then, having almost killed him, they'd turn on each other. An hour of wrestling and fighting would ensue, which led to whingeing, crying and tantrums. Why did anyone have kids, I wondered, at least ten times a day.

When it was sunny we went to the park and they played in the playground with other kids, and by the time we went home they were tired and happy . . . bliss. Although I did have to deal with a lot of dirty looks from mothers of gentle children, who were mown down when the twins threw themselves on to the swings, slides and climbing-frames. I spent a lot of time apologizing and dusting sand off bewildered little girls and boys who had been casualties of the twins' enthusiasm and "high spirits", as Fiona liked to call it — hyperactivity was closer to the truth. I missed Mrs Foley and her grumpy face at the school gate, because at least it gave me the mornings off. Roll on autumn.

Fiona's last chemo session dawned and Mark — who had been around even less since he'd lost the precious competition — offered to take his wife and stay with her.

"About bloody time," I mumbled, when Fiona told me. I'd tried not to give out about him or interfere in their relationship, but he was being ridiculously unsupportive and it bugged me that Fiona never said anything.

"Leave Mark alone. He's under a lot of pressure," she said, using her standard answer.

"That's it," I snapped. "What the hell is going on? How can you not be angry with him? He's never around. He's been really unsupportive. This all-forgiving, saintly stuff is wearing thin. You should be furious. We are."

"Mark does his best," she said.

"That is such bullshit, Fiona! He does nothing for you or the boys. What type of a human being is absent at his family's time of need? He checked out emotionally the minute you got sick. He called me up and passed all of his responsibilities over. Jesus, you're his wife and they're his kids. How can he not want to be with them more?"

"They're not his kids," Fiona said quietly.

"What?"

"Mark isn't the twins' father."

I stared at her. "I don't understand."

She took a deep breath and, with a quavering voice, said, "The twins are the result of a one-night stand."

"What?" I gasped.

"Yes, Kate. Before I became a frumpy mother I was attractive to other men and I had an affair with a chemistry teacher I met at a conference in Cork."

A maths teacher meets a chemistry teacher — it sounded like the beginning of a joke, but it wasn't. It was real.

"I can't believe it. It's so unlike you . . . You're so responsible and caring and a devoted wife . . . and I just . . ." I couldn't find the words to explain how shocked I was. Fiona? My elder sister? The family's rock? The person we all went to in a crisis? The perfect wife and mother? Women like Marilyn Monroe had affairs. Women like Fiona baked bread.

"Well, that was exactly why it happened. I was sick of being responsible. Mark and I had been married a couple of years and he was working all the hours in the day to further his career. He was distracted, distant and unaffectionate. The fun and passion were gone. I was only thirty and the idea that this was going to be my life for ever terrified me. So, I did something completely out of character when I met a man who lavished me with attention. He was good-looking, charming, sexy and completely unsuitable. He told me I was beautiful and desirable, so I got drunk and slept with him. It was the exact opposite of what everyone would expect me to do and it was incredibly liberating."

"Liberating?"

"Don't you dare judge me. You're in no position to judge anyone," she said, beginning to cry.

"I'm not judging you. I'm trying to understand — but however you look at it, you cheated on Mark."

"I'm perfectly aware of what I did. Obviously I felt absolutely awful about it afterwards, and when I discovered I was pregnant, I knew Mark couldn't be the father because we hadn't had sex in months. So I had to confess — Mark's a maths professor so he can count," she said, with a watery half-smile.

"What did he say? He must have gone mad."

I tried to picture Mark coming in from a day of solving maths problems or whatever he did: "Hi, honey, how was your day?" "Fine, by the way we're having twins and they're not yours. Cup of tea?"

"It was horrible," Fiona sobbed, bringing me back to reality. "He was shocked. He felt betrayed and humiliated, and threatened to leave me. But I spent weeks on my knees begging him to forgive me, and eventually he did. The strange thing about it was that it brought us closer together for a while."

"But what happened when the twins were born? It must have been weird for him. Does he consider them his own?"

"At first he pulled away. He couldn't cope with the babies and he got angry with me, and bitter. He kept being reminded of what I'd done when he looked at them. But they were so sweet and affectionate that after a few months, almost despite himself, he grew to love them."

"Does anyone else know?"

"Only us and now you."

"Is Mark's name on the birth cert?"

Fiona nodded. "Yes, it was a hard thing to do, but he agreed to it. He's a really good person, Kate."

I never thought I could feel sorry for Mark but . . .

"Whatever happened to the chemistry teacher? Does he have any idea that he has two kids running around?" I asked.

"No. As I said, it was a one-night stand and he was married with kids of his own. He wouldn't want to know. As far as I'm concerned they're Mark's children."

"I don't know what to say."

"I regret hurting Mark more than anything, but those boys are the loves of my life and, in a strange way, they saved our marriage." She blew her nose and wiped her eyes.

"Does Mark want to have kids of his own?"

"The twins are his children," Fiona said defensively.

"Well, technically, they aren't."

"He's their father in every way. But to answer your question, yes, he would like more children, as would I, but we tried for a couple of years after the twins were born with no success. It began to drive us apart so we stopped for a while. When I got sick it made us face the issue again and that's why I was so desperate to freeze some eggs. I want to give Mark a baby. But he said my health was more important and I'm to concentrate on getting better, but we've agreed to try again when my treatment is over — if I have any eggs left."

"Do you ever think about the other man?"

"Never."

"Do the boys look like him?"

"No, they look like Mark."

In a strange way, they did. Maybe they had morphed into him so it was easier for him to love them. I looked at Fiona, my sister, the scarlet woman, and shook my head.

You think you know someone — and *bam*! They shock you to the very core.

I couldn't sleep that night. I kept thinking about Fiona, the affair and the twins. She couldn't totally regret being unfaithful because the twins were the result of it and they were her pride and joy. If she hadn't had the affair, would she and Mark have had children of their own? Maybe, but they'd have been different kids. Not the Jack and Bobby we all love. Maybe they'd still be trying and have no kids. Maybe they'd have separated. It seemed strange that something as wonderful as the boys could come out of something that was morally wrong. But Fiona was such a good person and had sacrificed so much for everyone else in her life — maybe God and Fate had decided to give her a break on this one, a sort of payback for having been so selfless for so long. I tried to imagine a chemistry teacher who looked like George Clooney, but I kept coming up with the image of Albert Einstein. Eventually I fell asleep and dreamt of women in négligées dancing around Bunsen burners.

The next morning, thankfully, was sunny. When I arrived to take the boys off to the park Mark was reading the paper and finishing his coffee while Fiona was upstairs getting them ready.

"Hey, Mark, what are you reading? Anything interesting?" I asked, in an over-enthusiastic manner.

He glanced at me suspiciously. "Just the news."

I sat down opposite him. "How are you? How's life, work, fatherhood?"

"Kate, is something wrong?"

"No, why?"

"You usually only manage to grunt at me. Why the sudden interest in my state of health and what I'm reading?"

He really didn't make it easy to like him, but I was determined to try. This was, after all, a man who had adopted two children and raised them as his own after his floozy of a wife had slept with another man — and a chemistry teacher at that. I wondered if that had bothered him. It might have been easier if she'd slept with the geography teacher — less competition.

"Is it so unusual for a sister-in-law to ask after her brother-in-law?" I said, smiling at him, in a slightly demented way.

"In this case, yes."

The twins came running in and I stared at them, scrutinizing their faces.

"Why are you looking at me funny?" asked Bobby.

"Yeah, your eyes are all wide and scary," giggled Jack.

"I'm not staring."

"Yes, you are," said Bobby.

"Your aunt is behaving very strangely today, boys," said Mark. "Are you feeling all right, Kate? Do you need to go home?"

"Oh, for goodness' sake, I'm fine. I was just admiring my two beautiful nephews."

Fiona came into the room.

"Kate's looking at us funny, Mummy," said Jack. "Like this," he added, opening his eyes wide.

Fiona glared at me. "Is she? Why on earth would she do that?" she barked.

"She's been gawping at us all since she arrived," said Mark.

"I have not," I said, defending myself. "I'm just excited because it's Fiona's last chemo session and the end is nearly in sight."

"Yeah, Mummy's nearly finished with the nasty medicine," said Jack, cheering and hanging on to Fiona's leg.

"Dad?" said Bobby. "You won't get sick, will you?"

Mark leant over so he was at eye level with his son. "I'll try very hard not to. Now, who invented the first calculating machine?"

"William something," said Bobby.

"William Burns," said Jack.

Mark shook his head. "No, it was William Seward Burroughs. He was working in a bank and he came up with the idea of a mechanical device that would relieve accountants and bookkeepers of the monotony of their tasks and ensure that a smaller percentage of their time was spent correcting errors . . ." On and on he droned as the boys' eyes glazed over.

No wonder Fiona had an affair, I thought. Mark might be a nice person underneath but he'd bore you into an early grave. "I've got a good inventor question," I said, trying to lighten the mood.

Mark looked surprised.

"Which inventor has kept a mouse alive for seventy-three years?"

The twins brightened up.

"Walt Disney." I laughed. "Mickey Mouse is seventy-three years old."

The twins giggled and even Mark cracked a smile. Maybe there was hope for him.

# CHAPTER
# THIRTY-ONE

A few days later I was sitting at home, eating dinner, while Derek and Gonzo tried out new lyrics at the table beside me.

"'Machete' doesn't rhyme with 'ghetto'," Derek pointed out.

"Dude, it doesn't always have to be an exact match. It just has to be a good story like 'Stan'," said Gonzo.

"Who's Stan?" I asked.

"Duh, Eminem's, like, most famous song," said Derek, appalled by my ignorance. "You do know who *he* is, right?"

"Don't diss your sister," said Gonzo, leaping eloquently to my defence.

"Yes, Derek, I do know who Eminem is. I just happen to think he's overrated."

"You're too old to appreciate the lyrical genius of the white king of rap," said Derek.

"I'm not old, thank you."

"I think you're the perfect age," said Gonzo, gazing at me. "They say that chicks get really horny in their thirties. Are you feeling it?"

I looked down at my jeans, which were covered in muck and sand from my day in the park with the boys.

I felt about as sexy as a hippo. "To be honest, I think that's a myth."

"Obviously you're not having your buttons pressed properly. That dude is way too old for you."

"Who?"

"The journalist guy. Derek said you went out with him."

"Sam's thirty-two, Gonzo. It's not exactly ancient."

"Doesn't seem to be lighting your fire, though, does he?"

"He's in Australia so there's not much he can do."

"Yeah, well, he shouldn't be there. He should be here looking after his woman like a real man."

"He's working. It's a concept you may not be familiar with."

"Nothing would get between me and you. I'd never leave the crib."

"Gonzo, you don't have a house. You still live with your parents. It's not an ideal set-up for a relationship."

"I'll get a crib soon. When Rap-sodie get signed. It'll be big and bold."

"Let's say you don't get signed," I said, then seeing him bristle, I added, "because your genius isn't recognized. What are you planning to do with your life?"

Gonzo stared at me as if I was mad. "My man Derek, a.k.a. the Poet, writes the edgiest lyrics in town. There's no way we won't get signed."

Derek nodded.

You had to hand it to them, they had great self-belief. But was it delusional? Before I got the chance to probe any further about their future plans, my phone beeped. It was a text from Tara: *Early arrival this afternoon of beautiful baby girl. Kerrie Quinlan 7 pounds 3 ounces. Mother and baby doing well.*

"Oh, my God!" I squealed, jumping up. "Tara's had her baby early. It's a girl."

"I can't believe she has a kid," said Derek, who had known Tara since as far back as he could remember. "That's, like, really weird. She doesn't seem that old."

"She's not old. She's the same age as me."

"Yeah, but now she's a mother."

"And your point is?"

"Mothers look kind of wrecked."

"Except foxes like Angelina Jolie," said Gonzo.

"Dude, she adopted."

"Not the kid she had with Brad Pitt," said Gonzo.

"Oh, yeah, I forgot about that. How good-looking is that chick going to be?" said Derek.

"Off the Richter scale," said Gonzo, almost salivating.

"Well, I think it's great news. She'll be a brilliant mum," I said.

"You're not getting broody, are you?" asked Derek.

"If you are, I will be more than happy to provide the seed," offered Gonzo.

"Thanks, but no, I'm not getting broody and, tempting though your offer is, I'll pass."

"We'd make beautiful babies," Gonzo said.

I looked at him and, for the first time ever, envied him. It must be great to have such confidence and self-belief. He should bottle it and sell it.

Roxanne strolled in wearing one of Derek's T-shirts and a pair of knickers. She opened the fridge and yawned as she rummaged for something to eat. I peered at my watch. It was 8p.m.

"Any more of that?" she asked, eyeing my plate of pasta.

"No," I replied. "Where are your clothes? It's eight o'clock in the evening."

"I was out all night partying, so I'm wrecked."

"Were you there too?" I asked Derek, who was looking remarkably fresh-faced.

"No." He shrugged. "It was some friend of Roxie's from work."

"A tattoo person?" I asked.

"No, JJ does piercings," said Roxanne, putting on some toast.

"So you went to a party without Derek, then came here to sleep all day?" I asked, annoyed. It seemed to me that Derek was being taken for a complete ride.

"No, I went to work first, then came here to crash."

"Shouldn't you be going to parties together? Wouldn't that be normal?"

"If you're mutually exclusive maybe, but we're not," replied the harlot.

Fiona was like Mother Teresa compared to this girl. "This whole open-relationship thing is bullshit," I snapped.

"For your generation maybe, but for us it works."

Cheeky cow. I was only four years older than her. And Derek didn't look like a man who felt good about his girlfriend playing away. I decided to push it. Maybe then he'd see what a waste of space she was. "Were you with anyone else last night?" I probed.

"I snogged a couple of girls, no big deal."

"Well, now, isn't that lovely?" said Dad, walking into the room. "My son's girlfriend's a lesbian."

"I'm not a lesbian. I prefer men, but women can be cool too," said Roxanne, yawning.

"I see. So you like all God's creatures, then," said Dad. "Animals too?"

"Dad!" said Derek.

"There's no need to be gross," said Roxanne. "Only really sick fuckers are into bestiality."

"Well, it's nice to know there are limits to your extracurricular activities," said Dad. "Now, if you don't mind, Roxanne, I'd appreciate it if you got dressed when you're in my house. I have no desire to see so much flesh at any time of the day or night."

She wandered out of the room as Derek complained, "There's no need to be rude, Dad."

"Rude?" exclaimed Dad, sitting down at the table opposite Derek. "Lookit, son, I don't know what you think is normal, but let me tell you this. Going out with a girl who's unfaithful to you with anything in a pair of trousers or a skirt is demeaning. She's not welcome in this house any more. She's making a right eejit of you and I won't have it. Go out and find yourself a nice girl who likes wearing clothes, understands the meaning of monogamy and doesn't deface people's bodies for a living," he said, slamming his hand on the table to emphasize the point.

"So I guess I won't be seeing you," Roxanne said, from the open door. "Good luck finding a boring new girlfriend who works in a bank. I'm outta here."

Derek got up to follow her.

"Bit harsh, Bill," said Gonzo. "She's a cool chick."

"Well, then, why don't *you* go out with her?" said Dad.

"I'm holding out for Kate," he said, leering at me.

"Tara had a baby girl," I told Dad, eager to change the subject.

"Well, isn't that marvellous?" he said. "You wouldn't want to leave it too late, Kate — you don't want to be too old to pick your children up."

"I'm not old and, in case you haven't noticed, I don't have a boyfriend."

"Over here," said Gonzo, waving.

"I thought you were back with Sam," Dad said.

"We had one date and he disappeared to Australia."

"You've been in touch, though, haven't you?"

"Yes, but he's still smarting from his wife leaving him, so he's not in any rush to throw himself into another relationship."

"Tosser," said Gonzo. "The guy's obviously gay."

"No, he isn't." I sighed.

"Definitely a homo."

"Gonzo! Sam is not gay. He's just been badly burnt by his ex-wife."

"I get burnt every week. When you dig a chick, you take risks."

He had a point there. Maybe Sam was dragging his feet because he just wasn't keen enough.

288

"All I'm saying is that you're not getting any younger," said Dad, like a dog with a bone.

"Well, me and my ticking clock are going to visit Tara," I said, running out the door before I was put in a retirement home or, worse, forced to wed Gonzo in an arranged marriage and spend my days listening to badly rhyming rap.

Tara was sitting up in bed with baby Kerrie fast asleep on her chest. She looked elated and exhausted.

"How are you?" I asked.

"Shattered," she said, beaming.

"She's gorgeous," I said dutifully, although I could only see the side of her face and it was all red and scrunched and she had coagulated gunk matted into her thin strands of hair.

"Isn't she? She's the image of Tom," said the proud new mother.

I was thinking more Winston Churchill myself, but I just nodded. "Nice hair," I noted.

"Yes and she'll be getting a bath tomorrow to wash all that afterbirth away," said Tara.

Thank God for that, I thought. I was worried that she was so besotted she hadn't noticed it. "How did it all go?" I asked.

"Well . . ." Tara gave me chapter and verse on the labour. From waters breaking to pushing, shoving, snipping, sewing and placenta expulsion. ". . . and there she was, perfect," she finished, as I tried to contain the bile in my throat. Why do new mothers feel it vital to share the gory details with others? It's way too much information. Maybe if you have kids yourself and you've gone through the whole birth saga it's OK, but for a novice like me, it was very off-putting.

"Lovely," I said, smiling at her.

"Would you like to hold her?" she asked, as if it was a treat akin to inviting me to New York on an all-expenses-paid shopping trip.

I really didn't want to hold the baby because I was afraid I'd get the gunk on me. I was used to mess with the twins, but not this kind of stuff. However, I knew that to refuse would be the most grievous of insults.

"Sure," I said, trying to position the back of the baby's head away from my clothes. As I was manoeuvring her, she opened her eyes and stared right at me. The intensity stopped me in my tracks. It was as if she was looking into my soul. Her little blue eyes bored into me, then all of a sudden she yawned — a tiny, perfect, rosebud yawn — and promptly fell asleep in my arms, curled up against me — matted hair and all.

I felt completely overcome. It was as if the baby knew what I was thinking. The way she had looked at me, I could almost hear her saying, "I know my mother's a bit long-winded but give her a break. It's a big day for her and you're her best friend. By the way, I'm pretty great — you should think about this yourself. Here, let me show you how nice it feels when a newborn falls asleep in your arms . . ." I gazed down at her, so small and perfect and peaceful. What the hell was wrong with me? I'd never felt like this before.

"Kate," Tara whispered, as I tried to regain my composure, "what you're feeling is totally normal. It's instinctive and natural."

"This is not normal. I'm a mess," I said.

"No, you're not. Looking after the twins has brought out a maternal instinct in you, and it's lovely to see. You'd be a great mother."

"I don't know about that. It's just that sitting here seeing you with a baby, and you have a husband and a house and a proper, grown-up life, makes me realize that my life is going nowhere. I'm babysitting my sister's kids, hanging around for an ex-boyfriend who is emotionally scarred by his separation, and I've no job. After eight years in London, what have I got to show for it? Nothing."

"A glittering career in TV," said my loyal best friend.

"A very mediocre career in TV on a channel no one watches, and a string of broken relationships. It's a bit sad."

"Come on, Kate —"

I cut across her. "No, Tara, it's OK. I'm not looking for you to boost my morale. I guess I'm just thinking out loud. I was so desperate to get to London and be successful that I lost myself along the way. The things I thought I wanted so badly didn't bring me the happiness and fulfilment I expected. Sure I had good times and met interesting people, but I was living a false life. My flat was rented, my friends came and went, as did boyfriends and jobs. Having my own show was an achievement, but it was only a matter of time before a younger, brighter presenter knocked me off my stool. You and Fiona have homes, babies and husbands. If it wasn't for Dad, I'd have nowhere to live."

"But you followed your dream. I admire you for that," said Tara. "I took the safe option and stayed at home, going to the same pub every Friday night, seeing the same friends every weekend. Your life seemed so glamorous and exciting, and mine was so mundane."

"But it wasn't, it was real. I loved the travel and doing live broadcasts is a huge adrenaline rush, but I spent too much time on my career and too little on my life. Look, I'm not saying I'd do anything differently, I'm just in limbo at the moment and Fiona finishes her treatment soon, so I need to sort myself out."

"What do you think you'll do?" Tara asked.

"Go back to London and try to live a more balanced life," I said.

"Why don't you stay in Dublin?"

"Because I feel less like a freak over there. Everyone here has moved on. Over there it's normal to be married to your job and have a social life that revolves around colleagues. Most of the people I work with are either single, gay, divorced or recovering addicts. If you're married with children you're an anomaly."

"Will you get your job back?"

"I spoke to Donna last week. She said the girl presenting my show is pulling in good viewing figures so I may have lost that, but she said she'll try to sort me out with something else and my agent is putting out feelers for me. Nothing concrete yet, but he's pretty confident something will turn up. I feel useless here. Everyone has their own lives and I'm treading water until Fiona's better. I don't fit in. I'm too old for the single scene and too single for the married one. I'll go back to London, give it a year, and if nothing really good comes up I'll reconsider my options."

"What about Sam?"

"I still have feelings for him, but he's reeling from Nikki's affair, so I don't think he's likely to rush into another relationship. I'm seeing him in a couple of days when he gets back from Oz. We'll see how it goes."

Tara rested her head back on the pillows, "You guys were made for each other. I just know it's going to work out."

I wished I had her optimism, not to mention Gonzo's self-confidence. Life would have been a lot rosier.

# CHAPTER
# THIRTY-TWO

In the five weeks Sam had been away, my hair had made a come-back. The patchy clumps had joined up and it now looked quite normal — if extremely short. He called a few days after he got back and asked if I wanted to go to a football match. Ireland was playing Sweden in a European Cup qualifier and he was covering it for the paper, but he'd be able to take me out for dinner afterwards.

I didn't know much about football but it wasn't as if my diary was full and I was dying to see him. I felt this date would be make or break. If we got on well and ended up together, I was willing to give it a go, but if he was still being cagey and careful I'd tell him to take the time he needed to sort himself out. There was no point in trying to go out with him if he was still getting over Nikki. It would be a waste of time.

I was praying it would work out. I couldn't believe how strongly I still felt about him. Even though we'd been apart for so long, he had never left my thoughts. No guy had ever matched up to him and, looking back now, I could see what a good thing I'd had. I was too young to realize it at the time — too young, ambitious and stupid. Would I get a second chance?

Fiona was in much better form. She was over the moon to be finished with her chemo, and although she was apprehensive about the radiation treatment, she had been told the side effects were much less drastic. "Besides," she said, "it's only five weeks and then I'm finished with it all. I can have my life back, my hair, my energy and, hopefully, my body."

"How soon after the end of radiation do you get the all-clear?" I asked.

Fiona smiled. "I like your choice of words. I get tested six weeks after my last session and they should tell me within days."

"God, that'll be such a relief," I said, refusing to allow a negative thought to enter my mind.

"Or it'll be back to square one, which I'm not sure I'd be able for. The beauty of getting cancer for the first time is that you don't know what to expect. Now I know how awful chemo is, I don't know if I could face it again."

"You won't have to," I said, willing away her doubts.

"Careful, Kate, you're beginning to sound like Dad."

"Maybe he's got the right idea. If you refuse to believe something bad can happen, it won't."

"That didn't work with Mum," Fiona said quietly.

"I know." I wished she'd stop bringing that up. It was hard not to, when our mother had died of the same disease at the same age, but it didn't help to keep going back to it. "You're not Mum, so stop thinking that."

"I'm trying to be positive, but I have to be prepared for the worst. Which is why I need to ask you another favour."

Oh, God, what now? I didn't want to do any more favours. I was all out of goodwill and payback. It had been almost eight months. I just wanted my sister to get better, be happy and have her old life back (minus any more extra-marital affairs and love-children).

"Sure, anything," I lied.

"I want you to be the twins' guardian if I die."

"What about Mark?" I asked, shocked. He might not be their biological father, and he might not be the best father in the world, but he loved those boys in his own way. And, after all, this was the man who had stepped up to the plate, even when the plate wasn't his.

"Mark is their father," Fiona said, frowning. "I want you to be their female guardian. So if anything happened to him they'd have you."

From that moment on, I was determined that Mark would live a long and healthy life. I'd steam his vegetables for him myself. I'd hire him a personal trainer. I'd personally wrap him in cotton wool. I loved the twins but I had no desire to raise them on my own.

"I don't want some bimbo raising my kids."

"Who's the bimbo?"

"Mark's new wife."

"You think if you died Mark would marry a bimbo?" I asked her.

"It's possible."

"Jesus, Fiona, the man doesn't speak English, he speaks in maths terminology. His only interest is work.

It's highly unlikely that a bimbo would be interested in listening to the history of theorems. It may turn you on because you're a genius too, but to a normal average female, it's coma-inducing. Besides, can we please stop assuming that you're going to die?"

"I want to be prepared," said Fiona. "And should anything happen to me, I want the boys to spend time with you, their aunt, who can answer any questions they have about me and what I was like growing up."

"OK, I promise. Now can we please drop it?"

"Are you sure?"

"Yes, I'd love to be their guardian. I'm honoured, and I promise to tell them only the good stuff about you."

"Thanks, Kate, for everthing," said Fiona.

"No problem," I said, busying myself with the boys' laundry so she wouldn't see me welling up. My God, I was turning into a basket case.

I wasn't sure what I should wear to a football game, so I opted for jeans and a halterneck top. Kick-off was at eight and it had been a really sunny day, which in Ireland meant that everyone at the match was burnt to a crisp.

When the sun came out in Ireland people ran screaming from their houses to the beach, stripped off and lay out for hours. For some unknown reason they never applied sun cream because of the myth that you couldn't get burnt in the Irish sun — it wasn't strong enough. The fact that there is only one sun, worldwide, didn't come into the equation. You could get burnt in

Spain all right, but not in Ireland — don't be silly, sure the sun is too weak here. On sunny days, the hospitals would call in extra staff as hundreds of people came staggering through the A and E doors with sunstroke and severe burns. The men were the worst: "real" men didn't wear sun cream, it was for women. Real men just lay out and fried.

So, as I looked around me at the mainly male crowd, I saw bright red faces everywhere. The empty seats scattered around the stadium belonged, no doubt, to the fallen friends, who were currently on drips with sunstroke.

Sam had left tickets for Dad and me at the entrance and he was going to meet me afterwards for dinner in a new restaurant down the road. Dad was delighted to be at the match as tickets had been hard to come by.

"You should stick with this fella," he said. "There's a lot to be said for going out with a sports journalist. Will you ask him if he can get me tickets for the hurling semi-final next week?"

"We're not even dating yet. I can't start asking him for favours. Let's just see how it goes."

"Fair enough, but if it goes well, you might ask him for three tickets. I'd like to bring Paddy and Dave."

"Dad!"

"Lord, you're very touchy. What happened with Derek and Roxanne? Is it off?" he asked.

"Well, I haven't spotted her walking around the house half naked lately so I think he might have finally got sense, or else he was dumped after your outburst."

"I really don't know what he saw in that girl," said Dad.

"Flesh."

"Apart from that."

"She's sexy and wild and she did seem to appreciate his music."

"Jesus, that music'll be the end of us all. He has only a few months left before his birthday and that's it. I'm not having any more of this rubbish. He'll come and work for me and learn what a proper job is. I was running a business at his age, not writing about imaginary gangs. I was too easy on that fella. After your mother died I let him away with murder."

"He was four, Dad."

"The Jesuits always say, 'Give me the child until he's seven, and I'll give you the man.' I wasn't strict enough with him and now he lives in a delusional world where he thinks he's going to be the next Elvis Presley."

"He'll be fine, and he does work hard at his music. He probably won't get anywhere but at least he's giving it his best shot. There's no point in looking back and having regrets because you never tried."

"Pah! The music industry is as fickle as they come. Fiona's the only one of you who got a sensible job with a pension and medical insurance — thank God."

"My job may not be sensible, but it's a good job," I said, prickling a bit because it really bugged me that Dad never took what I did seriously.

"Media's the same as music. Here today, gone tomorrow. No security in it. It's a young person's game."

"What about Terry Wogan? He's ancient and still going strong."

"You need to settle down, Kate, and have a family," he said, ignoring me. "That's what life's about. Find yourself a nice lad who'll support you and have children."

"Like Fiona?"

"I don't think you'd last ten minutes with someone like Mark."

"He's not so bad," I said.

Dad's head snapped round. "Mark? Who, according to you, was the root of all evil?"

I nodded. "Yes, Dad, I know I gave out about him a lot, but I've seen a different side to him and he's not the worst in the world. He has some good traits."

"Like?"

"Well, he's loyal and he loves Fiona and the boys."

"Loyal?" said Dad. "He's never around to take Fiona to chemotherapy, and he hardly sees the boys, he's in work so much."

"He's taken her twice and when he comes home in the evenings he spends quality time with the boys."

"Quality time!" spat Dad. "Modern mumbo-jumbo. Time is quality. Quality time is a phrase made up for people who spend no time with their kids and claim that the five minutes they do is of such high quality it makes up for all the hours they're not present."

"Bit harsh."

"I'm sick of seeing these kids on television shooting people in schools and then the parents saying they don't understand how little Johnny turned into a psychotic murderer. It's because he had no supervision and no discipline in his life. Parents today don't take responsibility for their children. If you're going to have children, look after them and don't be down in the pub drinking pints while they're at home poisoning their little minds watching violence on television."

"OK, but Mark isn't in the pub, he's at work, and Fiona is there most of the time, and the twins don't watch TV and aren't about to mow down everyone in their Montessori school, so you can relax."

"The point is he's a fair-weather father."

"That's not true," I said. If there was one thing Mark wasn't it was fair weather. The weather had been about as bad as it could be from where he was standing, and he had taken on two children who weren't his.

Dad looked at me. "I don't understand the sudden turn-around. You were the very one slating Mark last week."

"Yes, I know, but I've realized that, actually, he's fundamentally a good person. He just hides it well."

"When did you discover this?"

"Recently."

"How?"

Bloody hell it was like the Spanish Inquisition. "I dunno. I just noticed that he really does care about the twins and he loves Fiona."

"What did he do to make you realize this all of a sudden?" asked the inquisitor.

I was terrified of letting something slip and I was beginning to sweat under the pressure. "Jesus, Dad, what's with all the questions? I just told you I realized over the last few days that Mark isn't such a bad guy. Obviously he can't be that bad if Fiona married him. It just took me a long time to see it. So I think we should try and cut him some slack."

"Women!" huffed Dad. "You change your minds like the wind."

"Let's watch the match," I said, desperate to change the subject before I unwittingly revealed that Dad's eldest and finest had had a dangerous liaison, and that if the twins ever went to school and shot anyone, it might be due to the chemistry teacher's genes, not because Fiona and Mark were bad parents. DNA can work in mysterious ways . . .

# CHAPTER
# THIRTY-THREE

Ireland lost by two goals to nil. All around me grown men, who were probably responsible citizens in their everyday lives, screamed and roared like bloodthirsty hyenas. The referee was a "blind wanker", the Irish players were "useless fuckers", the opposition were a "bunch of cheating bastards" . . . and on it went until the final whistle blew and everyone began speaking in normal tones and stopped cursing like drunken sailors.

Dad, who was disgusted by the team's lame performance, went home in a grump and I, who hadn't cared who won, as long as my date wasn't cancelled, skipped off to meet Sam.

I arrived at the restaurant first and went to the bathroom to fix my makeup and hair. I put lipstick on, then rubbed it off. I put gel in my hair and tried to create that just-got-out-of-bed style but it just looked as if I'd had an electric shock, so I rubbed it off with toilet paper, which got stuck in the gel and I had little bits of white tissue all over my head. Then I spent five minutes picking it out, by which stage I had two wet patches under my arms, which I tried to dry under the hand-dryer, but ended up burning myself and getting sweatier. I was a mess. Before I could do any more damage, I went to sit at the table and ordered a large glass of wine, which I proceeded to gulp down.

"Thirsty?" asked Sam, smiling, as I choked on my drink. He looked incredible — tanned after his trip to Australia, and his green eyes were even more piercing than usual. I pinned my arms to my sides so he wouldn't see the damp circles and tried to look relaxed.

He bent down to kiss me — on the cheek, sadly, but it was early in the night — and his lightly stubbled face, with the scent of aftershave, had me reeling. I took another glug of wine to steady myself. No other man had ever had this effect on me.

"How was your trip?" I asked, attempting to be breezy.

"Long," he said, and ordered a beer.

"Poor you. Five weeks' travelling around Australia watching sport."

"I know it sounds great, but the reality is that you're watching games, staying up all night writing copy, then up again chasing interviews and trying desperately to get some fresh angle in a one-to-one with the coach you've talked to a hundred times already. You have dinner alone most nights, and the nights you go out it's with the other journalists, who you're sick of after a week or two. Honestly, I'd much rather have been back here sleeping in my own bed. The novelty of hotels wears off pretty quickly. How've you been?"

"Well, while you've been off having a terrible time in Australia, I've been trying to entertain two hyper boys. With school over for the summer, they seem to have even more energy and be even more demanding than ever. I'm in bed by nine every night."

"How's Fiona?"

"Better, now that her chemo is finished. She starts radiation tomorrow. But she's not able for the boys yet. They're too full-on. She gets exhausted after an hour with them."

"Is she feeling positive about the end result?" Sam probed.

"Well, she's organized everything so that if she dies the boys will be OK. I got landed with looking after them if Mark snuffs it, so I'm hoping he lives a long and healthy life. I love them, but I really don't think I could bring them up on my own."

"So she thinks the treatment's going to fail?"

"No, it's not that, she just wants everything to be set up in case she doesn't get better. She doesn't want to leave chaos behind like there was when Mum died, and none of us really knew what was happening and Dad had a meltdown and she ended up looking after Derek and me."

"Do you think she'll get better?"

"She has to. Life can't be that cruel. Those boys are still babies, really. It would be too unfair to take her away from them."

"I'm sure she will. From what I remember, she's a fighter."

"Yes, she is, and she deserves to be happy and live to see her boys grow up. Everyone deserves that."

Sam smiled at me.

"What?" I asked.

"Nothing. It's just you've changed. You're a lot more mellow and reflective."

"I'm eight years older. Of course, I'm mellower."

"It's not that, you seem more content, not so restless."

"I haven't got the energy to be restless," I said, laughing.

"It's good to see you, Kate," he said. "I've missed you."

"Are you over Nikki?" I blurted. It was a hell of a moodbreaker but I needed to know before I allowed myself to plunge back in. I loved Sam and I didn't want to let myself fall if I was going to land flat on my face.

He nodded. "Yes, to be honest we never should have got married."

"So why did you?"

"I told you at the awards ceremony — because she was the opposite of you. It took me a long time to get over you leaving and I was determined never to go for anyone like you again. So I went for Nikki. She was the perfect girlfriend."

"In what way?" How could she have been the perfect girlfriend? She was a cow.

"She cooked me dinners, read all my articles, got on with my sister and my mum, never complained when I went out with the lads, good in bed —"

"Excuse me, how is that the opposite to me?"

He smiled. "I was only winding you up. She wasn't a patch on you."

"I should think so too. Anyway, how could she have been so perfect when she went off and shagged her boss?"

"I was coming to that. She seemed great, and it was easy, and we got on well, and she wanted to get married, so I agreed. And then she got bored and had an affair."

"How'd you find out?"

"Text."

"No!"

"She was in the shower when her phone beeped and I picked it up. I never normally read her texts, but something made me do it, so I must have suspected it subconsciously. Anyway, it was pretty graphic, so there was no room for denial."

"Were you shocked?"

"I was shocked because I didn't think she was the type."

"Well, in my experience there is no 'type'," I said, thinking of Fiona.

"Anyway, once she was gone all my mates told me I was better off without her and that they'd never liked her and she was always a bit of a gold-digger," he said. "I think they were right. And she wasn't the one for me," he added, staring at me.

"I see. Do you think you've ever met anyone who was right for you?" I asked, with about as much subtlety as an elephant in a teepee.

He grinned. "Actually, I do. I always thought this particular girl was the one, but now that she's older, wiser and more mellow I'm sure she is."

My stomach was doing back-flips. I willed myself not to jump on top of him. "Really? Even with the horrible hair?"

He took my hands, pulled me closer and kissed me — on the lips, this time. I melted. "*Because* you shaved your hair," he said.

The lump in my throat was now enormous.

"Shall we give it another go?" he asked.

"I'd love to," I whispered, as he leant in and kissed me again.

All was well with the world until we got to dessert. We had strolled hand in hand down Memory Lane through the starter. We had kissed and cuddled and had eyes only for each other through the main course, and then he had to go and ask me what my plans were for getting a job in Dublin.

"There are no jobs in Dublin," I said.

"What do you mean? You did that live show with Peter."

"Yes, and that was it. One show."

"Have you called him and asked him for work?"

"I rang him a few weeks after the broadcast and he said he'd be in touch if anything turned up and I never heard from him again. That was about four months ago so, clearly, there's nothing out there."

"So — what? You're going back to London?"

"I have to go back and try to salvage my career. I'm living with my father here and sponging off him. I need to get my independence back."

"Jesus, I don't believe this!"

"I'll fly back whenever I'm not working and you can come over. It'll be fine. Loads of people in relationships commute. We'll work it out."

"Why can't you try to get a job here so we can give this relationship a proper chance?"

"I've just told you — there are no jobs here."

"How many producers have you contacted apart from Peter?"

"I've been in touch with everyone who deals with light-entertainment shows, quiz shows, travel shows — you name it, I've covered it. The slots are filled, there's no chance of work here for me. It's much easier for me in London. I have a profile over there and a really good agent."

"I thought you'd changed," he said angrily. "It's still about your bloody career."

"Why can't *you* move to London? Your editor told me you'd been offered jobs there, so why not come over for a while and see if you like it? What's the big deal about staying here?"

"I like my job and I don't need to work for an English broadsheet to feel I'm succeeding. I love living in Ireland and I have no interest in moving to London now or ever."

"What are you so scared of? Why is success abroad so distasteful to you?"

"I'm sick of seeing the Irish run away to other countries because they don't feel validated unless they make it elsewhere. What's wrong with staying at home and being the best at what you do? Why is it not enough to be successful in your own country?"

"God, you're impossible! You just don't get it. Some people find Ireland claustrophobic and insular. It's liberating to go away and reinvent yourself."

"Is that what you did?"

"In a way, yes."

"Was it all that you thought it would be?"

"Some of it was fantastic and some of it was really hard. But I'm glad I went. I've learnt how to fight my own battles without leaning on Dad or Fiona. I proved to myself that I can survive on my own and I've had some of the success I craved."

"OK. So you've proved you can do it, why not stay at home now?"

"How am I supposed to live if I can't get work?"

"You'll find something."

"What? Where? There are no jobs for presenters here. Too many presenters and not enough shows."

"So do something else for a while."

"Like what?"

"Childminder?"

"Hilarious, Sam."

"Look, Kate, you're the most content I've ever seen you. Why go back?"

"You've never seen me in London. I'm content there too, and I'm fulfilled. I've been here for eight months looking after the twins, while my career flounders. And you know what? I'm not happy and I'm not fulfilled. I have no identity. I may not have the perfect career, but at least when I'm presenting I'm a person in my own right. Not just filling in time until Fiona gets better and looks after her own kids."

"A job doesn't define you. It's just a job."

"So give up yours and move over with me."

"I have no desire to move."

"Well, I have no desire to stay. So why don't we commute?"

"Because it doesn't work like that."

"Why not? If you'd stop being so pig-headed and accepted commuting it'd all be fine."

"It's always been about you. You do what you want to do and everyone else is expected to slot in. You decided to break up with me and go to London and I had no say in the matter. Then you came back, just when I was getting over you, told me you missed me, and disappeared for another seven years. And now you want to get back together but on your terms."

"It's not always about me. Haven't I just spent eight months doing everything for everyone except me? Jesus, is it too much to want some kind of a life for myself, an identity I can call my own? Can you not understand that I can't give up everything on the hope that this relationship works? If in a year's time we're still together, well, we can re-evaluate the situation."

"So you're not willing to stay here and give it a go?"

"I want to be with you, Sam, but I want to work and I can't here. Please commute and let's see how it goes."

"I'm not getting into another relationship with someone unless I really think it's going to work. If you go back there's no point. It won't work."

"I'm going back and it could work."

"Nothing's changed, after all. I was wrong. You're still the same," said Sam, bitterly.

"No, I'm not but you're too blind to see it, and if you weren't so bloody set in your ways we could make this work, so don't blame me. I want to try."

"On your terms."

"There's no talking to you."

"I hope the job's worth it. You're giving up a lot."

"No, you're giving up a lot."

"Have a nice life," he said, and stormed out the door.

I couldn't believe it. We'd got back together for precisely one hour and we'd broken up again over the same stupid argument. Why the hell couldn't he give commuting a go? I couldn't keep living with Dad and not working. Granted, my job hadn't been the most amazing, but I was proud of what I'd achieved, and I wanted to see if I could get the presenter slot back or else another show, maybe a better one. Was it so selfish to want a career, to want to do something I enjoyed? Was I mad? But I loved Sam. Should I stay and give it all up? What if it didn't work out? If I stayed in Dublin much longer I'd never get back into presenting. I had to go to London as soon as possible to let people know I was still alive and available for work. Why the hell couldn't he compromise? Wasn't that what relationships were about? Oh, God, I thought, slumping into the chair. Back to square one. My life is a joke.

I couldn't face going home, so I drowned my sorrows in another bottle of wine. The rest of the evening is a blur.

When I woke up the next morning I could hear breathing beside me. We must have patched things up. How fantastic, I thought, through my fuzzy hung-over brain. He must have come back and apologized. I don't remember it, but never mind, it's all sorted. God, I hope I didn't pass out before we had sex!

I looked down. I was naked, good sign. I must remember not to drink so much the next time, though. I'd like to remember the first bit of passion I'd had in a year.

I rolled over to give Sam a kiss.

"Dude, how drunk were you last night!" said Gonzo, grinning at me.

*Fuuuuuuuuuuuuuuuuuuuuuuuuuuuuuuuuck.*

# CHAPTER
# THIRTY-FOUR

"*Get out!*" I shouted, as Gonzo jumped ten feet in the air.

"That's not what you said to me last night," he said, put out.

"How did this happen? How on *earth* could it have happened?"

"Simple. You jumped my bones," said my little brother's friend, as I put the pillow over my head and stifled a scream.

"How drunk was I?" I asked, coming up for air.

"On a scale of one to ten, I'd say fifteen."

"You shouldn't have taken advantage of me."

"I was the one who was taken advantage of," said Gonzo, scratching his emaciated hairless white chest as I winced.

How in God's name could I possibly have let this happen? No matter how many drinks I'd had, there was no way I could have done it. There's a survival instinct in all of us, and sleeping with Gonzo was akin to self-mutilation.

"But I was an emotional wreck — I'd just broken up with Sam," I said, trying to make sense of it all.

"Yeah, yeah, I know all about it. You went on for hours about him and how he won't commute and he doesn't understand that you've changed, ya-di-ya. If you ask me, you're well shot of him. He's a tosser. I want you to know right now that I have no problem commuting to London. In fact, I'd be happy to move over there with you."

Oh, God, what had I done? Now Gonzo wanted to move in with me.

"I'm not looking for a boyfriend," I said firmly.

"Unlike your journalist friend, I'm flexible. I'll settle for being your sex slave."

"Gonzo, what exactly happened last night?"

"You staggered in all boo-hoo about the guy and Derek and I tried to calm you down, but you were ranting and raving about commuting and careers and all that stuff and you kept banging into the furniture and falling over. After telling us about the fight you'd had — like twenty times — you passed out and Derek went to bed. I was on my way home but I put a blanket over you before I left and you woke up and saw me leaning down and grabbed me and started kissing me. Man, I thought all my Christmases had come at once."

"Did I? Really? *I* kissed *you*?" I couldn't believe I'd done that. I was never, ever drinking Pinot Grigio again. "And then?" I asked, feeling ill at the thought, but needing to know.

"I carried you upstairs, kissing all the way, and when we got to your bedroom you took all your clothes off and jumped under the duvet. So I thought, Fuckin' A, it's finally going to happen, and I ripped my kit off and jumped in beside you."

My hand flew to my mouth. I was beginning to panic. Sex with Gonzo? What was wrong with me? How desperate was I?

"And when I turned around to get me some lovin', you'd passed out. What a let-down! But now you're awake, I reckon we can pick up where we left off," he said, leaning in and breathing stale cigarettes all over me.

"I passed out?" I screeched. "Oh, thank God for that. I knew it couldn't have happened. There's no way I could have slept with you, no matter how drunk I was. Hurrah, nothing happened."

"Jeez, there's no need to lay it on so thick. I know I don't have pecs like Justin Timberlake but I'm big where it matters. Besides, if the thought of shagging me is so offensive to you, you shouldn't have kissed me first. It's called prick-teasing and it isn't cool."

I felt a surge of affection for him — of the sisterly kind. "I'm sorry, you're right. Gonzo, thanks for being a gentleman last night, and I promise I never meant to lead you on. I was drunk and emotional and I'm sure lots of girls want to jump your bones, but it wouldn't have been a good idea for us to have sex. You're my little brother's friend. You need to be with someone your own age."

"You're right. There are a lot of chicks out there who'd jump me, but I dig the older more mature woman."

**316**

"OK, well, I'm sure you'll find one who appreciates you soon."

Gonzo got up and began to stride about the room, putting on his clothes. I didn't know where to look, but I opted to keep my eyes down.

"So I'll be seeing you," he said, as he opened the door. "Now you know what you're missing, you might change your mind."

And with that my knight in shining armour strolled out the door — and bumped straight into Dad.

"Well, well, well," said Dad, taking in Gonzo's dishevelled clothes and my open bedroom door.

"Morning, Mr O'B."

"Good morning, Frank," said Dad, who refused to call him Gonzo. "Good night?"

"So-so," shrugged the rap artist, as he slunk off down the corridor.

Dad came into my room and sat on the bed. "Would you like to explain exactly what's going on under my roof?"

"Nothing is going on."

"If I'm not mistaken, young Frank just came out of your bedroom half dressed at eight in the morning."

"True, but it was all very innocent."

"Did he stay the night?"

"Yes, but I wasn't aware of it."

"Not aware there was a fella in the bed with you?"

"Exactly."

"I didn't come down in the last shower, Kate."

"I know, Dad. Look, I had too much to drink and I came home and passed out. Gonzo carried me to bed and ended up crashing out."

"So there was no funny business?"

"I can assure you there was none."

"How can you be sure, if you didn't even know he was there?"

"Trust me, nothing happened. Come on, Dad — Gonzo?"

"Stranger things have happened. Anyway, I'm confused. What happened to Sam? I thought you were meeting him last night."

"I did. We got back together for an hour, had a blazing row and broke up," I said, feeling a bit weepy. The elation of finding out I hadn't slept with Gonzo was wearing off.

"I see. Did you get a chance to ask him about those Hurley tickets before the row?"

I rolled over and buried myself under the covers.

Half an hour later I dragged myself out of bed and stood under the shower with the worst hangover of my life. I felt as if I was going to die. I had promised to take the boys to the zoo as it was Fiona's first day of radiation treatment, and although the procedure only took a matter of minutes, I wanted to give her the house to herself for the day, so she could rest afterwards.

I threw on some clothes and walked gingerly down the stairs, each step making my head pound even harder. I went to grab some coffee and Panadol. Derek and Dad were having breakfast.

"Gonzo?" said Derek, accusingly.

"Nothing happened."

"Find a guy your own age."

"Hello! Are you deaf? Nothing happened," I said.

"That's not what Dad said."

I glared at Dad. "Well, Dad doesn't know what he's talking about."

"All I said was I saw him coming out of your room."

"You expect me to believe he stayed and nothing went down?" sneered Derek.

"I wouldn't touch Gonzo with a barge-pole. I passed out and he stayed the night."

"You shouldn't get so drunk. It's not pretty. You were a state last night, falling all over the show. It was embarrassing."

"Embarrassing? That's rich coming from you who spends most of his life stoned and speaking in riddles."

"I'm not a thirty-something chick. It's just . . ." Derek searched for the appropriate word.

"Unbecoming?" ventured Dad.

"Fucked up," said Derek.

"Eloquently put," said Dad.

"It was neither fucked up nor unbecoming. It was heartbreak. OK? I am heartbroken, in case anyone gives a shit, and I drowned my sorrows in wine. Big fucking deal." I stormed out of the house, slamming doors as I went.

Thankfully I wasn't stopped by the police and breathalysed on the way to Fiona's because I have no doubt I was still drunk. When I got there I drank several more cups of strong coffee and ate some toast. I told Fiona the date had gone well and I was a bit hung-over. I didn't want her worrying about my fiasco before she went in for radiation.

She went off to the hospital, and after I'd splashed my face with cold water, I put the boys into the car and we headed off to the zoo.

The forty minutes it took us to get there were torture. The boys were hyper at the prospect of seeing the animals in their "natural" habitat. The truth is that the animals in Dublin zoo are a bit like human beings in a Wendy house. There's no room and they look squashed and miserable. Chimpanzees shuffle around on small patches of grass with a token tree in the middle for them to climb — it's not exactly re-creating the jungle. The polar bears roll in and out of a paddling pool that barely covers their arses, never mind affords them a few laps. Kenya need not worry that people would be travelling to Dublin to go on safari any time soon.

"How many hours does a lion sleep a day?" Jack asked.

"Uhm, ten?" I answered, narrowly avoiding crashing into the car in front of me. My spatial awareness when hung-over was not good.

"No, they sleep for twenty hours and go hunting at night," said Jack.

"Penguins are birds but they can't fly," said Bobby, not to be outdone on the information front. "Guess how many types of penguin there are?" he asked me.

I was finding it difficult enough to drive in a straight line. Being distracted by questions about animals was turning the boys into an endangered species. I wanted to get to the zoo alive so I fobbed him off.

"I don't know. Ask Jack."

"No, I want you to say."

"I don't know, Bobby."

"Seventeen," shouted Jack.

"How do you know?" asked Bobby.

"Dad told me."

"Well, he told me that giraffes are the tallest animals in the whole world."

"I know. He told me too," said Jack.

"Did he tell you where the kangaroo keeps her baby?"

"No," said Jack, sounding annoyed.

"Ha! He told *me*."

"Where?"

"In a purse in the front of her tummy."

"You made that up," said Jack.

"Did not."

"Did."

"Did not," said Bobby, and hit his brother.

Jack kicked him and a fight ensued. I thought my head was going to explode. "Stop fighting," I said, as I swung the car into the car park.

They continued to bicker, as I took them out of the car and all the way into the zoo, until I blew up.

"*Enough!*" I shouted. "If you don't stop fighting we're going home. Kate has a sore head and she can't listen to any more of this. Do you want to go home?"

They shook their heads.

"OK, be good, then."

"Can we have ice-cream now?" Bobby asked.

"No. I'll get you some later if you behave."

"Can we go and see the snakes first?" asked Jack.

"I want to see the penguins," whined Bobby.

I could see it was going to be a long day. Why, oh, why did I have to drink so much?

We went from animal to animal and they bombarded me with questions, which I tried to answer by reading the information sheets, but it was endless. Their thirst for knowledge was boundless and exhausting. I reached breaking point on the nineteenth question, about why zebras had stripes and horses didn't, and why people rode horses but didn't ride zebras, and decided we'd go for an early lunch. At least while they were eating they couldn't ask any questions.

As it was warm we sat outside. They gobbled their chicken nuggets and chips — thrilled to be allowed forbidden food. And for ten whole minutes I wasn't having to be David Attenborough. After lunch we went to get ice-cream.

"What would you like?"

"A cone with the flake in it," said Bobby.

"I want a Loop the Loop," said Jack.

"No Loop the Loops," the ice-cream man said.

"OK, two cones, then," I said.

"No, I want a Loop the Loop," whinged Jack.

"They don't have any. Have a nice cone."

"I don't want a smelly cone. I hate cones."

"What else have you got?" I asked the ice-cream man.

"Soleros, Magnums and Cornettos."

"No, no, no!" said Jack, stamping his foot. "I hate them. I want a Loop the Loop."

"They don't have any bloody Loop the Loops, so just get something else. I've no patience for whingeing today."

"You're mean and grumpy."

"Well, you're a pain in the neck. Now, decide what you want or else I'm getting you nothing."

"*Nothing!*" he shrieked.

I sighed and turned back to the vendor. "One cone, please."

I paid the man and turned to hand Bobby his cone. "Where's Jack?"

"He ran away," said Bobby.

"Where did he go?" I asked, looking around, expecting to see Jack sulking somewhere.

Bobby pointed. "Over there."

We went to look for him and then I heard a loud scream. My heart stopped.

# CHAPTER
# THIRTY-FIVE

"*Jack!*" I yelled, as I sprinted in the direction of the noise. I could hear him sobbing.

A small crowd had gathered round him. I pushed my way through it and saw his little body lying on the ground, blood streaming down the side of his head. A lady was trying to soothe him, but when he saw me he pushed her away and reached up to me.

"*Kaaaaaate*, uh, uh, uh, *Kaaaaaaate!*" he sobbed, as I picked him up and wrapped my arms around him.

"Oh, Jack, I'm sorry, honey. I'm so sorry," I said.

"He came charging around the corner, tripped and banged his head off the bench, poor mite," said the lady, who had tried to calm him down.

"Looks bad," said a man with a beard, standing to my left. "Needs stitches."

"All head wounds have to go to hospital," said the security guard, coming up behind me. "I've called an ambulance."

"Can't take your eye off them for a second," said another lady, patting my back as I began to sob almost as much as Jack.

How could I have been so cruel? Shouting at a five-year-old because I was hung-over and had been dumped the night before. I was a wretched human being.

"I'm sorry, Jack, please forgive me," I said, hugging him tighter. He snuggled into my shoulder and whimpered with pain.

I felt a tug on my leg. It was Bobby. He was crying too. "Why is Jack sad?" he asked.

"He's OK. He just bumped his head and it's sore," I said, trying to lean down and comfort him, but with Jack in my arms I had to make do with patting his head.

"He's bleeding pretty heavily," said the beardy man.

I could have done without the voice of doom. I was tempted to tell him to sod off and mind his own business, but decided I'd done enough shouting for one day. "Does it hurt?" I asked Jack.

He nodded, face streaked with blood and tears. I felt physically ill. This was all my fault. Would he have a bad scar? I tried to make out how deep the cut was, but it was hard to tell: when I tried to push Jack's hair back to look, he squealed.

"Sorry, pet," I said, kissing his cheek. "We're going to take you to the doctor to make you better."

Within minutes the ambulance arrived and Bobby and I climbed into the back while the two cheery ambulance men — George and Simon — helped Jack in after a preliminary examination.

"It doesn't look serious, but you can't be too careful with head injuries, especially with kids," said George.

"Needs a couple of stitches, all right," said Simon, as I choked back a sob.

We were all securely strapped in before Simon drove off. Bobby was in seventh heaven. A ride in a real ambulance. He asked them to put on the "nee-naw" noise, which they did briefly to entertain him.

Jack, meanwhile, held my hand tightly and nuzzled into me. His face was deathly pale and he looked so small and vulnerable in his Shrek T-shirt and shorts. It took every ounce of willpower I had not to fall apart and throw myself at his feet to beg his forgiveness.

When we got to the hospital and it was established that I wasn't his mother, they suggested I call a parent. I didn't want to ring Fiona because it was her first day of radiation so I phoned Mark. I was crying so much that it took him a while to figure out what I was saying. Eventually he got the message and said he was on the way.

Jack was examined straight away and when it was established that the injury was not serious, we were asked to wait in A and E until a doctor became available to put in some stitches.

Jack sat on my knee never letting go of my hand, while Bobby, high as a kite from his real-life ambulance ride, ran around in circles singing songs from *Shrek* to the other poor sods waiting to be seen.

"Are you OK, Jack?" I asked him, for the hundredth time. "Would you like a drink?"

He shook his head. "No, thank you," he whispered. Then, resting his head on my shoulder, he said, "Auntie Kate?"

"Yes, honey?"

326

"I'm sorry for being bold and shouting cos the man didn't have any Loop the Loops."

"Oh, Jack, you have nothing to be sorry for. You're my little angel. I promise you that when we get out of here I'll buy you ten of them. I was mean to give out to you. I'm so sorry. Your dad's on the way here to see you."

Jack's face lit up. "Is Mummy coming too?"

"No, she has to have her new medicine today, so we'll see her when we get home. I know you wish she was with you now, but you can tell her all about it later and she can kiss you better."

"Will you kiss it better?" he asked.

I bent down and kissed his face.

"I love you, Auntie Kate," he said, and fell asleep.

Twenty minutes later, Mark rushed through the doors. I waved to him and he charged over to see Jack, who woke up. When he saw his dad, he reached out to him. Mark lifted him carefully from my arms and examined his head. "I think you'll survive," he said, smiling at his son. Jack leant into his father and closed his eyes.

"Dad!" said Bobby, who had just finished singing "Livin' La Vida Loca" from *Shrek 2* for a drunk with a bandaged head, who had dutifully clapped and slurred along.

"Ssssh, Jack's resting," said Mark, sitting Bobby up beside him. "We have to be very quiet now."

"I'm bored," said Bobby.

"Let's go and find a coffee-machine and get Dad a drink," I said, taking his hand, glad to do something useful.

We wandered around, looking for coffee.

"Is Jack going to be OK?" Bobby asked.

"Yes, he is, although he may have a little scar," I said, voice quavering.

"Then why are you crying?"

I bent down and hugged him. "Because I love you both very much and it makes me sad when you're sick or have a sore head."

Bobby stared at me. "Girls are weird," he said.

We came back with coffee, and Mark told us that Jack was next in line to be seen. Bobby wandered off to entertain the other patients and I told Mark what had happened. I didn't lie about being a narky cow and shouting at Jack — I told him everything. ". . . and so, you see, it's all my fault. I'm not fit to look after your kids," I said, dissolving again. "I'm such a loser and I feel so guilty because it was my stupid hangover making me impatient and horrible. How could I have shouted at him like that? Poor Jack."

"You're not a loser."

"Yes, I am. You were right. I'm selfish and useless. What if he'd fallen badly and broken his neck? He could have died in my care, and it's because I was feeling sorry for myself about my stupid non-relationship with Sam. I'd die if anything happened to the twins — I'd never forgive myself," I said, overcome at the thought.

I knew then just how much I loved them. They were so sweet and innocent, and although they'd drive a saint to drink at times, they'd got under my skin and into my bones. I loved every part of them and would have laid down my life for them. I stroked Jack's cheek. "I really love them, you know."

"I can see that," said Mark. "Look, Kate, children fall over all the time. Jack'll be fine tomorrow. These things happen, don't blame yourself. And, for the record, I don't think you're selfish any more. You've been a great help to Fiona and the boys. You've changed a lot. You've grown up."

"Really?" I was shocked. All Mark had done since I moved back was bark at me. It felt strange to be having a conversation with him where we weren't shouting abuse at each other.

"You've so much energy with them. Taking them out to the park and the zoo, playing football with them. It's been nice for the boys to have you around, with Fiona being so ill. I'm better at education and learning, but the boys need exercise too."

"I've enjoyed it," I admitted. "I've loved spending time with them and not just being a vague aunt they see twice a year. They're fantastic kids and, let's face it, they're probably the closest I'll ever get to having kids of my own. You're lucky to have them." I stopped dead and went puce. Shit! What was I saying?

Mark looked at me and shook his head. He checked to make sure Jack was asleep, then said, "It's all right. I know Fiona told you about the affair."

I didn't know what to say. What's the protocol when your brother-in-law admits his children aren't his because your sister slept with someone else? I opted for a sympathetic nod. After all, I wasn't going to start slagging off Fiona for being unfaithful and, to be honest, if I'd been married to Mark I'd have been shagging everything that moved.

"It was a really difficult time, but I decided to be the bigger man and I'm glad I did. The boys are my pride and joy."

"It's a wonderful thing to have done and you're their dad, as far as they or anyone else is concerned."

"Kate, I presume I don't need to tell you that this information is never to be repeated to anyone. I'm not happy Fiona told you, but I appreciate that she had to as she was making you their female guardian."

"Of course I won't tell anyone. I wouldn't dream of it."

"In fact, I never want it mentioned again," he emphasized.

"Not a word from me."

"With Fiona being ill and life suddenly seeming more fragile, I've taken the precaution of leaving a very precise list of instructions as to how I want the boys to be raised, should both Fiona and I die. I've listed the schools they're to go to, the subjects they must take and the extra-curricular activities I'd like them to focus on."

It didn't take a rocket scientist to know that if Mark snuffed it, I'd be spending a lot of time driving the boys to extra maths tuition and sitting through chess competitions, pretending I'd a clue what was going on. I prayed for Fiona and Mark to live long, healthy lives.

"OK, I'll do my best."

"If you follow the instructions properly you won't have any problems."

I was really trying to like Mark. After all, he had stood by my wayward sister. I knew there was a good side to him but, my God, he hid it well.

Thankfully, before I told him I thought Bobby was going to be more into Broadway than physics, we were called in for Jack to be examined. He needed three stitches and he held on to Mark for dear life as they were administered. I had to look away. Every time he whimpered I felt as if a knife was being twisted in my stomach. Bobby thought it was great fun and insisted that I lift him up so he could watch.

The doctor reassured us that Jack would be fine, that it was a minor injury and no damage had been done to the skull. He told us to give him a good dose of Calpol before we put him to bed and to keep an eye on him over the next few days in case he suddenly became drowsy or his speech slurred.

Mark carried him out to the car as I hovered behind, fussing over him, still riddled with guilt.

"Are you feeling better?" I asked him, for the zillionth time.

He gave a weary little nod.

"Will I get you a Loop the Loop now?"

"No, I want a cone with a chocolate flake in it, like Bobby had."

Kids. Go figure.

# CHAPTER
# THIRTY-SIX

By the time we got back to the house, Jack had recovered fully and was merrily chomping down the ice-cream cone I'd stopped to get him. Mark had gone back to work and had promised to call Fiona to tell her what had happened so she wouldn't get a shock when we arrived through the door and she saw Jack's bloodstained T-shirt.

Needless to say, a forewarned but worried Fiona was waiting at the door when we arrived. She scooped Jack up, kissed him all over and examined his head. "Are you feeling better, pet?" she asked, kissing him again.

"Yes, and Kate bought me ice-cream," he said.

"Fiona, I'm so sorry," I said. "It's totally my fault."

"Kate," she said firmly. "You have nothing to apologize for. I owe you an apology. I haven't properly thanked you for looking after the boys all these months. You've been incredible. I really don't know what I'd have done without you. The boys will always take tumbles and Jack's fine. I'm sorry for lumbering you with the job of supernanny. It's not easy looking after them, especially when they're off school. And I know you'd had a bad night — Dad's been on about Gonzo," she said, beginning to laugh.

"Nothing happened!" I protested.

"Sounds suspicious."

"Come on, Fiona — Gonzo?"

"I have to admit I would have been surprised. What happened with Sam?"

"Fuck Sam."

"Kate said 'fuck'," squealed a recovered Jack.

"OK, boys, go into the playroom and get out the abacus," said their mother. "Go on, what happened?" she asked me.

"First and foremost, I'd like to hear how your radiation went. It's a little more important than my stupid love life."

"It was fine, actually," said Fiona, looking genuinely relieved. "It was over in ten minutes, and although it's a drag having to go every day for five weeks, I feel pretty good. It's nothing like chemo, thank God."

"Are you sore?"

"It feels a bit like I'm sunburnt in the area they zapped. But other than that, and feeling a bit tired, I'm OK."

"Thank God it's going to be easier than the chemo."

"I don't think anything could be worse. Anyway, I'm bored with talking about my cancer. Tell me about Sam."

"There's nothing to tell. We had a great night, all loved-up and happy, and then he said he presumed I was going to stay in Dublin and I said no, because my job is in London, and we had the same argument all over again."

"Wouldn't you stay and give it a go?"

"What if we break up in six months and I have no job, no boyfriend and am still living with Dad? I said I'd fly back every chance I got. We could probably manage to see each other at least once every two weeks and then, if it goes well, in a year's time we can reassess the situation. If I felt then that we were going to make it long term I'd consider moving back. But we can't even go out for dinner without breaking up, so it's too big a risk to give up my career until I know we can make it work."

"What did he say about commuting?"

"He's dead set against it. Says there's no point in having a half-arsed relationship with someone you never see. It's all or nothing with him. He said I haven't changed, I'm still the same self-obsessed person I was when I was twenty," I said, suddenly feeling worn out. Between the hangover, the shock of finding Gonzo in my bed, Jack falling down, hospital and the fiasco with Sam, I was completely wiped out. I needed to lie down.

"Bollox," said Fiona. I started — she never cursed. "You *have* changed, and if he can't see it he's a blind fool who doesn't deserve you. You're a different person."

God, how bad *was* I? With Fiona *and* Mark emphasizing how much I'd changed, there must have been a lot of changing to do.

"Different how?" I asked.

"Calmer, kinder, nicer."

"What was I like before?" I ventured, not sure if I wanted to hear the truth.

"Well, you always seemed dissatisfied and ill-at-ease. As if you wanted to be somewhere else all the time."

She was right. I *had* wanted to be somewhere else all the time. I'd always felt uncomfortable when I came home to Dublin. The minute I stepped off the plane I wanted to be back in London. I felt hemmed in and claustrophobic. The things that Dad, Fiona and Derek talked about seemed mundane compared to my jetting around interviewing stars — even though most of the time that had meant sitting outside hotel rooms for hours to get a three-minute slot with an inarticulate tosser about their latest film that you thought was absolute tripe.

I had felt restless at home and was always relieved to get on the plane and back to my apartment. I was in control of my life in London. I never thought too much about things. I lived from day to day, breezing along. In Dublin I had to answer questions. How was I? What was happening with my job? Did I have a boyfriend? Who did I see over there? Where did I go? Why hadn't I been in touch? When was I coming home?

The when-are-you-coming-home question really got to me. No one ever thought that when you emigrated you'd stay away. Everyone always assumed you were desperate to get home, that it was just a matter of time . . .

Sure the quality of life "over there" — regardless of whether you lived in a penthouse in New York or a bedsit in London — was rotten. Ireland had the best of both worlds. Sure you couldn't raise a family "over there". Big cities were a young person's game. You went abroad for work experience but you'd never stay. God, no, only poor sods who "got stuck" stayed. And you'd "get stuck" if you didn't come home before you were thirty. Lord save us if you were still there when you were thirty-five — sure you'd no hope!

But the saddest of all were the "lifers". The poor eejits who fell in love "over there" and married a local! They were trapped for ever. That was the worst that could happen. Parents throughout Ireland were on their hands and knees, praying that their beloved children wouldn't become lifers. Everyone felt most sorry for Australian lifers — sure you'd never see them again. It was a three-day camel ride to get to the other side of the world where those Australians lived. Those lifers were gone for good. Come home and marry the one-legged hunchback next door, but whatever you do, DO NOT MARRY A LOCAL.

So, every time I came home, I'd spend a lot of time answering questions — or avoiding them — and it made me take stock of my life, which I didn't like doing. It freaked me out. I didn't know where I was going or what the future held. All my schoolfriends were married or in serious relationships, and I wasn't. It made me question my decisions. I used to wonder if I was doomed never to meet someone. Maybe I should have stayed with Sam. But I hadn't: I had chosen this road and it had brought me fulfilment of a sort, and when I was immersed in my London life I was content. So Fiona was right: I did feel edgy when I came home. I didn't like reflecting on where I was going because I didn't know where that was. I had no plan.

But this time it had been different because I knew I had to stay for a while, and I had a purpose. I had come back to help Fiona and mind the boys. And it had been fun — difficult, trying and absolutely exhausting, but I was enjoying it and I did feel different, in a good way. It had been nice to focus on others for a change, and I loved spending time with the boys, becoming an important person in their lives. It had been lovely to finally give back something to Fiona too.

"I suppose I have changed a bit. At least it's for the better," I said, with a smile.

"Don't worry, Kate. Things will work out."

"Isn't that what I'm supposed to be saying to you?"

"You have, a thousand times. Now, why don't you go home and get some sleep? You look exhausted."

"Are you sure you're able for the boys?"

"Absolutely. I feel fine."

"OK, well, I'll see you tomorrow."

"Kate?"

"Yeah?"

"You've been really amazing. Thanks."

"It's a pleasure."

When I got home I went to grab something to eat before I crashed out. Derek was in the kitchen. I looked around suspiciously.

"He's not here," said Derek.

"Thank God for that," I said, sitting down with a bowl of corn flakes. I couldn't have faced Gonzo. I was too tired.

"I hear Jack ended up getting stitches."

"Yes, and it was my stupid fault."

"Is he OK?"

"He's fine, thank God."

"Scar?"

"Tiny one, but it's hidden in his hair."

"Cool."

"Derek?"

"Yo."

"Do I seem different?"

"Did you get a boob job?"

"No!"

"Lips?"

"I haven't had any plastic surgery. I'm talking about different in personality."

He shrugged. "Like how?"

"Calmer."

"Nope."

"Fiona said I am," I said, put out that Derek hadn't spotted my new Zen-like personality.

"You didn't seem too chilled this morning when you were freaking out about being heartbroken and stuff."

"Yeah, well, you accused me of being with Gonzo so naturally I flipped. What about before this morning? Have I changed over the last few months?"

"I suppose you're less all about you."

"Was I very self-obsessed?"

"Kinda."

"In what way?"

"You weren't interested in other people's shit."

338

"Yes, I was," I said, offended. I might not have been very relaxed, but I was always concerned about my family and what was going on.

"No," said Derek, firmly. "You weren't. When I got into all that trouble in college, Fiona was the one who bailed me out. You just told me I was a gobshite."

Derek hadn't done too well in his school exams — he had problems applying himself, the teachers said — so Dad had got him into this small private college to study marketing. He had been desperate for Derek to get some kind of third-level qualification and was convinced that it would stop him obsessing about a career in music.

Needless to say, Derek had had about as much interest in marketing as he did in chess. He continued not to apply himself and was lucky to scrape through the first year. In year two, he had been caught smoking dope at the back of a lecture hall and had been given a warning by the dean: clean up your act or you're out. A couple of weeks later he got caught again and was asked to leave.

The expulsion had happened a few days before I flew back for Tara's wedding, and the night I got home he confessed to Fiona and me that he was no longer in college. A letter was on its way to Dad.

I told him he was a gobshite — something he had clearly not forgotten — and that he deserved to be expelled for behaving like an idiot. Fiona told him he was irresponsible, but that if he promised to behave and study hard, she'd do everything she could to help him. The next day she went to see the dean and somehow managed to persuade him to give Derek another chance, while I skipped off to Tara's wedding.

Derek had spent the next two years keeping his head down and muddled through his exams, helped and tutored by Fiona.

"You're right. I was no help to you. I'm sorry about that." It looked like I was going to be spending this entire day apologizing to people.

"'S OK, I'm over it. Besides, you're not like that any more. You actually seem to give a shit now and you've stopped dissing my music all the time."

"Well, I think you have talent but you need to face the fact that you may not get signed and think about possible options for the future," said the new mature, caring, subtle me.

"You went to London to follow your dream, right?"

"Yes, but —"

"I always thought that was cool. You know, you went over there, took a chance and it worked out. You made it. You got your own show. I respect that. You chased the dream. That's what I'm doing with my music."

"Well, thanks. But all I'm saying is that you need to think about alternatives in case it doesn't work out."

"I have," he said, grinning.

"Good for you."

"If I don't get signed before my birthday when the old man pulls the plug on my finances, me 'n' Gonzo are going to crash with you in London and try the

340

scene over there. I was thinking your agent could maybe sort us out with some auditions."

The old me would have said, "Hell will freeze over first."

The new me said, "Over my dead body."

# CHAPTER
# THIRTY-SEVEN

Although Fiona hated having to go to the hospital every day for the radiation, which tired her, the queasiness and mouth ulcers were gone and she could see that the end was near. She was in much better form and more able for the boys. As a result I had more time on my hands, which was not necessarily a good thing: I had time to brood about Sam. I was staying in Dublin until Fiona was finished with the radiation and then I was going back to London. She'd be having her remission tests six weeks after that and I was planning to fly home when she got the results. We were all holding our breath and watching the calendar as time dragged on towards that date.

On one of my afternoons off from minding the boys I had decided to contact Sam. I was desperate to talk to him and try to sort things out. I wanted to show him what a mistake we were making by not giving it a go.

I sent him a text: *Can we talk?*

Sam: *Unless uv changed ur mind about London there is nothing 2 say.*

Me: *U r a stubborn git.*

Sam: *Pot — kettle — black.*

I was bashing my head off a brick wall so I didn't contact him again. In the meantime I decided to get in touch with a few more people in Irish television to prove to Sam there was nothing for me in Dublin. Maybe if he saw that I'd tried every angle possible, he'd consider commuting.

I got my agent to track down a few names and put out a few feelers in Dublin for me. I was still waiting to hear back. She said she was on the case but she was definitely keener to find me a good job in London where her commission would be higher. I had called Peter Kildare from TV3 again, just to say I was still alive and available for work, and he had given me the names of two other Irish producers to contact. They had both told me the same thing: there were no jobs going. Once people had a presenting job in Ireland, they stayed in it for ten years. Movement and job-hopping were not common.

With a few days to go before Fiona's treatment ended, my agent rang. She only ever rang if it was good news. "Kate, are you sitting down?" she asked.

"Yes — go on, what is it?" I said, holding my breath . . .

"Your agent *extraordinaire* has landed you a presenting job on Sky One." She paused for maximum effect.

"What show?" I urged, my heart pounding. Sky One was great. It was a big step up from the Lifechange channel.

"*Reality Stag Party*," she announced breathlessly.

"Excuse me?"

"It's going to be fantastic and so much fun for you. You travel to different places each week with different stag parties and talk to the groom about his relationship and talk to his friends about him and if they think his wife-to-be is Mrs Right. It'll be great! The first stag is fourteen lads from Newcastle going to Benidorm for a week, so you'll even get a tan while you're working — and, you never know, you might find yourself a man while you're at it."

"You got me a show following a bunch of men around Benidorm, watching them eat eggs and chips in the local pub and getting plastered watching football, then going to a nightclub with them while they grope every girl in sight? Jesus, Jackie, are you insane?"

"Joking!" She cackled. "I've got you series two of *Eating-disorder Camp*."

"Really?"

"Yes!"

This was a big deal. The girl who had presented the first series was now presenting the hugely popular *So You Think You Can Sing*. It was a big step up for me and I knew the competition would have been fierce.

"How did you manage to get it for me?"

"I told the producer you'd rushed home to nurse your sick sister and look after her kids, and he thought you'd be perfect for the job because you're obviously good with sick people. So the stick-insects will be able to talk to you about their problems. By the way, I told him your sister had teenage-girl twins and one was refusing to eat since her mother got sick. It sealed the deal."

"You cunning thing, I love it. God, this is brilliant. When do I start?"

"Filming kicks off in a month, but I need you over here next week to talk to the producer and do some schmoozing. How's your hair?"

"Short, but it looks OK."

"Let me be the judge of that. Bring a wig with you. Got to fly."

"Thanks, Jackie, I really appreciate it," I said, hanging up and hugging myself.

This was huge. I was on the road to serious stardom now. All my hard work had paid off. This was my big break and it felt fantastic. I was over the moon. I had to tell someone, so I jumped in the car and called over to Tara.

After I'd rung the doorbell for five minutes she finally appeared in her pyjamas. She looked shattered.

"Hi," I said, bounding in. "You'll never guess what!"

"Can you hang on a sec," she said, rushing into the house to pick up a screaming baby.

I followed her and watched her settle Kerrie on her breast. The baby stopped crying instantly.

"Impressive," I said.

"She's a very hungry baby," said Tara, wearily. "It's non-stop and I'm wrecked. Look at me! It's eleven o'clock and I'm still not dressed. She was up four times last night and it's nearly an hour every feed by the time you burp her —"

I decided to interrupt. I didn't want to hear about the feeds again — she'd talked of nothing else since the baby was born. While I realized it was pretty much the only thing she did all day, it was pretty boring to hear about every feed, how long it took, how many burps and how long the child slept — or, rather, didn't sleep — in between. I wanted to tell her my news.

"My agent just called — I've got a great job!" I blurted out, but Tara didn't hear me: she was busy manoeuvring the baby.

"It's easier to feed her if she's comfy," she said, putting a cushion under Kerrie's bum. "Now, what were you saying?" she asked.

"I've got a new job."

"Great. Doing what?"

"You're looking at the new presenter of *Eating-disorder Camp*," I announced.

"What's that?" she asked.

"It's one of the top reality TV shows. And Terry Halfpenny, who presented the last series, is now presenting *So You Think You Can Sing*."

"I like that show," said Tara, absent-mindedly. "But I never get to watch TV, these days. Ouch, Kerrie, easy there, pet," said the earth-mother, as she adjusted her breast again.

"So, I'm really excited about it and I start filming next month. God, it'll be great to have my life back."

"Mmm, sounds amazing. Could you pass me that muslin square? Thanks. She's not eating so I need to burp her first."

"OK. Well, you seem kind of busy here so I'll talk to you later," I said, trying not to snap. I had been so excited to share my good news with my best friend but

346

she couldn't concentrate for more than five seconds on anything that wasn't baby-related.

"Don't go — I'm sorry, Kate. I know I'm distracted. Look, let me stick Kerrie in the swing chair and hopefully she'll nod off. She doesn't seem hungry."

After fifteen minutes of swinging, rocking, music and soothers, Kerrie fell asleep.

"Come on," whispered Tara. "Let's go into the kitchen so we don't disturb her. Now, tell me everything."

Once we were in the kitchen, Tara gave me her almost undivided attention. She leapt up every five minutes to check on Kerrie, but in between she managed to focus on the conversation.

"So this show is a big deal and may lead to prime-time TV?"

"Exactly."

"What's the show about?"

"Kids with eating disorders."

"Yes, I got that part, but what happens? Do you watch people throwing up all day?"

"You do see the odd puke, but it's basically a group of teenage girls — although they usually throw in a token boy or two — who are food-averse and they send them to this camp with nutritionists and psychiatrists and fitness trainers to try to help them."

"So the winner is the one who puts on the most weight?"

"Yes."

"How much did the last winner put on?"

"Well, she got a bit carried away and put on four stone, so she's now going to be starring in *Get Fit Camp*. The kids on the show can't be badly anorexic or bulimic because they'd be in hospital on drips if they were. This is for kids in the early stages of eating disorders. It got really good viewing figures last time, almost as many as *Celebrity Dancing on Roller Skates*."

"No wonder you're excited. So you'll be going back to London soon?"

I nodded. "Fiona finishes her treatment next week, then she and Mark are having an end-of-treatment plus Derek's twenty-seventh birthday dinner on the Saturday night. I'll head back on Sunday or Monday."

"I don't mean to be a kill-joy, but what if she's not in remission?" Tara asked.

"She will be," I said.

"But what if she isn't?"

"She has to be, Tara. I can't even contemplate it, if she isn't. Life can't be that cruel and, selfishly, I don't think I can do another eight months as a surrogate mother. I want my life back."

"Of course you do. It's not selfish, it's normal. I'm sure she's really grateful for all your help. You were there when she needed you, and that's what matters."

Yes, but what if she needed me again? Could I do it? I really didn't know that I could. I was so looking forward to having my own place, job and income again. I felt lost and useless without it. I blocked the thought out. It wouldn't happen. She'd be fine.

"Any word from Sam?" Tara asked.

"Not since the disastrous texts."

"Does he know about the new job?"

"There's no point in telling him. He doesn't care about my career — he thinks I'm a selfish cow."

"Are you sure you want to give him up?"

"That's just it. I don't have to give him up. If he'd meet me half-way it would all be fine. What's the big deal about commuting?"

"It's just putting off the inevitable decision that one of you will have to move," Tara said gently.

"Only if the relationship works out," I reminded her.

"Do you honestly think it wouldn't?"

"Not if we really gave it a go."

"Can you do that while you're living in two different countries with separate lives?"

"Lots of people do."

"Like who?"

"Posh and Becks. When he first went to play in Spain she was still in England."

"Until she moved over to save her marriage," Tara reminded me.

"I can't let this opportunity go. It's a really big deal. I've been working towards it for years."

"Look, Kate, it's your decision and it sounds like a great job, but you should really think about the bigger picture."

"What d'you mean?"

"What do you want to be doing in five or ten years' time? Do you want to have a successful career and no private life, or a relationship with someone you love, kids, a house and to be near your family and loved ones?"

"I want it all. I want the guy and the job and maybe the kids."

"Life is about compromise," Tara said.

"Why does it have to be *my* compromise? Why can't he get a job in England?"

"He loves his job. His mum and sister live here. His whole life is about Irish sport. Why does he have to give it up to move over there when the only thing keeping you both in London would be your job?"

"I've looked into getting a job here but there are none going."

"Something's bound to come up."

"When? And in the meantime what am I supposed to do?"

"If you go back to London you'll lose yourself again, and it's been so nice having you around."

"I've enjoyed being back, but I've had enough."

"He's a really great guy, Kate. They don't come along very often. Think very seriously about it before you jump on the plane."

Kerrie started to bawl again so I took my leave, and spent the rest of the day trying to figure out how to have my career *and* Sam.

# CHAPTER
# THIRTY-EIGHT

Over breakfast the next day, Dad reminded Derek that he had only a few days to get a record deal or the game was up. "Your twenty-seventh birthday will be a turning point in your life. Reality will finally reveal itself to you in all its glory and you'll understand and appreciate hard work," said Dad.

"There's no need to gloat over the fact that my dream is about to be shattered into a thousand pieces. Besides, a lot can happen in a few days." Derek began to rap:

"It ain't over till I'm one year older
And you can sit there and be all smug
About working real jobs and pullin' the plug
On my financial assistance but don't y'all worry cos
I got me a plan B cos entertainment's in my blood, see?"

"Very nice, son, get it all out of your system now, because there'll be no need for any of that lark when you come to work for me."

"What plan B?" I asked, hoping he wasn't referring to his suggestion that he and Gonzo move in with me.

"All will be revealed on Saturday night. If there's anything to reveal, that is," he added.

"I won't hold my breath so," said Dad.

"Hey, Dad, who won the Oscar for Best Original Song in 2003?" Derek asked.

"That eejit you think is so great who named himself after a chocolate bar or something."

"Eminem for 'Lose Yourself'. And his old man didn't believe in him either."

"Very apt title," said Dad. Then, turning his attention to me, he asked, "What was wrong with you last night? I heard you pacing at three in the morning."

"Couldn't sleep," I said.

"Are you stressed about the new job?" Derek asked.

"Pah," muttered Dad, from behind his paper.

"Do you have something you'd like to say, Dad?" I inquired.

"A programme about girls who won't eat — I never heard such rubbish in my life. I don't see why you can't stay at home with your family and get a decent job."

"Thanks for the support, Dad. It's a big deal for me."

"Nonsense. You need to settle down with a nice lad and have children. That's what life's about. Not filming girls being sick. I never heard the like."

"Gonzo wants to know if he stops eating now can he be one of the people on the show?"

"No," I said.

"I hope that wasn't your plan B," said Dad, as Derek walked off in a huff.

Later that day I was in Fiona's kitchen, helping her tidy up after the boys' dinner. I handed her a plate to put away and she dropped it.

"Fuck fuck fuck fuck fuck fuck *fuuuuuuuuuuuck!*" she shouted.

The twins, Teddy and I almost jumped out of our skins.

"Jesus, are you OK?" I asked, looking for blood on her hands.

"No, I'm not OK. I'm not fucking OK at all," she sobbed, dropping to the floor as her body shook with grief.

The twins, shocked to see their mother crying so violently, began to get upset. I ushered them out and put on the TV to distract them.

Then I came back in to my sister and sat down with her on the floor among the bits of broken plate. "What's up? Was it a favourite plate?"

"I don't care about the stupid plate!" she cried, as Teddy licked her face. "I just can't keep it in any more. I've tried so hard to be calm and in control during chemo and radiation and I'm sick of it. I'm sick of being sick. I'm sick of trying to pretend everything's OK, I'm sick of having my body ravaged by drugs and burnt by radiation. I have cancer. I'm a cancer victim. Mum was a cancer victim and she died. God didn't give a shit about leaving her three children with no mother. He took her anyway. Why should I be any different? Why should I be luckier than Mum? Why should my boys be luckier than we were? I could die — I really could actually *die* — and not see my boys grow

353

up. Never see them become the wonderful human beings I know they'll be. Never see them get married and have children of their own. They'll be the poor Kennedy twins, just like we were the poor O'Brien kids. It's not fair, it's not bloody fair, and I'm furious. I'm furious with life and Fate and God and everyone. I hate having this disease inside me. I want to rip it out and smash it into little pieces. I don't want my boys growing up without a mother. I can't bear that." She covered her face with her hands.

"Fiona, please listen to me," I begged. "What's happened to you over the last eight months is unspeakable. You've been so brave and wonderful. I'm in awe of you. The way you've handled it is incredible. You're always so cheerful around the boys, making sure their lives were disrupted as little as possible. You're an amazing mother and an inspirational person. I believe, with every bone in my body, that you're going to be OK. You'll be around till you're ninety, I know it."

"How?"

"Because you deserve to be."

"So did Mum."

"That was really bad luck and, besides, the treatments then were nothing like they are now. I *know* you'll be fine, I promise."

"You can't promise that, Kate," she said sadly, patting Teddy as he nuzzled into her.

"Yes, I can," I insisted.

"No, you can't. No one deserves to die of this horrible disease. Some get lucky and most don't. It's a lottery. There are no guarantees. The thing that really scares me is that, if I die soon, the boys won't remember me. They won't have a clue what sort of person I was or how much I loved them."

"Of course they'll remember you," I said.

"Does Derek remember Mum?"

"I'm sure he does."

"Do you?"

"Yes."

"You don't really, Kate, you've told me so before. You said that the worst part of Mum dying young is that you don't remember what she was like."

Typical! Me and my big mouth, and Fiona with her elephant memory. She was right, though. I didn't really remember Mum. I was eight when she died, and although I have some memories of her, they're blurred and I don't know if they're real memories or if I think I remember things because I've heard Dad tell the stories. It was awful to lose my mother so young: I had felt a gaping hole in my life for as long as I could remember. I would have given anything for one conversation with her, one hug, one kiss.

I looked at my poor sister and felt a pang of anguish. "Come on, Fiona, the statistics are really good for your recovery."

"Kate!" she snapped. "Let me be miserable. I need to let this out. I need to feel the fear of death. I'm sick of being upbeat. I want to be allowed to wallow and rant and rage against the world. I might die and you can't change that. Even if I do go into remission now, there's no guarantee it won't come back in a couple of years. It's a life sentence."

"It's so unfair," I said, unable to stop myself getting emotional. "I wish I'd got the cancer, not you. I swear I'd take your place if I could. It should have been me."

"Oh, don't be so melodramatic," said the woman who'd just had a nervous breakdown over a broken plate — well, OK, over cancer, really, but it had started with the plate.

"I mean it," I said, insulted. "Your kids need you, I'm not leaving anyone behind. In fact, apart from my family no one would notice."

"Well, instead of feeling sorry for yourself why don't you do something about it?" said a recovering Fiona, dishing out advice as she cleared up the plate shards.

"Like what?"

"Like stop messing about and give your relationship with Sam a go. You love him, it's as plain as the nose on your face and no job should stand in your way. If I've learnt one thing from this stupid disease it's to value what matters in life and that's people, Kate, not things. No one wants 'Here lies Kate O'Brien: she had a successful career' engraved on their headstone. It's sad and soulless."

Before I had a chance to answer, the twins came in with Mark, who had just arrived home.

"Is everything all right?" he asked, taking in the two blotchy red faces and the broken plate. "I found the twins gawping at *Baywatch*."

"Kate and I needed to have a heart-to-heart," said Fiona.

"Are you OK?" Mark asked his wife, putting his arm around her. "The boys said you were upset."

356

"Fine, thanks. I just needed to blow off steam."

"What happened to the plate?"

"She threw it at me for being melodramatic," I said, laughing when Mark looked shocked.

"She's joking. I dropped it and it set me off," Fiona admitted. Then, as the twins appeared, she said, "Mummy's better now, boys. I'm sorry if I scared you. I got a fright when I dropped the plate."

They snuggled into her, glad to see her back to normal.

"Did you get a fright too?" Jack asked me.

"No, honey. I'm sad because I'm going back to London soon and I won't see you every day," I said, as Fiona tried frantically to stop me.

"I haven't prepared them for this," she hissed.

Their little heads snapped around. "Going back? But you live here now, with Granddad," said Bobby.

Damn. I'd assumed they knew it was only temporary.

"I was staying with Granddad for a few months while Mummy was sick. But now she's better I'm going back to London."

"But I don't want you to go," said Bobby, and burst into tears.

"Me neither," said Jack coming over and hugging me.

"Stay with us, Auntie Kate. Don't go," said Bobby, as I struggled to control myself. I hadn't thought they'd care. They had Fiona back now, their mum, the love of their lives.

"But you don't need me now. Mummy's better."

"Mummy, don't let her go back to horrible London!" pleaded Jack.

"I'm sorry, sweetheart, I want her to stay too, but that's where Kate wants to go," she said pointedly.

"But who's going to watch *Shrek* with us?" asked Bobby. Mark looked surprised: *Shrek* was not on his list of appropriate viewing.

"Who's going to take us to the zoo and buy us ice-cream?" said Jack, thankfully remembering the fun part of that day rather than the splitting-his-head-open bit.

"I'll be back all the time to see you," I said.

"No, you won't," said Bobby. "We never saw you before. I hate London."

"I hate London too," said Jack, and kicked the table.

"Don't leave us," begged Bobby.

But that was exactly what I did do: I ran out the door, tears streaming down my face.

I drove down to the seafront and parked the car. What was I doing? Why was I running back to London when everyone I loved was here? Was my career that important? Could I make it work in Dublin with no job? What if Fiona got a bad result? Would I come back? Was I mad to give up Sam, the only man I'd ever loved? Could it work out?

I rested my aching head on the steering-wheel. I felt completely drained. The last eight months had been an emotional rollercoaster. What was I going to do?

My phone rang, and suddenly everything seemed clearer.

# CHAPTER
# THIRTY-NINE

In honour of Derek's twenty-seventh birthday and as a thank-you to the family for helping out during her treatment, Fiona and Mark were having us all over for dinner. As we were getting ready to go to their house, Gonzo called in.

"Hey, Mr O'B, just calling in to see my man Derek," he said, as Dad opened the door.

"OK. Be quick about it — we're off to dinner in Fiona's and don't be making any more music plans. That part of Derek's life is over as of now."

"It's a sad day for music lovers worldwide to lose a poet like D-Rek."

"I've a sneaking suspicion they might get over it," said Dad.

"Get over what?" I asked, walking into the kitchen.

"Derek getting a real job."

"*Maaaaaaaaaaan!*" said Gonzo. "You look fine."

"Thanks." I smiled.

"Steady now, the pair of you, I don't want any more shenanigans like there were the other night," said Dad, with a wink.

"If only," sighed Gonzo.

"'Sup?" asked Derek, shuffling in.

"Just saying to your old man that it's a sad day for the rap industry."

Derek shrugged. "At least we tried."

"Can't say we didn't follow our dream," agreed Gonzo.

"Fun while it lasted," said the poet.

"It's been an honour," said Gonzo.

"Couldn't have asked for a better wing man," said Derek.

"Means a lot," said Gonzo, thumping his heart.

"Keep it real," said Derek.

"So long, partner," said Gonzo, handing Derek a bag.

"For God's sake, he's not going the electric chair. He's going to work down the road — you'll still see him every day," said Dad.

"'S not the same, though," said Gonzo.

Derek pulled a T-shirt out of the bag and put it on. "Dude, I'm speechless," he said, as Dad and I read the words.

Across the front in red letters it said, "Talent will triumph. Keep the faith."

"There may be more than one poet after all," said Dad, snorting into his tea.

"We'd better go — we don't want to be late," I said, forcing back a giggle.

"When are you off?" asked Gonzo.

"In a couple of days," I said.

"If you ever get lonely —"

"I'll know who to call."

"Right, that's enough emotion for one night. Into the car with you," said Dad, ushering us out the door.

When we arrived the twins were in their pyjamas chasing Teddy. They weren't their usual selves with me. They were obviously still annoyed that I was leaving them. I tried to overcompensate by singing songs from *Shrek* and feeding them contraband biscuits, but they were having none of it. I was *persona non grata*.

Fiona and Mark were busy cooking, so they asked me to put the twins to bed. As I tucked them in I kissed them.

"Yucky wet kiss," said Jack.

"Here's another one," I said, as he squealed and dived under the covers.

"Night night, boys, I love you," I said, and sadness flooded me.

"Why are you crying?" Bobby asked.

"Because I love you and I've loved getting to spend so much time with you. You're very special boys."

"I love you too," said Bobby.

"I love you more," said Jack.

I closed the door, dried my eyes and composed myself before heading down to dinner.

Fiona and Mark had pulled out all the stops. The table was set with their best china, and the wine glasses twinkled in the candle-lit room. When we had sat down, Mark opened a bottle of champagne and proposed a toast.

"Fiona and I would like to thank you all for having been so supportive to us during the last year. We owe a special debt of gratitude to Kate, who gave up her job to help us with the boys. So here's to you, Kate, and we wish you every success back in London."

"Thanks," I said, flustered by his unexpected praise. "And you're welcome."

Then Dad jumped up and said he'd like to say a few words. Derek and I groaned. Dad's speeches went on for five or fifty minutes, depending on his mood.

"You can stop your moaning, I'll be brief," he said. "Tonight is a very special night for many reasons. First and foremost, it brings to an end Fiona's long and arduous journey through her cancer treatment. Throughout the last year she has been — as always — an example to all of us. Fiona, pet, you have been a credit to me and your mother all your life. When I found out you'd got the same cancer as her I was so angry I wanted to kill someone. Life couldn't be this unkind, I thought, and now I believe it isn't. I know you'll get better. The treatment and care you've had is in a different league to your mother's and we got the cancer earlier this time. I lost your mother far too young. There's no way I'm letting you go too.

"Hindsight is a wonderful thing, and I can see now how useless I was when your mother died. I left you to cope with Kate and Derek, and it wasn't fair. I'm sorry for that. My only excuse is that I was heartbroken. Your mother was an incredible woman and I couldn't imagine life without her. I stuck my head in the sand and it meant you had to grow up too soon. I won't let that happen to your boys, I promise you that."

I realized then that Dad probably still missed Mum. You never really get over losing the love of your life and he had compared every woman he had met since to her. They'd never come close. She was his soul mate. How could anyone compete with that? The bendy Sheryl had had no hope.

"Out of every bad thing comes something good — or so they say. I didn't believe that anything positive could come of this until Katie came home. And for once, Katie, you weren't rushing back to London. You stayed and we got to spend time with you and get to know you again, and it's been lovely. I've enjoyed having you around very much, and I'm sorry to see you go back. I hope you're making the right decision. I'd like to see you stay here and settle, but you're big enough and bold enough to make your own decisions, so I'll just say we'll miss you and the door is always open for you, if you change your mind.

"And that leaves young Derek here, except he isn't young any more. You're twenty-seven now, Derek, and it's time to grow up. I've indulged you long enough, the music hasn't worked out so now you'll come and work for me, and I think you'll enjoy it once you get over not being a pop star."

"Rap artist." Derek sighed.

"Whatever it is, you haven't made it, so it doesn't really matter. Anyway, in fairness to you, Derek, despite your knock-backs you've tried hard to make it work and I take my hat off to you, but there comes a stage where you have to accept defeat and that's now. So I'm asking you from today forward to speak in normal English, leave off the big tent-like T-shirts and saggy-arsed trousers and wear decent clothes — and for God's sake, no more tattoos."

At this point Fiona and I cheered. It was a welcome relief from the emotion that was flooding the room.

"When a man looks at his children and tries to remember the time he was proudest of them, it usually conjures up memories of graduations or wedding days. But for me it's been the courage and grace Fiona has shown through every day of her ordeal this year, and for Kate and Derek, it's the day you shaved off your hair. That's solidarity, that's kinship, that's love, that's family. I've never been more proud of my three children than this year," he said, choking up. "So here's to you all, and to a long, happy and healthy life."

We threw back our champagne and tried not to cry. This was the most touchy-feely we'd ever been. It was uncomfortable and wonderful at the same time.

Just as we were all catching our breath, Fiona stood up. "I'd like to say a few words now. First of all, thanks, Dad, for what you just said and for everything. You've had to be father and mother to us, and you've done a great job. You don't have to apologize to me about falling apart after Mum. I understand better now and I wouldn't change a thing. My life is what it is and having cancer has made me realize how lucky I am. I have a wonderful family, husband and children."

Then, turning to me, she said, "I'd like to take this opportunity to thank Kate properly. You dropped everything to come home and help me and the boys. I know how much your career means to you and I know how hard that must have been. I don't think you'll ever know how deeply grateful I am. I couldn't have got through this without you, Kate. You've been amazing to me and the twins. They adore their auntie Kate. It's been so lovely having you around every day and getting closer again. I'm really going to miss you. I wish you weren't going, but if this is what you want, I wish you every success. If I can ever do anything to help you out, just pick up the phone."

I knocked back another glass of champagne to stop the lump forming in my throat making me bawl — at this rate I'd be plastered before dinner.

Turning to the birthday boy, Fiona added, "Derek, you've been brilliant too. You've always managed to make me laugh, even on my really bad days, so thank you. And finally, Mark, I couldn't have got through this without you. Thank you for everything, but most of all thanks for being such a wonderful father," she said, and bent to kiss him. He looked chuffed, and I almost liked him again.

"Kate, do you want to say anything?" Dad asked. I shook my head. I didn't trust myself to speak.

"Birthday boy? Anything you'd like to add?" Dad asked Derek.

Derek shuffled to his feet. "OK, so this is weird, everyone being all nice to each other and shit. All I've got to say, really, is that turning twenty-seven sucks because I've got to give up music, but the fact that you're all here is making it a bit less shitty. I never really said any of this mushy stuff before but, Fiona, I want you to know that I appreciate everything you've done for me, like for ever. You've been like a mum and a sister, and you've always been there when I've fucked up and helped me out and never judged me. It's pretty rare.

"Dad, I promise I'll try to fit in with your office people but I can't guarantee I'll totally blend. Kate, it's a bummer that you're going back. It's been fun having you around. You used to be all stressed out when you came home and snappy and distracted, but this time you were cool. So it's farewell to music and hello, real world."

"What happened to plan B?" Dad asked

Derek shrugged. "The guy never got back to me so I guess he thought the idea sucked."

The doorbell rang. I stood up abruptly. "Actually, Derek, I have some good news for you. Just hang on a second."

They all stared at me as I ran out to answer the door.

"What's going on?" asked Sam, as I pulled him in.

"Thanks for coming. I promise it'll all make sense in a minute," I said, ushering him into the room and thrusting a drink into his hand.

Everyone was puzzled.

"I've asked Sam to be here because what I've got to say affects him too." I cleared my throat and took a deep breath. "It would appear that I used to be a royal pain in the arse. Self-obsessed, self-important and full of hot air. I admit that coming home to help Fiona was one of the hardest things I've ever done and, without a shadow of a doubt, the best and most rewarding. I've loved getting to know the twins and seeing them grow and develop. They're a credit to both of you," I said, to Fiona and Mark. "You've done a really great job, and they're amazing kids. I've also really enjoyed spending time with all of you. I forgot how important family is. I'd lost my way and it's a pity that something so awful had to happen to give me the slap in the face I needed, but I guess that's life. I owe Fiona so much for having looked after me so well as a kid. With only four years between us in age, there was a generation between us in maturity. You were incredible, Fiona, always putting me and Derek first, and I'm sorry it's taken me so long to give something back to you. The best thing about coming home this time was that it gave me a chance to help my sister, the most selfless person I know. It's been lovely to spend time with you guys, too," I added, smiling at Dad and Derek.

"Over the last eight months I've had time to reassess my life, where it was going, what I really want for my future and the type of person I want to be, and I realized that a lot of changes needed to be made. I've had a long hard look at myself, and there was a lot I didn't like, so I'm trying to change and make better decisions. Fiona, you said something to me the other day that really struck home. I couldn't stop thinking about it and it helped me make some tough choices. You said, 'No one wants "She had a successful career" engraved on their headstone. It's sad and soulless.' And you were right. So —"

"Yo, nice speech and all, but what's the good news you have for me?" interrupted Derek.

I smiled and proceeded to explain what had happened three days earlier when I'd received a phone call out of the blue . . .

"Hi, Kate, Peter Kildare from TV3 here. I've had another call from Sam Taylor offering me tickets to the All-Ireland hurley final if I could find you a job. He must be very keen on you — those tickets are like gold dust. I told him I don't have any presenting jobs coming up, but I did have something turn up on my desk that might be a possibility, if you'd agree to do it. I've been toying with the idea of running fly-on-the-wall documentaries about people trying to make it as musicians, actors, chefs, artists, writers and that kind of thing. If you get the right people, it can make great TV. Anyway, the other day these two lads arrived into my office and tried to sell me the idea of a reality TV show based around them trying to make it as rap artists. The singer's old man was going to pull the plug on their cash-flow and they were desperate not to have to give up the dream. They were hilarious — unintentionally so — but a riot none the less. They take themselves very seriously, so I asked them for a sample of their songs — which weren't all that bad. I'm thinking of starting the series with a documentary on them. They're such characters that it should be very entertaining. They talk like hard-core gangsters — it's priceless. I'd need someone good to steer the documentary, though, and I couldn't pay much, which is the problem so far. None of the presenters I've approached will do it because the pay is so bad, and you're talking at least six months to make a decent documentary — but if you'd consider it, maybe we could work something out . . ."

Derek jumped up from his chair. "NO WAY!"

"So," I said, smiling at him, "it looks like I'm going to be making a documentary about you and Gonzo. Which means I'll be staying in Ireland. Although I may have to live at home for a while longer, Dad. The money *is* pretty awful, but if it's a success I get a cut of the profits."

"Awesome! Wait'll I tell Gonzo," whooped Derek, dialling his band mate's number.

"Excuse *me*," said Dad. "I'd like to complain. After twenty-seven years I finally get my son to agree to give up trying to be a rapper and get a proper job and you've just given him another six months of tormenting me with bad grammar and looking at the crack of his arse! Get away over to London with you."

"Sorry, Dad, but as the T-shirt says, 'Talent will triumph.'"

I sat down and looked at Sam. "Thanks for coming."

"Your message said it was life or death."

"It is to me. So, can we give it a go? I really want this to work,"

"It *has* to work. Do you have any idea how difficult it was to get those tickets for Peter Kildare? I'm all out of favours," he said, smiling.

"I'll take that as a yes." I laughed, and he kissed me.

"Sorry, bro," said Derek, into the phone. "Judging by the tonsil-tennis going on here Kate's back with the journalist dude. But, hey, we're going to be famous so you'll have your pick of the ladies."

"Someone shoot me now," said Dad, putting his head in his hands. Teddy put a comforting paw on his lap.

"Why is Granddad crying?" asked Jack, who had appeared out of nowhere with his brother in tow.

"Boys!" said Fiona. "It's way past your bedtime."

"We heard Uncle Derek shouting," said Bobby.

"Guess what, boys?" I said. "I'm not going back to England! I'm staying here with you."

They yawned and climbed on to their mother's lap.

# Acknowledgements

Sincere thanks go to:

My editor, Patricia Deevy, for her patience and guidance with this book.

All at Penguin Ireland, especially Michael McLoughlin, Cliona Lewis and Brian Walker.

All at Penguin UK, with special mention to Tom Weldon, Becke Parker, Naomi Fidler and the wonderful sales, marketing and creative teams; Hazel Orme, for her excellent copy-editing.

My agent Gillon Aitken, Ayesha Karim, Lesley Thorne and everyone at the agency.

All my friends, for their support and encouragement.

Monica McInerney for the long lunches and emails that keep me sane.

My uncle, Michael Moriarty, for his great help and patience in talking me through the treatment of breast cancer — any mistakes that remain are my own.

Mum, Dad, Mike, Sue, and all the nephews, nieces, in-laws and out-laws for being so generous of spirit and endlessly enthusiastic.

Troy most of all — I couldn't do this without you.

My two little miracles, Hugo and Geordy, who make every day feel like Christmas.

# Any Way You Want Me

## Lucy Diamond

On paper, Sadie's got it all — the partner, the children, the house. But Sadie can't help harking back to the time when she was a career woman by day and a party animal by night. The only sleepless nights she's getting now are due to the baby. Maybe a little reinvention is the answer . . .

Sadie can't resist creating a fictitious online identity for herself as a hot TV producer. It's only a bit of harmless fun . . . until truth and fantasy become dangerously tangled. It isn't long before she's wondering if the exciting alter ego she has dreamed up really is the kind of person she wants to be after all . . .

**ISBN 978-0-7531-7922-2 (hb)**
**ISBN 978-0-7531-7923-9 (pb)**

# The Truth About Ruby Valentine

## Alison Bond

When Hollywood legend Ruby Valentine shocks the world with her mysterious suicide, Kelly's father reveals something even more shocking — she's Ruby's daughter.

So Kelly sets off for Tinseltown to find some answers, diving head first into Hollywood society with her new family of jet-setters and fashionistas. But she soon discovers that Ruby's real life was laced with more drama, tragedy and intrigue than any screenwriter could imagine.

When Ruby's fortune turns out to be non-existent, and Kelly learns of the intense relationship her mother had with her slick, powerful agent, she begins to get suspicious about what's really going on. And the more she digs, the closer she gets to uncovering the most unbelievable secret of them all.

ISBN 978-0-7531-7866-9 (hb)
ISBN 978-0-7531-7867-6 (pb)

# Rescuing Rose

## Isabel Wolff

Rose Costelloe has more than a few thorns in her side. Despite dishing out advice as an agony aunt, she hasn't practised what she preaches. Her new marriage is in tatters, she's had to move house and the bills are piling up. Her scatty best friends, twins Bella and Bea, make the unusually sensible suggestion that she lets out her spare room. Geeky accountant Theo promises to solve one of her problems. Quiet and reclusive with a passion for star-gazing, he seems the perfect lodger for Rose's spare room.

Her romantic dilemmas are another matter. Just when she thinks she's over Ed the ex-husband, her universe is thrown into chaos. And unexpectedly, only Theo seems able to grasp what really matters to Rose beneath her prickly exterior. If she's to find happiness, should she take his advice?

ISBN 978-0-7531-7864-5 (hb)
ISBN 978-0-7531-7865-2 (pb)

# The Playground Mafia

## Sarah Tucker

Meet Caroline Gray: divorcee and newly-single mother. Caroline and son Ben have moved to the trendy town of Frencham where they join Caroline's long-time best friends, Heather and Eva. Settling into their new life is easy, but nothing has prepared Caroline for the demands of motherhood at The Sycamore, the school the trio's beloved offspring attend. Forget classroom bullies, this is full-scale adult playground politics. This is battle with the mothers who won't take no for an answer — the Playground Mafia.

Amidst the four-wheel drives, Ben's complicated afterschool play-date schedule and her friends' extra-marital affairs, Caroline tries to keep a low and very single profile. But it's not long before she too finds herself under the mafia's scandal-radar, and her life takes an unexpected turn . . .

ISBN 978-0-7531-7812-6 (hb)
ISBN 978-0-7531-7813-3 (pb)

# Lucky Girl

## Fiona Gibson

Everyone always told Stella Moon how lucky she was to have a famous dad.

She just wished he was more like everyone else's. And when her mum died, and he withdrew to his allotment leaving Stella and her brother alone to play in rusty cars and exist for a whole week on Black Forest gateaux, she didn't feel lucky at all.

Now in her thirties; Stella has made sure her life couldn't be further from her chaotic upbringing, with a strict routine as a music teacher and a peaceful, tidy home. Until two noisy little girls move in next door.

At first, she feels besieged. The girls hound her, bearing sticky gifts of edible jewellery and firing personal questions about her mum, her dad and her love life. But it's their friendship that helps her to confront the truth about her own childhood and start living life to the full.

**ISBN 978-0-7531-7778-5 (hb)**
**ISBN 978-0-7531-7779-2 (pb)**

ISIS publish a wide range of books in large print, from fiction to biography. Any suggestions for books you would like to see in large print or audio are always welcome. Please send to the Editorial Department at:

**ISIS Publishing Limited**
7 Centremead
Osney Mead
Oxford OX2 0ES

A full list of titles is available free of charge from:

**Ulverscroft Large Print Books Limited**

**(UK)**
The Green
Bradgate Road, Anstey
Leicester LE7 7FU
Tel: (0116) 236 4325

**(Australia)**
P.O. Box 314
St Leonards
NSW 1590
Tel: (02) 9436 2622

**(USA)**
P.O. Box 1230
West Seneca
N.Y. 14224-1230
Tel: (716) 674 4270

**(Canada)**
P.O. Box 80038
Burlington
Ontario L7L 6B1
Tel: (905) 637 8734

**(New Zealand)**
P.O. Box 456
Feilding
Tel: (06) 323 6828

Details of **ISIS** complete and unabridged audio books are also available from these offices. Alternatively, contact your local library for details of their collection of **ISIS** large print and unabridged audio books.